THE BEAST MUST DIE

Nicholas Blake was the pseudony[illegible] [illegible]oet Laureate Cecil Day-Lewis, who [illegible] County Laois, Ireland, in [illegible] [illegible]er died [illegible] 190[illegible], he was brought up in London by his fath[illegible] [illegible]ending summer holidays with relatives in Wexford. He was educated at Sherborne School and Wadham College, Oxford, from which he graduated in 1927. Blake initially worked as a teacher to supplement his income from his poetry writing and he published his first Nigel Strangeways novel, *A Question of Proof*, in 1935. Blake went on to write a further nineteen crime novels, all but four of which featured Nigel Strangeways, as well as numerous poetry collections and translations.

During the Second World War he worked as a publications editor in the Ministry of Information, which he used as the basis for the Ministry of Morale in *Minute for Murder*, and after the war he joined the publishers Chatto & Windus as an editor and director. He was appointed Poet Laureate in 1968 and died in 1972 at the home of his friend, the writer Kingsley Amis.

ALSO BY NICHOLAS BLAKE

A Question of Proof
Thou Shell of Death
There's Trouble Brewing
The Widow's Cruise
Malice in Wonderland
The Case of the Abominable Snowman
The Smiler with the Knife
Minute for Murder
Head of a Traveller
The Dreadful Hollow
The Whisper in the Gloom
End of Chapter
The Worm of Death
The Sad Variety
The Morning After Death

NICHOLAS BLAKE

The Beast Must Die

London

Published by Vintage 2012

6 8 10 9 7

First published in Great Britain in 1938 by Collins

Vintage
Random House, 20 Vauxhall Bridge Road,
London SW1V 2SA

www.vintage-books.co.uk

Addresses for companies within The Random House Group Limited can be found at: www.randomhouse.co.uk/offices.htm

The Random House Group Limited Reg. No. 954009

A CIP catalogue record for this book is available from the British Library

ISBN 9780099565383

Printed and bound in Great Britain by Clays Ltd, Elcograf S.p.A.

FOR
EILEEN AND TONY

Contents

Part One

The Diary of Felix Lane

20 June 1937

I am going to kill a man. I don't know his name, I don't know where he lives, I have no idea what he looks like. But I am going to find him and kill him . . .

You must pardon me this melodramatic opening, gentle reader. It sounds just like a first sentence out of one of my own detective novels, doesn't it? Only this story is never going to be published, and the 'gentle reader' is a polite convention. No, not perhaps just a polite convention. I propose to commit what the world calls 'a crime'. Every criminal, who has no accomplice, needs a confidante; the loneliness, the appalling isolation and suspense of crime are too much for one man to contain within him. Sooner or later he will blurt it all out. Or, if his will stands firm, his superego betrays him – that strict moralist within who plays cat-and-mouse with the furtive, the timorous or the cocksure alike, forcing the criminal into slips of the tongue, luring him into overconfidence, planting evidence against him, playing the agent provocateur. All the forces of law and order would be powerless against one man absolutely without conscience. But deep inside us all there exists that compulsion to make atonement – a sense of guilt, the traitor within the gates. We are betrayed by what is false within. If the tongue refuses to confess, the involuntary actions will. That is why the criminal returns to the scene of his crime. That is why I am writing this diary. You, my imaginary reader, *hypocrite lecteur, mon semblable, mon frère*, are to be my confessor. I shall keep nothing back from you. It is you who will save me from the gallows, if anyone can.

It's easy enough to envisage murder, sitting here in the bungalow James lent me so that I could recuperate after my nervous breakdown. (No, gentle reader, I am not mad. You can dismiss that from your mind at once. I was never saner. Guilty, but not insane.) Easy enough to envisage murder, looking out of the window at Golden Cap glowing in the evening sun, and the crisped leaf-metal waves of the bay, and the curved arm of the Cobb enfolding the baby boats a hundred feet below me. Because, you see, they all say Martie to me. If Martie had not been killed, he and I would be going for picnics on Golden Cap; he would be splashing into the sea in that bright red bathing-dress he was so proud of; and today would have been his seventh birthday, and I had promised to teach him how to sail the dinghy when he was seven.

Martin was my son. One evening, six months ago, he was crossing the road outside our house. He had gone into the village to buy some sweets. For him it could only have been a paralysing blaze of headlights round the corner, a moment's nightmare, and then the impact turning everything to darkness for ever. His body was hurled into the ditch. He was dead at once, minutes before I got to him. The bag of sweets was sprinkled over the road. I remember I began to pick them up – there didn't seem to be anything else to do – till I found his blood on one of them. After that, I was ill for quite a time: brain fever, nervous breakdown or something, they called it. The fact is, of course, that I didn't want to live. Martie was all I had – Tessa died giving birth to him.

The motorist who killed Martie did not stop. The police have failed to trace him. They say he must have been going fifty round that blind corner, for the body to have been thrown and injured like it was. He is the man I have got to find and kill.

I don't think I can write any more today.

21 June

I had promised to keep nothing back from you, gentle reader, and I've broken my promise already. But it's a thing I have had to keep back from myself, too, till I was well enough to face it. *Was it my fault?* Ought I to have let Martie go into the village alone?

There. Thank God that's out. The agony of writing it down has nearly driven the nib through the paper. I feel faint, as if an arrowhead had been extracted from festering flesh; but the pain itself is a kind of relief. Let me look at the barb that was slowly killing me.

If I had not given Martie that twopence, if I had gone with him that night, or sent Mrs Teague, he would be alive now. We would be sailing in the bay, or fishing for prawns from the end of the Cobb, or scrambling down the landslide among those huge yellow flowers – what are they called? – Martie always wanted to know the name of everything, but now that I'm by myself there doesn't seem any point in finding out.

I wanted him to grow up independent. I knew that, when Tessa died, there was the danger of my swamping him with my love. I tried to train him to do things by himself and for himself: I had to let him take risks. But he had been down to the village alone dozens of times; he used to play with the village children all the morning when I was working. He was sensible about crossing the street, and anyhow there's very little traffic on our road. Who could have known that devil would come smashing round the corner? – showing off to some bloody woman passenger, I suppose, or drunk. And then he hadn't the guts to stop and take his medicine.

Tessa darling, was it my fault? You wouldn't have wanted me to wrap him in cotton wool, would you? You didn't like to be cosseted and looked after either; you were independent as hell. No. My reason tells me that I was right. But I can't quite get out of my head the hand clutching the burst paper bag. It doesn't accuse me, but it won't let me rest – it's a gentle, importuning ghost. My revenge will be for myself alone.

I wonder did the coroner make any censorious comments on my 'negligence'. They didn't let me see the paper in the nursing home. All I know is that a verdict of manslaughter was brought in against some person or persons unknown. Manslaughter! Baby-killing. Even if they had caught him, he'd only have got a term of imprisonment, and then he'd have been free to run amok again – unless they suspended his licence for life, and do they ever do that? I've got to find him and put him out of harm's way. His murderer ought to be crowned with flowers (where have I read something like that?) as a public benefactor. No, don't start kidding yourself. What you intend has nothing to do with abstract justice.

But I wonder what the coroner said. Perhaps it's this that has kept me lingering on here, when I'm really quite well again, nervous of what the neighbours may be saying. Look there goes the man who let his child get killed: coroner said so. Oh, damn them and the coroner! They're going to have some reason for calling me a murderer before long, so what in God's name does it matter?

The day after tomorrow I'll go home. That's settled. I'll write to Mrs Teague tonight and tell her to get the cottage ready. I have faced the worst thing about Martie's death now, and I honestly believe I have nothing to blame myself for. The cure is completed. I can devote my whole heart to the one thing that is left for me to do.

22 June

James paid me a flying visit this afternoon, 'just to see how you're getting on'. Nice of him. He was surprised that I looked so much better. All due to the salubrious situation of his bungalow, I said. I could scarcely tell him that I'd found something to live for – it might have led to awkward questions. One of them, at least, I couldn't answer myself. 'When did you first decide to murder X?' is the sort of question (like 'when did you first fall in love with me?') which needs a whole treatise to answer it adequately. And would-be murderers, unlike lovers, are not so keen on talking about themselves – in spite of the evidence of this diary to the contrary. They do their talking after the event – too much of it, poor wretches!

Well, my ghostly confessor, I suppose it's time you had some personal details about me – age, height, weight, colour of eyes, qualifications for the post of murderer, that kind of thing. I am thirty-five years old, five foot eight, brown eyes; usual expression of face – a kind of sombre benevolence like the barn owl – or so Tessa used to tell me. My hair, by some odd freak, has not yet turned grey. My name is Frank Cairnes. I used to occupy a desk (I will not say 'work') in the Ministry of Labour, but five years ago a legacy and my own laziness persuaded me to hand in my resignation and retire to the country cottage where Tessa and I had always wanted to live. 'She should have died hereafter,' as the bard says. Pottering about in my garden and my dinghy was too much of a good thing for even my capacity for idleness, so I started writing detective novels – under the name of 'Felix Lane'. They are rather good ones, as it happens, and bring me in a surprising amount of cash, but I am unable to convince myself that detective fiction is a serious branch of literature, so Felix Lane has always been absolutely anonymous. My publishers are pledged not to disclose the secret of his identity. After their initial horror at the idea of a writer not wanting to be connected with the tripe he turns out, they quite enjoyed making a mystery of it. Good publicity, this mystery stuff, they thought, with the simple credulity of their kind, and started whacking it up into quite a stunt. Though who the hell of my 'rapidly growing public' (the publishers' phrase) cares two hoots who Felix Lane is in reality I should very much like to know.

Still, no harsh words about Felix Lane; he's going to come in very useful in the near future. I should add that, when my neighbours inquire what I'm scribbling at all day, I tell them I'm working on a Life of Wordsworth. I do know quite a lot about him, but I'd as soon eat a hundredweight of solid glue as write his life.

My qualifications for murders are, to say the least, meagre. As Felix Lane I have acquired a smattering of forensic medicine, criminal law, and police procedure. I have never fired a gun or poisoned so much as a rat. My studies in criminology have suggested to me that only generals, Harley Street specialists and mine owners can get away with murder successfully. But here I may be doing the unprofessional murderer an injustice.

As to my character, it can best be deduced from this diary. I like to think that I think it a pretty inferior kind of character, but this is probably just the self-deception of the sophisticated . . .

Forgive all this pretentious garrulity, gentle reader who will never read it. A man has to talk to himself when he is alone on the drifting floe, in the dark alone, lost. Tomorrow I go home. I hope Mrs Teague has given all his toys away. I told her to.

23 June

The cottage looks just the same. Well, why not? Did I expect the walls to have been weeping? It's typical of human impertinence – this pathetic fallacy of expecting the whole face of nature to be changed by one's own squirming little agonies. Of course the cottage is the same. Except that the life has gone out of it. I see they've put up a danger sign at the corner. Too late, as usual.

Mrs Teague very subdued. She seems to have felt it; or maybe her funereal tones are just sick-room stuff for my benefit. Looking at that sentence again,

I find it peculiarly nasty – jealousy at someone else's having been fond of Martie, having had a share in his life. Good God, was I on the way to becoming one of those I-want-you-all-to-myself fathers? If so, murder is certainly all I'm fit for.

. . . Just as I was writing that, Mrs Teague came in – a sort of apologetic but determined expression on her huge red face, like a timid person who has screwed himself up to lodge a complaint, or a communicant returning from the altar. 'I just couldn't do it, sir,' she said, 'I hadn't the heart' – and to my horror started blubbering. 'Do what?' I asked. 'Give them all away,' she sobbed. She threw down a key on my table and rushed out of the room. It was the key of Martie's toy-cupboard.

I went upstairs to the nursery and opened the cupboard. I had to do it at once, or I could never have done it. I stared at them for a long time, unable to think: the model garage, the Hornby engine, the old teddybear with only one eye; his three favourites. Coventry Patmore's lines had come into my head –

He had put, within his reach,
A box of counters and a red-vein'd stone,
A piece of glass abraded by the beach
And six or seven shells
A bottle with bluebells
And two French copper coins, ranged there with careful art,
To comfort his sad heart.

Mrs Teague was quite right. It needed that. It needed something to keep the wound open. These toys are a better memorial than the tombstone in the village, they will not let me sleep, they are going to be the death of someone.

24 June

Had a talk with Sergeant Elder this morning. Fourteen stone of bone and muscle, as 'Sapper' would say, and about one milligram of brain. The fishy, arrogant eyes of the stupid man invested with authority. Why is it that one is always infected with a kind of moral paralysis when one encounters a policeman, as though one were on board a pinnace about to be run down by the *Rodney*? Probably just a case of fear being catching; the bobby is always on the defensive – against the 'upper classes' because they can make things so darned uncomfortable for him if he takes a false step, against the lower classes because he is the representative of the 'law and order' which they have every reason to suspect of being their natural enemy. However.

Elder gave a display of the usual pompous, official reticence. Has a habit of scratching the lobe of his right ear and at the same time staring at the wall about six inches above one's head, which I find insanely irritating. Investigations were still being pursued, he said, every channel would be explored; a mass of information had been sifted, but they had no lead as yet. That means, of course, that they've come to a dead end and don't like to admit it. Which leaves the course clear for me. A straight fight. I'm glad.

I gave Elder a mug of beer, which unbuttoned him slightly. Managed to prise some of the details of the 'investigations' out of him. They're certainly thorough enough, the police. Apart from the BBC appeals for witnesses of the accident to come forward, it seems that they visited pretty well every garage in the county and enquired about dented wings, bumpers, damaged radiators, etc., brought in for repair; all the car owners within a wide radius were investigated, more or less tactfully, to find out if they had alibis for their cars at the time of the accident. Then there were house-to-house enquiries along the chap's presumed route in the vicinity of the village: proprietors of wayside petrol pumps and AA men were questioned, and so on. It seems that there was a reliability trial in progress that evening, and they thought the chap might have been one of the drivers who'd got off his route – he was certainly going the pace of someone trying to make up for lost time – but none of the cars was noticed to be damaged when they reached the next check. They also worked it out, on the basis of the times given by the officials at this check and the previous one, that none of the drivers could have made the detour needed to take him through our village. There may be a loophole here, but I should think the police would have found it if there was one.

I hope I extracted all this information without appearing too heartlessly inquisitive. Would the heart-broken father be expected to want to know all this? Well, I don't suppose Elder is particularly hot on the nuances of morbid psychology. But it's an appalling problem. Can I succeed where the whole police organisation has failed? Talk about looking for a needle in a haystack!

Wait a minute! If I wanted to hide a needle, I wouldn't hide it in a haystack, I'd hide it in a heap of needles. Now then: Elder was pretty definite that the impact of the collision must have caused some damage to the front of the car, even though Martie was only a featherweight. The best way to conceal damage is to cause more damage in the same place. If I'd knocked a child down and dented a wing, say, and wanted to cover it up, I'd fake an accident – run the car into a gate or a tree or something. That would cover up all traces of the previous collision.

What we've got to do is find out whether any cars were piled up in this way that night. I'll ring up Elder in the morning and ask him.

25 June

NBG. The police had already thought of that one. Elder's respect for the bereaved was severely tried, judging by his tone over the telephone. He made it politely plain that the police don't need to be taught their job by any outsider. All accidents in the neighbourhood were investigated, to establish their 'bona fides', as he put it – the pompous oaf.

It's bewildering, maddening. I don't know where to start. How did I ever come to think that I'd only to stretch out my hand and lay it upon the man I want? Must have been the first stage of murderer's megalomania. After my telephone conversation with Elder this morning, I felt irritable and disheartened. Nothing to do but potter about in the garden, everything reminding me of Martie, not least this silly business of the roses.

When Martie was a toddler, he used to follow me about the garden as I cut flowers for the table. One day I found he'd cut the heads off two dozen prize roses which I was keeping for the show – that superb dark red bloom, 'Night'. I was furious with him, though I realised even at the time that he had thought he was helping me. A bestial performance on my part. He wouldn't be comforted for hours afterwards. That is the way trust and innocence are destroyed. Now he's dead, and it doesn't much matter I suppose, but I wish I'd not lost my temper with him that day – it must have been like the end of the world for him. Oh hell, now I'm getting maudlin. I shall start making a catalogue of his babyish sayings next. Well, why not? Why not? Looking out on the lawn now, I remember how he saw two halves of a worm that had been cut in half by the lawnmower, trying to wriggle together, and he said, 'Look, Daddy, there's a worm shunting.' I thought that was pretty bright. He might have made a poet, with that gift for metaphor.

But what started this sentimental train of thought was my walking out into the garden this morning and finding that the top of every single rose had been cut off. My heart stood still (as I phrase it in my thrillers). For a moment I thought all the last six months had been a nightmare, and Martie was alive still. Some kid in the village up to a silly bit of mischief, no doubt. But it got me down, made me feel as if everything was against me. A just and merciful Providence might at least have spared me a few roses. I suppose I ought to report this 'act of vandalism' to Elder, but I just can't be bothered.

There's something intolerably theatrical about the sound of one's own sobbing. I hope Mrs Teague didn't hear me.

I'll do a pub crawl tomorrow evening, and see if there's any information to be picked up. I can't go on glooming around in the cottage for ever. Think I'll drop in on Peters for a drink now, before I go to bed.

26 June

There's a certain unique thrill about dissembling, the sensation of that man in some story or other who carried an explosive in his breast pocket, and in his trouser pocket a bulb which he only had to press and blow himself and everything within twenty yards to glory. I felt it when I was secretly engaged to Tessa – the dangerous, lovely, dynamite secret in the breast, and I felt it again last night talking to Peters. He's a good sort, but I don't suppose he's ever come up against anything more melodramatic than childbirth, arthritis and influenza. I kept on wondering what he'd say if he knew there was a prospective murderer sitting in the room with him, drinking his White Label. The compulsion to blurt it out became almost overwhelming at one point. I really will have to be very careful indeed. This isn't a game. Not that he'd have believed me; but I don't want him sending me back to that nursing home – or worse – for 'observation'.

Was glad to hear from Peters, when I'd screwed myself up to ask him, that nothing was said at the inquest about my being responsible for Martie's death. It still rankles in my mind a little, though. I look into the faces of the village people, and wonder what they're really thinking about me. Mrs Anderson, for instance, our late organist's widow – why did she deliberately cross the street to avoid me this morning? She always used to be so fond of Martie. Spoilt him, in fact, with her strawberries and cream and those queer gelatine lozenges and her furtive huggings of him when she thought I wasn't looking – he disliked the latter as much as I did. Oh well, the poor thing never had a kid herself, and Anderson's death broke her up for good. I'd much rather she cut me dead than came slobbering over me with sympathy.

Like many people who lead a rather isolated life – spiritually isolated, I mean – I'm abnormally sensitive to other people's opinion of me. I hate the idea of being the popular, hail-fellow-well-met type, yet the idea of unpopularity gives me a feeling of deep uneasiness. Not a very sympathetic trait – wanting to eat one's cake and have it, to be liked by my neighbours yet to remain essentially aloof from them. But then, as I said before, I don't set up to be a very nice person.

I'll go straight away to the Saddler's Arms, and beard public opinion in its den. I might get a lead there, too, though I suppose Elder interviewed all the chaps.

Later

I've drunk about ten pints in the last two hours, but am still cold sober. There are some wounds too deep for local anaesthetics, it seems. Everyone very friendly. I'm not the villain of the piece, anyway.

'A cruel shame,' they said. 'Hanging's too good for the like of them sort.'

'Us do miss the little lad – a regular peart 'un, he were' – this from old Barnett, the shepherd. 'These yurr automobiles are the curse of the countryside. If I'd my way, I'd pass a law against 'em.'

Bert Cozzens – the village wiseacre – said, 'The toll of the roads. That's what it is, see, the toll of the roads. Ar. Natural selection, if you take my meaning. The survival of the fittest – meaning no disrespect to you sir, who has all our sympathy in this shocking fatality.' 'Survival of the fittest?' young Joe piped up. 'What're you doing here, then, Bert? Survival of the fattest, more like.' This was considered a bit near the knuckle, and young Joe was suppressed.

They're grand chaps – neither smug nor cynical nor sentimental about death; they've got the proper realist attitude towards it. Their own children have to sink or swim – they can't afford nurses and vita-glass and fancy foods for them, so it would never occur to them to blame me for letting Martie live the independent, natural life their own children live. I might have known that. But they were no use to me otherwise, I'm afraid. As Ted Barnett summed it up, 'Us'd give the fingers off our right hands to find the B— who done it. Us seen a car or two come through village after the accident, but us had no call to notice 'em special, see, not knowing anything'd happened; and they headlights maze 'ee so, 'ee can't see number plates nor nothing. Reckon 'tes the job of the bloody police, only that Elder spends 'is time – ' here followed slanderous speculations about the spare-time activities, mainly erotic, it would appear, of our worthy sergeant.

Same at the Lion and Lamb and the Crown. Much goodwill but no information. I shan't get anywhere on this tack. Must try an entirely different line. But what? Too tired to think any more tonight.

27 June

A long walk over towards Cirencester today. Passed the ridge from which Martie and I catapulted those toy gliders. He was quite crazy about them; would probably have smashed himself up in an aeroplane if the car hadn't come first. I shall never forget the way he stood watching the gliders, his face ineffably solemn and tense, as though he could will them to keep soaring and flying for ever. The whole countryside is his memorial. As long as I stay on here, the wound will stay unhealed – which is what I want.

Someone seems to want me to clear out. All the madonna lilies and tobacco plants in the bed under my window were torn up last night and flung on to the path. Some time early this morning, rather; they were all right at midnight. No village kid would do a thing like that twice. There's a malevolence about this that worries me a little. But I'm not going to be intimidated.

An extraordinary thought has just struck me. Have I got some deadly enemy who killed Martie deliberately and is now destroying everything else that I love? Fantastic. Just shows how easily anyone's brain can be turned if he is too much alone. But if this goes on much longer, I shall be afraid to look out of the window in the morning.

I walked fast today, so that my brain couldn't keep up with me and I was free of its constant nagging for a few hours. I feel refreshed now. So, with your permission, hypothetical reader, I'll start thinking on paper. What is the new line that I must adopt? Better put it down as a series of propositions and deductions. Here goes:

(1) There's no use my trying the methods of the police, which they have far better means to carry out, and in any case seem to have failed.

 The implication is that I must exploit my own strong point – presumably, as a detective writer, the capacity to imagine myself into the mind of the criminal.

(2) If I'd run down a child and damaged my car, my instinct would be to keep off main roads, where the damage might be spotted, and get as quickly as possible to a place where it could be repaired. But, according to the police, all garages have been investigated, and all damages repaired during the days after the accident were found to have had some innocent explanation. Of course, they may have been diddled about this, somehow or other but, if they were, I couldn't possibly discover how.

 What follows from this? Either (a) the car was undamaged after all – but expert evidence suggests this is most unlikely. Or (b) the criminal drove his car straight into a private garage and has kept it locked up ever since; possible, but highly improbable. Or (c) the criminal secretly effected the repairs himself. This is surely the likeliest explanation.

(3) Assume the chap did his own repairs. Does that tell me anything about him?

Yes. He must be an expert, with the necessary tools at his disposal. But even a small dent in a mudguard has to be hammered out, and that kicks up enough din to wake the dead. 'Wake'! Exactly. He'd have to do the repairs the same night, so that there should be no trace of the accident next morning. But a sound of hammering at night would be bound to wake people and rouse suspicion.

(4) He did not do any hammering that night.

But, whether his car was in a private or a public garage, hammering the next morning would surely call attention to him, even if he could afford to put off the repairs till the morning.

(5) He did not do any hammering at all.

But we have to assume that the repairs were effected somehow or other. What a fool I am! Even to hammer out a small dent, *one has to take the wing off*. Now if – as we are forced to conclude – the criminal could not afford to make a noise while repairing his car, the deduction is that he must have removed the damaged parts and replaced them with new spare parts.

(6) Assume that he fitted another wing – perhaps another bumper too, and/or a new headlight, and got rid of the damaged ones. What follows?

> That he must be at least a fairly expert mechanic, and have access to spare parts. In other words, surely, he must work in a public garage. More, *he must own it* because, only the owner of the garage could conceal the fact that certain spare parts had disappeared from stores and were not accounted for.

By God! I seem to have got somewhere at least. The man I'm after owns a public garage, and it must be an efficient one, otherwise they would not stock the requisite spare parts; but probably not a very big one, for in a big garage it would be presumably some clerk or manager, not the owner, who would check the spare parts in store. Or the criminal might be manager of a big garage, or a clerk in it. That widens the choice again, I'm afraid.

Can I deduce anything about the car and the nature of the damage? From its driver's point of view, Martie was crossing the road from left to right. His body was flung into the ditch on the left-hand side of the road. This suggests that the damage would be on the left side of the car, particularly if it swerved out to the right a bit to avoid him. The left-hand wing, bumper or headlight. Headlight – that is trying to convey something to me. Think. Think . . .

I've got it! There was no broken glass on the road. What kind of headlight is least likely to be smashed by an impact? The kind covered with a wire grille, like you see on those low, fast sports cars. And it must have been a low-slung fast car (with an expert driver) to get round this corner at the pace it did, without going off the road.

Sum up. There's reasonable hypothetical evidence to suppose that the criminal is an expert, reckless driver, is owner or manager of an efficient public garage, and owns a sports car with wire-protected headlamps. It is probably a pretty new car, or the difference between the original right-hand mudguard and the new left-hand one would have been noticed, though I suppose he might have faked the new one to look as though it had been worn a bit – scratches, dust, etc. Oh, and another thing: either his garage must be in rather a lonely place, or he must have some efficient sort of dark-lantern; otherwise he might have been spotted doing the repairs at night. Also, he must have gone out again that night to get rid of the damaged parts he'd removed from the car; and there must be some river or thicket fairly near into which he could throw them – he couldn't afford just to put them on the garage dump.

Heavens – it's long after midnight. I must go to bed. Now that I've made a beginning, I feel a new man.

28 June

Despair. How flimsy it all looks in the morning light. Why, now that I come to think of it, I'm not even sure whether any cars have wire screens over the headlamps; the radiators, yes, but the headlamps? Still, that's easily enough verified. But even supposing my whole train of argument has by some miracle hit the truth, I am almost as far away from him as ever. There are probably thousands of garage proprietors who own sports cars. The accident occurred about six twenty in the evening. Assuming it took him a maximum of three hours to refit with new parts and get rid of the old ones, he would still have had ten hours of darkness to play about with, which means that his garage may be anywhere within a three-hundred-mile radius. A bit less, perhaps. He wouldn't be likely to stop anywhere for petrol, with the mark of the beast on his car. But think of all the garages within even a hundred-mile radius. Am I going round to each of these, asking the proprietor if he owns a sports car? And what if he says, yes? The prospect is as sickening as the endless reaches of eternity. My hatred for this man must have swept my common sense right off its feet.

Perhaps this is not the chief reason for my depression. There was an anonymous letter this morning. Left by hand, before anyone was awake – presumably the same maniac or filthy joker who has been destroying my flowers. It's getting on my nerves. Here is the letter – cheap paper, block capitals, all the usual.

YOU KILLED HIM. I WONDER YOU DARE SHOW YOUR FACE IN THE VILLAGE AFTER WHAT HAPPENED ON 3 JANUARY. CAN'T

YOU TAKE A HINT? WE DON'T WANT YOU HERE, AND WE'LL MAKE THINGS SO HOT FOR YOU THAT YOU'LL BE SORRY YOU EVER CAME BACK. MARTIE'S BLOOD IS ON YOUR HEAD.

Sounds like an educated person. Or people, if the 'we' means anything. Oh, Tessa, what am I to do?

29 June

The darkest hour comes before the dawn! The hunt is up! Let me salute the new day with a salvo of commonplace. This morning I took the car out. I was still in the depths of depression, so I thought I'd go over to Oxford and see Michael. I took a short cut from the Cirencester to the Oxford road – a narrow track over the hills I'd never been on before. Everything was alive and sparkling in the sunlight, after the recent rain. I was gazing out over the wolds to my right – there was an astonishing field of clover, the colour of crushed raspberries – when I ran slap into a watersplash.

The car crawled out to the other side and stopped dead. I don't know anything about what goes on under the bonnet but, when my car stops, the thing to do is to leave it for a while to recover its temper, and then it usually starts up again. I was outside the car, shaking the water off my clothes – a great fan of water had gone up and descended on me when I hit the splash – and a bloke leaning over a farm gate addressed me. We bandied a few wisecracks about shower-baths. Then the bloke remarked that just the same thing had happened here one night this winter. Idly, just to make conversation, I asked him what day that was. The question turned out to be an inspiration. He did some exceedingly complex calculations in his head, involving a visit of his mother-in-law, a sick sheep, and a wireless set that had broken down, and said, 'January the third. Ar, that's what it were, third of January. No mistake about it. After nightfall.'

At this point – you know the way idiotically irrelevant phrases come into one's head – I found that my mind's eye was staring at the words, 'Washed in the Blood of the Lamb' – I remember now I'd seen them on a poster outside a Methodist chapel on the way. The writing on the wall, in more senses than one. The next thing that happened was that the word 'blood' linked up with the anonymous letter I received yesterday – 'Martie's blood is on your head.' And in that instant the fog rolled away, and I saw a vivid picture of Martie's murderer driving fast into the watersplash, as I had done, but on purpose – *to wash Martie's blood off his car*.

My mouth was quite dry when I asked the man, as nonchalantly as I could:

'Do you remember by any chance exactly what time it was – when this other chap ran into the watersplash?'

He took his time about it. Everything trembled in the balance – how satisfactory these old clichés are – then he said:

''Tweren't seven o'clock. Quarter or ten to, I reckon. Ar, that'd be it. Round about quarter to.'

My face must have been, as they say, a study. I saw him looking at me rather curiously, so I burst out with great enthusiasm:

'Why, that must have been my friend, then! He told me he'd lost his way after leaving my house and run into a splash somewhere on the Cotswolds,' etc., etc.

Behind this smokescreen my brain was doing some lightning calculation. It had taken me just over half an hour to get here. In a fast car, if he'd known the roads and not had to stop to consult a map, X could have done it between six twenty, when the accident occurred, and six forty-five. Seventeen odd miles in twenty-five minutes, average of forty m.p.h. Just possible for a sports car. I risked everything on another question.

'A fast, low-slung sports car, was it? Did you notice what make? Or the registration number?'

'She came into the ford fast enough, but I don't rightly know about the make of cars. It were dark, see, and them headlights dazzled I. Saw 'em coming quite a way off. Don't rightly remember the number, either. CAD something, it were.'

'That's it!' I said. (CAD are the new Gloucestershire registration letters. It's narrowing down.) I was thinking – with good headlights only a lunatic would drive fast into a watersplash, unless he wanted to push up a wave of water that would surge over the front of the car and wash off bloodstains. I only hit the splash so hard because I was looking at the scenery, which nobody does on a dark night. Why had I left the question of blood right out of my calculations before? Obviously, if X were to be stopped anywhere on his return journey, bloodstains on the car might be noticed and would be much more difficult to explain away than a crumpled wing. On the other hand, there would be a certain risk attached to stopping the car and wiping the blood off with a cloth – blood-stained clothes are not so easy to get rid of. Much the simplest thing would be to drive hard into a ford, and let the water do the rest. He'd presumably stopped his car to make sure it had been done thoroughly.

I became aware that the man was saying, with a suspicion of a wink on his brown-corduroy sort of face:

'A rare pretty one, sir, isn't she?'

For a moment I thought he was talking about X's car. Then, to my horror, I realised he meant X himself – herself, rather. It had never occurred to me, for some reason, that the person I was after could be a woman.

'I didn't know my friend had a – er – a passenger with him,' I stammered, trying to make the best of it.

'Ooh-ar,' he said. (Reprieved! Thank God for that!) So there had been a man and woman in the car. The swine had been showing off to her, just as I thought. I tried to get the man to describe 'my friend', but it wasn't much use. 'A tidy big chap, he were, very civil spoken. His ladyfriend was in a proper taking, being as she was scared running into the ford like that. Kept on saying, "Oh, do hurry up, George. We don't want to be here all night." But 'e warn't in no hurry. Stood there, just like 'e might be you, leaning against the mudguard and talking affable like.'

'Leaning against this mudguard? Just here?' I asked, dazed with my good luck.

'Ar. That's right.'

You see, I was leaning against the front left-hand wing of my car – the very one that I calculated would be damaged on X's car – and X had been leaning against it to hide the damage from this chap I was talking to. I put some more questions, as tactfully as I could, but wasn't able to find out anything further about the man or his car. I was at my wits' end. For want of something to say, I assumed a hideously jocular tone.

'Well, I'll have to ask George about this ladyfriend of his. Can't have that sort of thing, eh? And him a married man. Wonder who she was.'

The jest struck oil. The chap scratched his head.

'Come to think of it, I know her name, only it have gone out of my head. Saw her at the pictures last week. In Chel'unham. She wor' in her undies – and not much of them neither.'

'In her undies at the pictures?'

'Ar. In her undies. Mother was proper shocked. Now what was her name? Hey, Mother!'

A woman came out of the farm.

'What were the name of the picture us saw last week, Mother? The first one.'

'The supporting picture? *Housemaid's Knees*.'

'Ar. That's it. *Housemaid's Knees*. And this young lady – she were Polly, the housemaid, see? Cor, she didn't 'alf show her knees, too.'

'Daft like, I thought it was,' said the woman. 'Our Gertie's in service, but her don't have no lace lingerie nor no time to flaunt 'er charms like that thurr Polly. Give her what for, I would, if her did.'

'You say the girl my friend had with him that night was the one who took the part of Polly in the film?'

'I wouldn't swear to it, sir. Don't want to get the gentleman into trouble, eh? Hurr, hurr, hurr. The lady in the car kept her face turned away, see, most of the time. Dessay her didn't want to be reckernised. In a fair rage her was, when the gentleman turned on light inside car – "Turn the damn' thing off, George," she says. That's how I caught a sight of her face. And when I sees this yurr Polly on the pictures, I remarks to Mother, "Hey, Mother, if that bean't the young lady was in that car what stopped at ford!" – didn't I, Mother?'

'You did.'

I left the couple soon after that, having thrown out some dark hints about the desirability of their keeping all this to themselves. Even if they do talk, they'll have nothing to go on but the idea of an illicit relationship between the two, which I think I fostered with some skill. They couldn't remember the name of the actress who played the part of Polly, so I drove straight to Cheltenham and found out. *Housemaid's Knees* is a British film. One might have guessed that from the title – typical of the British genius for cheap, vulgar indecency. The girl's name is Lena Lawson. She's what they call 'a starlet' (God, what a word!). The film is on at Gloucester this week. I'll go tomorrow and get an eyeful of her.

No wonder the police didn't get these people as witnesses. Their farm is in a deserted place, down a road where few cars come even in the daytime. They didn't hear the BBC appeal, because their wireless was out of action that week. And in any case, what was there to connect this couple in the car with an accident nearly twenty miles away?

Here's the new data about X. His Christian name is George. His car has a Gloucestershire registration mark. Taken in conjunction with his knowledge of the existence of the watersplash (he surely wouldn't have time to go hunting for one on a map), this strongly suggests that he lives in the country. *And*, Lena Lawson is his weak spot. And when I say weak spot – I mean it – the girl was obviously terrified when my friend accosted them at the ford; she said, 'Oh do hurry up,' and tried to keep her face hidden. My next step is to get in touch with her. She'll obviously crack under pressure.

30 June

Saw Lena Lawson tonight. Quite a cute number, I must say. I shall look forward to meeting her. But Gawd what a film! Spent quite a lot of time after breakfast looking up the names of all the garage owners in the county whose initials begin with G. Made a list of a dozen or so. It's a queer sensation, looking down a list of names and knowing that you're going to obliterate one of them.

My plan of campaign is beginning to occupy my mind. I'll not write it down till I've worked out the general line. I feel somehow that Felix Lane is going to be useful. But all the ridiculous, boring little details one has to attend to before one can get in touch with one's victim, let alone kill him! – one might almost be organising an Everest climb.

2 July

It is an interesting comment on the fallibility of human intelligence – even of an intelligence above the average

– that for two days I have been racking my brains to work out a really safe murder plan, and only this evening did I realise it was quite unnecessary. The point is this – since no one but myself (and presumably Lena Lawson) knows that 'George' was the man who killed Martie, no one can ever discover my motive for killing George. I realise, of course, that legally motive does not have to be proved against an accused man provided that circumstantial evidence proves him guilty. But in actual fact, where there appears to be no possible motive, only direct eyewitness of the crime could secure conviction.

Provided George and Lena do not connect Felix Lane with Frank Cairnes, the father of the child they ran over, nobody on earth can ever find any connecting link between me and George. Now, no photographs of me appeared in the press in connection with Martie's death. I made certain of that. Mrs Teague was giving the reporters no chance. And the only people who know that Frank Cairnes is Felix Lane are my publishers, who are sworn to secrecy. Therefore, if I play my cards sensibly, all I have to do is to get an introduction to Lena Lawson, *as Felix Lane*, get at George through her, and kill him. If by any chance she or George has read my detective novels and seen the 'mystery' stunt – the 'who is Felix Lane?' stuff – that my publishers have been running, I shall merely say that it was all a publicity fake and that I have really been Felix Lane all along. The only danger would be if someone I knew found me posing as Felix Lane with Lena, but I don't think that will be very difficult to avoid. For one thing, I shall grow a beard before I have any doings with the luscious starlet.

George will take the mystery of Martie's death to the grave with him (where he'll have all eternity to meditate on the bestiality of road hogs), and in the same grave will be buried therefore my own motive for the 'crime'. The only possible danger could come from Lena. It may prove necessary to get rid of her too, but let us hope not – though I've no reason at present to suppose that she'd be any loss to the world.

Are you commenting unfavourably, ghostly confessor, on my desire to save my own skin? A month ago, when first the idea of killing Martie's murderer began to insinuate itself into my mind, I had no wish to go on living. But my will to live somehow grew strong, as my will to kill flourished; they have grown up together, inseparable twins. I feel I owe it to my revenge that I should get away with this killing scot-free – as George so nearly got away with his killing of Martie.

George. I've already begun to look upon him as an old acquaintance. I feel almost a lover's impatience and trembling anticipation of our meeting. Yet I've no real proof that he is the man who killed Martie; nothing more than his odd behaviour at the watersplash, and a feeling in my bones that I am right. But how shall I be able to prove it? How shall I ever be able to prove it?

Never mind. I'll not cross my bridges till I've come to them. What I have to remember is that I can murder George, or X, or whoever he is, with absolute impunity – as long as I don't over-elaborate or lose my head. An accident, that's what it must be. No nonsense about subtle poisons and complex alibis, just a little push when he and I are walking along a cliff, or crossing a street, that sort of thing. No one will ever know my motive for wanting to kill him, and therefore no one will have any reason to doubt that it was a genuine accident.

Yet, in a way, I'm sorry it must be like this. I'd promised myself the satisfaction of his agony – he does not deserve a quick death. I'd like to burn him slowly, inch by inch, or watch ants honeycomb his living flesh; or, there's strychnine, that bends a man's body into a rigid loop – by God, I'd like to bowl him down the slope into Hell . . .

Mrs Teague came in just then. 'Writing at your book?' she said. 'Yes.' 'Well, you're lucky you've got something to take your mind off—' 'Yes, Mrs Teague, very lucky,' I said gently. She was fond of Martie, too, in her way. She's long ago given up reading the mss on my desk. I used to leave notes for my apocryphal Life of Wordsworth lying about – that put her off all right. 'I like a good read, mind you,' she said once, 'but none of your highbrow stuff. Gives me the bellyache, it does. My old man was a great reader – Shakespeare, Dante, Marie Corelli – he'd read 'em all. Tried to get me to. Said I ought to improve my mind. "You leave my mind alone, Teague," I says, "one bookworm's enough in this house," I says, "Dante won't butter your parsnips for you." '

However, I've always kept my detective mss locked up, and I'm keeping this diary locked up too. Though, if any outsider happened to find it, he can assure himself that it's just another of Felix Lane's thrillers.

3 July

General Shrivenham dropped in this afternoon. Engaged me in a long controversy about the heroic couplet. An admirable man. Why is it that all generals are intelligent, kindly, charming and knowledgeable, whereas colonels are invariably bores and majors for the most part unspeakable? A subject 'Mass Observation' might investigate.

Told the General I'd be going off for a long holiday fairly soon. Couldn't stand the way this place reminded me of Martie. He gave me an exceedingly sharp glance out of his guileless old blue eyes and said:

'Not going to do anything foolish, I hope?'

'Foolish?' I repeated stupidly. For a moment I thought he must have somehow read my secret. It sounded like an accusation, almost.

'Mm,' he said. 'Take to drink. Women. Pleasure cruises. Shooting grizzlies. Silly nonsense, all that. Work's the only cure, take my word for it.'

I was so relieved this was all he meant that I was seized by a rush of affection for the old man – wanted to confess something to him, to reward him for not having found out my secret as it were – an interesting reaction. So I told him about the anonymous letter and my ruined flowers.

'Really?' he said. 'Horrible. Don't like that sort of thing at all. I'm a mild-tempered man, you know. Hate shooting animals, and that sort of thing. Of course, I used to do a bit of shooting when I was in the Service, tiger chiefly – but that was a long time ago, in India – beautiful beasts, graceful, a pity to shoot 'em, I gave it up after a bit. What I mean is, the type of fella who can write an anonymous letter – I'd have no compunction about shooting him, none at all. Reported it to Elder yet?'

I said no. An unholy gleam of relish lit up in the General's eye. He insisted on my showing him the anonymous letter and the beds where the flowers had been destroyed and asked a lot of questions.

'Fella comes in the early morning, eh?' he said, gazing commandingly over the terrain. His eye finally came to rest on an apple tree and he gave me a leer of outrageous irresponsibility.

'Just right, eh? Sit up there quite comfortably. Rug. Flask. Gun. Get him as he comes out in the open. Leave it all to me.'

After a little, I gathered from him that his intention was to sit up in the tree with his elephant gun and loose it off in the direction of the anonymous letter-writer.

'No. Damn it all, you can't do that. You might kill him.'

The General was quite wounded. 'My dear fellow,' he said. 'Last thing I want – get you into trouble; just frighten him, that's all. Cowards, those sort of fellas are. Cowardly. You wouldn't be troubled with him any more, bet you a pony. Save a lot of fuss and bother – keep the police out of it.'

I had to be rather firm with him. As he was going away, he said, 'Perhaps you're right. Might be a woman. Don't care about shooting women – there's so much of 'em too, more easy to hit by mistake, especially in profile. Well, keep your pecker up, Cairnes. Come to think of it, what you want is a woman. Not a flibbertigibbet. A good, sensible woman. Look after you, and make you think you're looking after her. Someone to quarrel with – you fellas who live alone, like to think you're self-sufficient, living on your nerves – if you haven't someone to quarrel with, you start quarrelling with yourself, and then where are you? Suicide or the madhouse. Two easy ways out. Not good enough, though. Conscience doth make cowards of us all. Not blaming yourself, about the boy's death, I hope, eh? No need to, my dear fellow. Rrrm. Dangerous to brood about it, though. A lonely man's an easy target for the devil. Well, come over and see me soon. Magnificent crop of raspberries this year. Made a pig of myself yesterday. Goodbye.'

He's as sharp as a needle, that old boy. That rambling, abrupt stage-military idiom is all my eye. He probably adopted it as camouflage from behind which he could surprise and rout his less talented colleagues, or just in self-defence. 'You start quarrelling with yourself', not yet, at any rate. I've got another quarrel on hand, and bigger game to hunt than tigers or anonymous letter-writers.

5 July

Another anonymous letter this morning. Very disagreeable. I cannot have this person distracting my attention, just when I most need to concentrate on the main business. Yet I feel unwilling to put the matter into the hands of the police. I feel that, if I knew who it was, I should stop worrying about these stupid little pinpricks. Will go to bed early tonight and set my alarm for 4 a.m. That ought to be early enough. Then I'll drive in to Kemble and catch the breakfast train to London. Have arranged to lunch with Holt, my publisher.

6 July

No luck this morning. The anonymous ill-wisher failed to put in an appearance. A good day in London, though. I told Holt I wanted to lay my new detective novel in a film studio. He gave me an introduction to a chap called Callaghan, who is something or other in British Regal Films Inc – the company that Lena Lawson works for. Holt was mildly facetious about my beard, which is now at the awkward age – a kind of raw and gawkish stubble. Told him, equivocally, that it was for purposes of disguise. Since I should be looking over the studio in the character of Felix Lane, and might have to hang about there quite a lot for material, I didn't want to risk being recognised as Frank Cairnes. I might, after all, run into some acquaintance of my Oxford or civil service days. Holt lapped it all up, looking at me in the slightly worried, proprietary way that publishers do look at their more successful authors – as though one were a temperamental performing animal which might any moment begin to sulk or try to escape from their circus.

I'll get a bit of sleep now. The alarm is set for 4 a.m. again. I wonder what I'll find in the net.

8 July

No luck yesterday. But this morning the stinging fly walked into the parlour. And what a fly! – grey, draggled, winter-sleepy. Ugh. I'd speculated quite a lot, off and on, who could be the author of those letters. They're usually written either by subnormal illiterates (which mine obviously weren't) or by respected, 'respectable' people with a hidden kink. I'd thought of the vicar, the schoolmaster, the post mistress – even Peters and General Shrivenham; that's the detective writer's mentality – choose the most unlikely person. Of course, quite rightly and properly, it turned out to be the most obvious one.

The latch of the garden gate clicked faintly just after four thirty this morning. In the dim, shabby light I saw a figure coming up the path. It moved slowly at first, indecisively, as though plucking up courage or fearful of discovery, then it broke into a curious little sort of rapid, consequential trot, like the gait of a kitten carrying a mouse.

I could see now it was a woman, and it looked remarkably like Mrs Teague.

I hurried downstairs. I'd left the front door unlocked, and as the envelope dropped into the letter box I flung the door open. It was not Mrs Teague at all. It was Mrs Anderson. I might have guessed. That day she avoided me in the street, her widowhood and lonely life, her starved maternal instinct that had been poured out upon Martie. She was such a quiet, harmless, nondescript old thing – I'd never thought about her at all.

There was a very painful scene. I said some wounding things, I'm afraid. She'd made me lose a lot of sleep, so she might have expected me to be a bit irritable. But the sting of her letters must have gone deeper than I'd thought. I felt cold and furious, and I stabbed back very hard. There was a kind of bedraggled, stuffy air about her, like you get in a railway compartment full of women after a long night-journey, which filled me with angry disgust. She said nothing. She stood there blinking, as if she'd just woken up from an unrefreshing sleep. After a bit she began to cry – a thin, hopeless drizzle. You know how that kind of thing unleashes all the bully in oneself – one piles on cruelty on cruelty to bury the struggling reproach and self-disgust. I had no mercy at all. I am not proud of myself. In the end, she turned and crept away, without a word. I shouted after her that, if anything more happened, I'd turn her over to the police. I must have been beside myself. A very, very nasty exhibition. But she shouldn't have written that about me and Martie. Oh God, I wish I was dead.

9 July

Tomorrow I pack up and leave this place. Frank Cairnes will disappear. Felix Lane will move into the furnished flat I've taken in Maida Vale. There will be nothing (I hope) to connect the two except Martie's one-eyed teddybear, which I'm taking with me – a gentle reminder. I think I've arranged for everything. Money. Accommodation address for Mrs Teague to send on my letters to. I've told her I shall probably be in London for some time, or else travelling. She'll look after the cottage while I'm away. I wonder, shall I ever come back? I suppose I ought to sell the place, but somehow don't like to; a place where Martie was happy. But what shall I do – afterwards? What does a murderer do when his occupation's gone? Does he start writing detective novels again? It sounds rather an anticlimax. Well, sufficient unto the day.

I feel that things have now been taken out of my hands. It's the only possible course for a vacillating sensitive like myself – to arrange circumstances in such a way that they compel him into action. That must be the truth behind the good old phrases like 'burning one's boats' and 'crossing the Rubicon'. I imagine J. Caesar was something of a neurotic too – the Hamlet streak – most of the really great men of action had it – look at T. E. Lawrence.

I just refuse to envisage the possibility that the Lena–George tie-up is a dead end. I couldn't face having to start all over again from the beginning. In the meanwhile, there's plenty to be done. I've got to create the character of Felix Lane for myself – his parents, his characteristics, his life history. I must *be* Felix Lane, otherwise Lena or George may smell a rat. By the time Felix Lane is word perfect, my beard should have reached years of discretion. Then I'll pay my first visit to British Regal Films Inc. No more of this diary till then. I think I've worked out the right line to take with Lena. I wonder will she fall for my beard – one of Huxley's characters advertises the aphrodisiac virtues of beards – I'll see if he's correct.

20 July

What a day! Went down to the film studio for the first time. I'd rather work in hell, or even in an asylum, than in a film studio. The heat, the pandemonium, the fantastic artificiality of it all – everything is like a two-dimensional nightmare – the people no more solid or real than the sets. And one is perpetually tripping over things: if it's not an electric cable, it's the legs of one of a horde of extras, who sit about all day twiddling their fingers like the wretched creatures in Dante's Limbo.

But I'd better start at the beginning. I was met by Callaghan, the chap Holt gave me an introduction to – very pale, thin, almost emaciated face, and a curiously fanatical glitter in his eyes, horn-rim spectacles, grey roll-collar jumper, flannel bags, all very dirty, untidy and high-tension – just like a stage caricature of a film executive. Obviously efficient to the fingertips (which were stained bright yellow – he rolls his own cigarettes, and while he's smoking one he's starting to roll the next – the most restless fingers I've ever seen).

'Well, old man,' he said, 'anything particular you want to see, or shall we tour the whole dump?'

I indicated a preference for the whole dump. In my innocence. It seemed to take hours and hours and hours. Callaghan prattled technicalities without cessation all the time, till my mind was like a piece of post office blotting paper. I only hope my beard concealed the absolute incomprehension of my mind. They'll find 'camera angles' and 'montage' (whatever that is) written on my heart when I'm dead. Callaghan is certainly nothing if not thorough. What little receptive power I started with was soon exhausted after half an hour of being tripped up by electric cable, blinded by arc lights, and mown down by bustling operatives. Incidentally, the language in this place would make a bargee or a sergeant major sound like a representative of the Purity League. All the time, I was looking out for Lena Lawson, and finding it more and more difficult to mention her name in an innocent, conversational manner.

However, Callaghan gave me an opening when we stopped to have a bit of lunch. We talked about detective novels and the impossibility of making films out of the best ones. He had read two of mine but was completely incurious about their author; I'd expected to have to stave off some awkward questions. Callaghan, however, was only interested in technique (which, typically, he pronounces 'technic'). Holt had told him, of course, that I was on the lookout for the setting and detail of a new thriller. After a bit he asked how I'd happened to light on British Regal for my investigations. I saw my opportunity and said that the last English film I'd seen was one of theirs, *Housemaid's Knees*.

'Oh, that,' he said. 'I should have thought you'd run a mile from any company which produced that sort of tripe.'

'Where's your *esprit de corps?*' I said.

'Damn it all – underclothes and stockbrokers' humour? Why it isn't even tolerable cinema.'

'That girl – what's her name? – Lawson. She wasn't bad, I thought. Plenty of go.'

'Oh, Weinberg's building her up,' Callaghan said somberly. 'From the legs upwards, you know. Up and up and up. She's all right as a peg to hang lingerie on. Thinks herself a second Harlow, of course. They all do.'

'Temperamental?'

'No, just dumb.'

'I thought all these film stars were perpetually going into tantrums,' I said, casting – I flatter myself – a very delicate fly indeed.

'You're telling me? Oh yes, la Lawson used to throw her weight about all right. But she's sobered down a hell of a lot lately. Quite subdued and biddable.'

'How's that?'

'Dunno. Maybe Love has come into her life. She had a sort of breakdown – when was it? – last January. Held up the film we were making for nearly a fortnight. Believe me, old man, when the leading lady gets to sitting about in corners, just weeping quietly away to herself, it's a menace.'

'Bad as that, was it?' I said, trying to keep my voice normal. January. 'A sort of breakdown.' Another piece of circumstantial evidence! Callaghan stared at me, with that febrile glitter in his eyes which makes him look like a minor prophet working up to some outsize piece of denunciation, but in actual fact – I should think – is just part of the stock-in-trade of the high tension, 100 per cent efficiency fiend.

He said, 'I'll say it was. Gave us all the jim-jams. Weinberg told her to take a week off in the end. She's got over it now, of course.'

'Is she here today?'

'No. Out on location. Thinking of making a pass at her, old man?' Callaghan leered at me amiably. I told him that my intentions were relatively honourable: I wanted to study a typical film actress for my new thriller, also I'd got plans about making it the kind of story which could be turned into a film – the Hitchcock type – and Lena Lawson might be the right person to play the heroine. I don't know whether this carried much conviction with Callaghan, he looked at me a bit sceptically, but it doesn't much matter whether he believes my motives to be professional or erotic. I'm visiting the studio again tomorrow, and he's going to introduce me to the girl then. I feel absurdly nervous about it – I've never had anything to do with her sort before.

21 July

Well, I've got that over. What an ordeal! I didn't know what to say to the girl at first. Not that there was any need to. She gave me a perfunctory hand, shot a rather neutral sort of look at my beard, as though reserving judgement, and instantly launched forth into a long rigmarole to Callaghan and me about someone called Platanov. 'That fiend, Platanov!' she said. 'Do you know my dears he rang me up four times last night well I ask you what is a girl to do of course I don't mind attentions but when it comes to having one's footsteps dogged and being persecuted on the telephone well as I told Weinberg it'll drive me crackers. The man's a fiend incarnate my dears he actually had the nerve to turn up at the station this morning luckily I'd told him the train left at nine ten when it really goes out five minutes earlier so I saw him chasing it down the platform just like the Scissors' Man definitely a fiendish turn of speed and you know what he looks like my dears a positive nightmare and it's not as if I could have anything more to say to him is it?'

'No, of course not,' said Callaghan soothingly.

'I keep on telling Weinberg he must ring up the Embassy and have the man deported the country's not big enough to hold both of us either he goes or I but of course all these Jews are in league I must say we could do with a bit of Hitler here though I do rather bar rubber truncheons and sterilisation. Well now, as I was saying . . .'

She went on and on for some time longer. There was something engaging about the way she assumed that I knew the context of her speech. I've no idea – probably never shall –whether the fiend Platanov is a white slaver, a talent scout, and agent of the GPU, or just an infatuated admirer. It's all of a piece with this incredibly unreal world – there's simply no knowing where film leaves off and real life begins. However, Lena's monologue gave me an opportunity to study her in some detail. She certainly had got a not unattractive, vulgar, vivacity; if she's now 'quite subdued and biddable', as Callaghan said, she must have been a proper handful before. I was rather surprised that she should be so like the film Polly in appearance, but obviously the chap at the ford would not have recognised her otherwise. Tip-tilted nose, wide mouth, very thick white-gold hair rising in a sort of wave or tiara above her forehead, blue eyes. Her features, except for the mouth, are quite delicate, which contrasts oddly with her gamine expression. But these inventories are useless – I've never seen a physical description of anyone in a book which gave a clear mental pictue. To look at her, you'd never think she had anything on her mind. Maybe she hasn't. No, I refuse to admit that possibility.

I stared at her while she was talking, thinking, This is one of the last two people to see Martie alive. I didn't feel any horror or rancour against her – only a burning curiosity and impatience to know more, to know everything. After a bit she turned to me and said:

'Now you must tell me all about yourself, Mr Vane.'

'Lane,' said Callaghan.

'You're an author, aren't you? I love authors. Do you know Hugh Walpole? I think he's a lovely author. But of course you look much more like my idea of an author than he does.'

'Well, yes and no,' I said, rather overwhelmed by this frontal attack. I couldn't take my eyes off her mouth. She opens it eagerly when one begins to speak, as though she's about to guess what one is going to say. A not unattractive mannerism. I really can't imagine what Callaghan meant when he called her 'dumb': frivolus, no doubt, but not dumb.

I was floundering about, trying to say something to the point, when someone bawled out her name. She had to get back on the set. Despair. I saw it all slipping out of my hands. It was this that made me screw up my nerve and ask her if she'd have lunch with me some time soon, at the Ivy, I added, guessing her tastes. It worked like a charm. 'Little lambs eat ivy,' as the riddle goes. She looked at me, for the first time, as though I were really there and not an extension of her own fantastic little ego, and said Yes, she'd love to, what about Saturday? So that's that. Callaghan gave me an ambiguous look, and the party broke up. The ice – though that is scarcely the correct word where Lena's concerned – has been broken. But how, in heaven's name, am I to get any further? Lead the conversation round to motor cars and manslaughter? Transparent.

24 July

Well, say what you like, the expenses of this murder are going to be very heavy. Apart from the expense of spirit and the waste of shame involved in entertaining Lena, there are the actual bills. The girl eats with astonishing gusto – the little contretemps of last January does not seem to have impaired her appetite for long. Of course, I shall save a certain amount on ammunition and/or poison; I've no intention of using such crude and dangerous methods upon George. But the road to George, I can see, is going to be paved with five-pound notes.

You perceive, gentle but no doubt perspicacious reader, that I'm in good spirits as I write this. Yes, you're right. I believe I'm getting warmer, I believe I'm really moving in the proper direction.

She turned up at the Ivy today in a sophisticated dress, black with touches of white, and one of those cute little eye-veils, all set to absorb lunch and admiration in equal quantities. I think I played up to her pretty well. No, let's be honest, I had no difficulty at all in playing up to her, because she's really quite a fascinating creature in her way and it will obviously pay me to combine pleasure with business, as long as I don't get soft. She pointed out two famous actresses lunching there and said didn't I think they were divinely beautiful creatures, and I said Yes, not so bad, suggesting with a look that they couldn't hold a candle to Lena Lawson. Then I pointed out a bestselling novelist to her, and she said she was sure my books were much nicer than his. So that made us all square, and things were going famously.

After a bit, I found myself telling her all about myself – all about Felix, that is. My early struggles, my travels, my legacy and the fat income from my books (an important part of the saga, this). There's no harm her knowing the size of my bank balance; my brass may succeed where my beard fails. Of course, I kept the story as near to my real life history as possible. No point in gratuitous embroidery. I was chattering away – the solitary with an audience at last, quite an agreeable sensation – feeling no urgent desire to force the issue, when suddenly I saw an opening and took it. She asked me if I'd lived in London for long. I said, 'Yes, off and on. I find it easier to work here. I really preser the country, though – I suppose that's because I'm a countryman. I was born in Gloucestershire.'

'Gloucestershire?' she said, almost in a whisper. 'Oh, yes.'

I was watching her hands. They tell more than the face, especially when it's an actress. I saw the nails of her right hand – they are varnished red – bite into the palm. But that wasn't all. The point is, she didn't say anything more just then. There's no doubt she was seen near our village soon after the 'accident', and there's not much doubt that George lives in Gloucestershire. You see the point? If she hadn't something to conceal, the natural thing would be for her to have said, 'Oh, whereabouts in Glucestershire? I've got a friend who lives there.' Of course, it might be simply an intrigue with George that she's wanting to conceal. But I doubt it. Girls like her are not coverd with guilt and confusion nowadays by that sort of thing. What else but the fact that she had been in the car when Martie was killed could have made her go suddenly silent at the mention of Gloucestershire?

'Yes,' I went on. 'In a little village near Cirencester. I'm always meaning to go back there, but I've somehow never quite managed.'

I didn't dare mention the name of the village. That might have scared her off altogether. I watched her pinched nostrils and the strained withdrawn look in her eyes for a moment. Then I began to talk about something else.

At once she started chattering away faster than ever. Relief will loosen anyone's tongue. I felt oddly grateful and friendly towards her for that moment of self-exposure and laid myself out to please. Never in my wildest dreams have I imagined myself giggling and exchanging coy glances with a film actress. We both drank a goodish amount. After a bit of this, she asked me what my Christian name was.

'Felix,' I said.

'Felix?' She wiggled the tip of her tongue at me – 'roguishly' is the word, I believe. 'I think I'll call you "Pussy", then.'

'You'd better not, or I shall refuse to have anything more to do with you.'

'You do want to see me again, then?'

'Believe me, I don't intend to lose sight of you for a long time,' I said. The opportunities for tragic irony are becoming quite alarmingly plentiful; I mustn't get into the habit of it. There was a good deal more of this kind of badinage, which I won't embarrass myself by writing down. We're dining together next Thursday.

27 July

Lena is not such a fool as she looks – or rather, as people of her appearance are assumed to be. She certainly gave me a nasty shaking-up this evening. It was after the theatre. She asked me to come in for a final drink – I'd taken her back to her flat. She was standing by the fireplace, rather pensive, and suddenly she swung round to me and said point-blank:

'What's the idea of all this?'

'The idea?'

'Yes. Taking me around and spending your money? What's on your mind?'

I stammered out something about the book I wanted to write – getting ideas – the possibility of writing one suitable for film adaptation.

'Well, when are you going to get started?'

'Started?'

'That's what I said. D'you know, you've not said a single word about this book yet. Where do I come in, anyway? Am I meant to be the pen wiper, or what? I'll not believe in this book of yours till I see it.'

For a moment I was paralysed. I felt she must somehow have guessed what I was after. Staring at her, I thought I saw something like apprehension, distrust, fear in her eyes. Then I wasn't sure if it was that. But still, I think it was sheer panic which made me say:

'Well then, it wasn't just the book. It wasn't the book. When I saw you in that film, I wanted you. The loveliest thing. I'd never seen – '

The fright she'd given me must have made me sound exactly like the confused, timid lover. She raised her head, her nostrils distended, a different look on her face.

'I see,' she said. 'I see . . . Well?'

Her shoulders drooped towards me. I kissed her. Ought I to have felt like Judas? I didn't, anyway. Why should I, though? It's a business deal, give and take, we've both got something to gain by it. I want George and Lena wants my money. I realise now, of course, that the scene she was staging about the book was simpy a manoeuvre to make the timid admirer declare himself. She must have felt all along that the book was just a pretext on my part, and she wanted to bring me to the point. Where she went wrong was in her idea of what the book was a pretext for. Really, it's turned out very well. Making love to her was like a whetting of my revenge.

After a bit, she said, 'I think you'll have to shave your beard off, Pussy. I'm not used to them.'

'You'll get used. I can't take it off. It's my disguise. I'm really a murderer, you see, in hiding from the police.'

Lena laughed prettily.

'What a liar you are! You couldn't hurt a fly, Pussy darling.'

'If you call me that again, you'll see if I can't hurt a fly.'

'Pussy!'

Later, she said, 'It's queer, me falling for you. You're no Weissmuller, are you, my sweet? It must be the funny way you look at me sometimes, as if I wasn't there, or transparent, or something.'

What a transparent little hypocrite she is herself! But nice. As a pair, we should win the hypocrisy stakes against all comers.

29 July

She had dinner at my flat yesterday evening. A very unpleasant thing happened. Luckily it passed off all right in the end, and if we hadn't had the quarrel, maybe she wouldn't have told me about George. But it's a warning to me not to get careless. I can't afford to make slips at this game.

I had my back to her. I was rummaging in the cupboard for drinks. She was wandering about, giving one of her quickfire monologues.

'So Weinberg started to bawl me out, Whaddy'a think y' are? An actress or a stuffed eel? I don't pay you to go about looking like a stick of Edinburgh rock, do I? What's the matter with you? Fallen in love or something, you dumb cluck? Not with you Father Time I said not with you so there's no need to get all burned up I say Pussy what an angelic little room you do do yourself well don't you? And oh, *look*! if it isn't a teddybear – !'

I jumped up. It was much too late. She came out of my bedroom carrying Martie's teddybear, which I kept on the mantelpiece. I'd forgotten to put it away. For some reason, I lost my head completely.

'Give it to me,' I said, making a snatch at it.

'Naughty! Mustn't snatch! So little Felix keeps dolls. Well, we live and learn.' She made a face at the bear. 'So this is me rival!'

'Don't be such a damned little idiot. Put it back!'

'Oh, oh, oh. Ashamed because he plays with toys?'

'As a matter of fact, it belonged to a nephew of mine. He died. I was very fond of him. Now will you give—'

'Oh, so that's it.' Her face changed. I saw her breasts heaving. She looked a holy terror and quite amazingly attractive. I thought she was going to scratch my face. 'So that's it. I'm not good enough to touch your nephew's teddybear? Think I might defile it, do you? It's me you're ashamed of, is it? Well, take the bloody thing!'

She flung the teddybear down violently on the floor at my feet. Something flared up in me. I smacked her in the face, hard. She came at me and we fought. She was abandoned and furious, like an animal in a trap. Her dress got torn away from her shoulders. I was far too angry to feel any distaste for this extraordinary scene. After a while, her body went soft and she moaned, 'Oh, you're killing me,' and we were kissing each other. She was flushed, but I could still see the mark of my hand on her face.

Later she said, 'But you are ashamed of me really, aren't you? You think I'm a common little spitfire.'

'Well, you're quite at home in a rough house anyway.'

'No. I want you to be serious. You wouldn't introduce me into your family circle, would you? The old folks at home wouldn't approve. I know.'

'I haven't got one. For that matter, you wouldn't introduce me into yours. What's the point? We're much happier as we are.'

'What a cautious old thing you are! I do believe you think I'm trying to lead you up to the marriage lines.' Her eyes sparkled at me suddenly. 'Now that *is* an idea. I'd just like to see George's face when—'

'George. Who's George?'

'All right, all right. You don't have to jump on me, jealous. George is just – well, he's married to my sister.'

'So what?' (I'm learning the language, you see.)

'Nothing.'

'Go on. What's George to you?'

'Yes, you *are* jealous. A jealous, green-eyed Pussy. Well, if you must know, George used to try it on with me. I—'

'Used to?'

'That's what I said. I told him I didn't fancy myself as a home-breaker; though I must say Violet does ask for it.'

'You've not been seeing him lately? Is he worrying you?'

'No,' she said, in a queer, wooden, stilted sort of voice, 'I've not seen him for quite a bit.' I could feel her body rigid beside me. Then she relaxed, laughing audaciously, a little wildly, 'What the hell? It'd show George he's not ev— Look here, suppose we go down there this weekend.'

'Go down where?'

'Severnbridge. Where they live. In Gloucestershire.'

'But, my dear girl, I can't—'

'Of course you can. He won't eat you. He's a respectable married man, or supposed to be.'

'But why?'

She gazed at me seriously. 'Felix, do you love me? All right, don't look so alarmed, I'm not trying to string you up. Do you like me enough to do something without asking a lot of questions?'

'Yes, of course.'

'Well then, I've reasons for wanting to go back there, and I want someone with me. I want you with me.'

Her voice sounded a little harsh and uncertain. I wonder how near she was to telling me everything; about George, and the accident that must have been haunting her. But I couldn't trust myself to persuading her into a full confidence, and it would have been a bit too caddish just then, even for my present standards. Not that there was really much need. I seemed to sense behind her words a determination to have it out in the open, not with George, but with the horror she's been running away from all these months. What did I say at the beginning of this diary about the murderer's compulsion to return to the scene of his crime? She didn't kill Martie. But she knows who did. She was there. She feels impelled to exorcise the haunting, deadly fascination of that moment, and she wants me to help her. Me! Heavens, what a savage piece of irony on the part of the Doomsters!

I said, 'All right. I'll drive you down on Saturday.' I kept my voice light and uninterested. 'What's George? What does he do?' I asked.

'He owns a garage – in partnership – Rattery and Carfax. Rattery's his name. He's rather – it's sweet of you to say you'll come. I don't know whether you'll like him very much – he's not exactly your saucer of milk.'

A garage. She doesn't know whether I'll like him very much. George Rattery.

31 July

Severnbridge. I drove Lena down here this afternoon. I'd traded my old car in part exchange for a new one; undesirable to turn up with a Gloucestershire registration number. So here I am, in the enemy's citadel, my wits against his. I don't think there's any danger of recognition – Severnbridge is at the opposite end of the county from my village, and my beard alters me enormously. The difficulty is going to be to get a firm footing in the Rattery's' house, and to maintain it when I've got it. At present Lena is there and I'm staying at the Angler's Arms – she thought it best to break me gently to the Rattery household – for the moment I'm just a 'friend' who kindly brought her down in his car. I dumped her and her suitcase outside the house. She says she did not write to tell them she was coming. Is this because she was afraid George might refuse to have her here? Very likely. He might well be nervous, considering the secret they share together – nervous of her getting hysterical when she saw him again and was reminded of it.

When I'd unpacked, I asked the boots which was the most efficient garage here. 'Rattery and Carfax,' he said. 'That's the one near the river, is it?' I asked. 'Yes, sir, backs on to it; just this side of the bridge, going up the High Street.' Two more facts in the case against George Rattery. I'd worked it out that his garage must be an efficient one or it would not have in stock the necessary spare parts for replacing those damaged in the accident. And it backs on to the river – that's where the damaged parts disappeared, I knew he'd hidden them somewhere like that . . .

Just then, Lena rang me up. They wanted me to go round there for dinner. I feel desperately, miserably nervous. If I feel like this just because I'm going to meet him for the first time, what'll I feel like when I'm going to kill him? Calm as a nun, probably, familiarity with one's victim should breed contempt and I'm going to study George Rattery with the flaying eye of hatred. I shall take my time, I shall glut my hatred and contempt for him before he dies – feed on him like a parasite on its host. I hope Lena doesn't start getting too affectionate towards me at dinner. Now for it.

1 August

An obnoxious creature. A very, very objectionable man indeed. I'm glad. I had been more than a little afraid, I realise it now, that George might turn out to be a sympathetic character. But that's all right; he's not. I shall have no compunction at all about putting his light out.

I knew it the minute I went into the room, before he had said a word. He was standing by the fireplace, smoking a cigarette. He held it between first and second fingers, his elbow raised, his forearm horizontal – an unpleasingly self-important attitude – the attitude of a man who wants everyone to know that he is master in his own house. He stood there, a cock on a dunghill, eyeing me superciliously for a moment or two before he came forward.

After I'd been introduced to his wife and his mother, and given a peculiarly disagreeable cocktail, George went straight on with what he'd been saying before I came. Typical of his bullocking tactlessness, his innate bad manners. However, it gave me an opportunity to study him and I measured him like an executioner measures his man for the drop. He wouldn't need a big drop, he's so heavy: a big, fleshy man, his head recedes upward at the back, and the top of it slopes down to a low forehead. He has a pseudo-cavalry moustache, which does not succeed in hiding his arrogant, negroid lips. I should say he was in the middle forties.

I see the result looks like a caricature. I daresay some women – his wife, for instance – would think him a fine figure of a man. Admittedly, my eye is jaundiced. But there's a crass, over-bearing quality about him which would turn any sensitive stomach.

After he'd finished his monologue, he looked at his watch in a marked manner.

'Late again,' he said.

No one made any comment.

'Have you spoken to the servants, Vi? They're getting later with the dinner every day.'

'Yes, dear,' his wife said. Violet Rattery is a washed-out, dispirited, pathetically eager-to-please version of Lena.

'Huh,' said George. 'They don't seem to pay much attention to you. I shall have to speak to them myself, I suppose.'

'Please don't do that, dear,' his wife said, in a flustered voice: she blushed, smiling timidly. 'We don't want them to be giving notice.' She caught my eye, and flushed again, painfully.

She just asks for it, of course. George is the sort of man whose nastiness thrives on that kind of submissiveness from the people around him. He's an anachronism, really. His thick-skinned, brutal type was the natural thing in apeman days (Elizabethan days too; he'd have made a good sea captain or slave driver) but in a civilisation that gives no scope for those qualities, except an occasional war, his crude sort of power is confined to the bullying of his own household, and goes bad for lack of wider exercise.

It's extraordinary how hatred sharpens the eye. I feel I know more about George already than about people I've known for years. I gazed at him politely. I was thinking, There's the man who killed Martie, who ran him down and gave him no chance at all, who finished a life worth more than a dozen of his sort, the one thing left for me to love. Never mind, Martie. His time is coming too. Soon.

At dinner I sat next to Violet Rattery, with Lena opposite me and old Mrs Rattery on my left. George, I noticed, kept glancing from Lena to myself – trying to sum up the situation. I would not say he was jealous, he's too self-satisfied to imagine that a woman could prefer anyone else to himself, but he was obviously puzzled as to what Lena wants with an odd fish like Felix Lane. He treats her in an offhand, slightly proprietorial way, as though he was an elder brother. 'George used to try it on with me,' Lena had said that night at my flat. I wonder, was that only half the truth? There is a suggestion of intimacy in the very offhandedness of his behaviour towards her.

At one point he said, 'So you've taken to poodle-curls too, Lena?' He leaned over and ruffled the curls at the back of her head, glancing at me in a challenging sort of way and saying, 'They're slaves to fashion, the ladies, aren't they, Lane? If some pansy from Paris told them that bald heads were all the rage, they'd shave off their hair pronto, eh?'

Old Mrs Rattery, who sat beside me surrounded by a faint aura of censure and mothballs, said:

'In my young days a woman's hair was considered her crowning glory. I'm glad all this Eton-crop nonsense has gone out.'

'You standing up for the younger generation, mater? What's the world coming to?' said George.

'The younger generation can stand up for themselves, I fancy – some of them at any rate.' Mrs Rattery was staring straight in front of her, but I got the impression that the second part of her remark was aimed at Violet, also that she conceives George to have married into a lower social stratum – which is true enough. She treats Violet and Lena with a kind of patient, grande dame tolerance. Not a very nice old lady.

After dinner the womenfolk (as no doubt George would call them) left him and me over the port. He was evidently ill at ease – didn't know what to make of me at all.

He tried the usual gambit, 'Heard the one about the Yorkshire woman and the organist?' he asked, drawing his chair confidentially nearer. There were a good many more where that one came from. I listened to it and laughed as convincingly as possible. Having thus, in his sly, hippopotamus manner, broken the ice, he proceeded to pump me for details about myself.

I've got the Felix Lane saga by heart now, so there was no difficulty about that.

'Lena tells me you write books,' he said.

'Yes. Detective novels.'

He looked a bit relieved. 'Oh, thrillers. That's different. Don't mind telling you, when Lena said she was bringing an author down here, I was a bit alarmed. Thought you'd be one of those highbrow Bloomsbury sort of fellows. Got no use for them myself. D'you make a good thing out of it – the writing game?'

'Yes, I do pretty well. Of course, I've got some money of my own. But I suppose I make betwen £300 and £500 on each book.'

'The devil you do!' He looked at me almost with respect. 'A bestseller, eh?'

'Not quite that yet. Just a moderately successful hack.'

His eyes shyed away from me a little. He took a gulp of port and said, with over-deliberate insouciance, 'Known Lena for long?'

'No. Just a week or so. I'm thinking of writing something for the films.'

'Nice girl. Plenty of spirit.'

'Yes, she's a fetching number.' I said it quite unthinkingly. George's face went all shocked and incredulous, as if he'd suddenly caught sight of a viper in his bosom. Dirty stories are one thing, it seems, and levity about his own 'womenfolk' another. He suggested, very stiffly, that we should join the ladies.

Can't write more now. Just off for a drive with my prospective victim and his family.

2 August

As we walked out of the front door yesterday afternoon – Lena, George, his son Phil, a schoolboy about twelve years old, and myself – I could have sworn that Lena stopped dead for an instant in a kind of panic. I've gone over the scene again and again, trying to visualise it clearly. It all happened so quickly that I had not time to realise its implications at the moment. On the surface, there was nothing in it at all. We came out on to the steps, in the sunlight. Lena paused for a fraction of a second, and said, 'The same car?' George who was a little behind her, said, 'What d'you mean?' Am I just imagining an undertone of fear, of menace in his voice? Lena replied, with a touch of confusion, I think, 'You've still got the same old car?' 'Same old? – I like that! She's not done ten thousand yet. What d'you think I am – a millionaire?'

The whole thing could be susceptible of a perfectly innocent interpretation, that's the trouble. We got in; George and Lena in front, Phil at the back with me. Phil slammed the car door behind him, and George slewed round and exclaimed angrily, 'How often do I have to tell you that these doors don't need to be slammed? Can't you shut the thing quietly?' 'Sorry,

Dad,' Phil said, looking hurt and resentful. Of course, George *may* have been in a bad temper before we started, but I suspect that he was shaken up by what Lena had said – or not quite said, and took it out on Phil in consequence.

George is certainly a pushful driver. I can't honestly say he drove recklessly yesterday afternoon, but he shouldered along through the Sunday traffic as though he had a sort of right of way, like a fire engine. There were numbers of cyclists three abreast. He didn't abuse them, as I rather expected him to do, but shaved past very close and cut in sharply in front of them – obviously trying to panic them or force them to collide with each other. At one point he said to me, over his shoulder, 'Know this part of the world, Lane?' 'No,' I said, 'I've always been meaning to come back here, though. I was born at Sawyers Cross, you know, the other end of the county.' 'Really? Pretty little place. Been through it once or twice myself.'

He had a nerve all right. I was watching the side of his face, the jaw muscle didn't even tighten when I mentioned the name of the village where he had killed Martie. Shall I ever make him betray himself? Lena was staring straight in front of her, hands clasped over her knees, immobile. I risked a lot when I said, 'Sawyers Cross'; suppose he were to become suspicious, or just out of idle curiosity make enquiries? He'd find that there had been no family called Lane in Sawyers Cross for fifty years. When we got out of the car, Lena seemed to avoid my eyes, she had been silent for the last quarter of an hour – since I mentioned Sawyers Cross – and that's pretty unusual for her, but not incontrovertible evidence of anything.

We got out, and I asked George to show me the points of his car. This was just an excuse, of course, to have a good look at it. It's got stone-guards all right, but there was no indication – to my novice eye, at any rate – that a wing or a bumper had been removed and a new one fitted. But after seven months, there wouldn't be; the trail (as I hope I always avoid expressing it in my detective novels) is cold. The only clues left are inside the heads of George and Lena; or maybe Lena alone – George has probably forgotten all about the incident by now. I can't believe that an odd killing here and there would rankle with him very long.

The question is, how am I to get at it? And, more important at the moment, what plausible reason can I give for staying on here? Lena will be going back to town tomorrow. Perhaps I'll find an opening this afternoon; we're all supposed to be playing tennis at the Ratterys'.

3 August

That's settled, anyway. I'm here for a month – on George's invitation, more or less – which ought to be long enough. I'd better begin at the beginning.

When I got there, none of the people they'd invited had arrived yet, so George suggested he and I should have a knock-up with Lena and Phil. We waited on the court for a little and then George started to bawl out for Phil who was somewhere in the house. This brought Violet running out. She tried to draw George aside, and I heard her whisper something about 'doesn't want to play'.

'What's wrong with the boy?' George exclaimed. 'I don't know what's come over him lately. Doesn't want to play? Go and tell him he's damned well got to play. Sulking about upstairs! I never—'

'He's a bit upset, George dear. You know, you were rather unkind to him this morning over his report.'

'My dear good girl, don't talk nonsense. The boy's been slacking this term. Carruthers says he's got plenty of ability, but if he doesn't pull up his socks he'll stand no chance for Rugby next year. Don't you want him to get a scholarship?'

'Of course, dear. But—'

'Well then, somebody's got to tell him to buck up. I will not have him mooning about all the time at school and wasting my money. He's thoroughly spoilt, if you—'

'There's a wasp on the back of your shirt,' Lena interrupted, gazing at him with quite fictitious concern.

'You keep out of this, Lena,' he said dangerously. I thought I really couldn't do with any more of the squalid scene, also, I was a bit sorry for Phil if his father went to lug him out in this mood, so I said I'd go and say we wanted him to play. George looked distinctly taken aback, but he couldn't very well forbid me to go.

I found Phil lurking in his bedroom – in a very obstinate frame of mind indeed at first. However, we had a talk – he's really not a bad kid at all – and after a bit it all came out. He hadn't been slacking last term, but there was a boy at the school who'd made a dead set at him and this got on his mind (don't I know how!) so that he couldn't concentrate on his work. Phil was in tears by this time. For some absurd reason, it reminded me of the day I'd ticked Martie off for ruining my roses, and I suggested, quite impulsively, that perhaps he'd like me to give him a few lessons in the holidays – a couple of hours a day, say, so that he could make up the lost ground.

It was only when Phil was in the middle of a stammering and most embarrassing display of gratitude that it occurred to me that here was an excellent pretext for staying on at Severnbridge. A nice example of doing good that evil may come of it – if one can call the removal of George an evil. I waited till George was in good humour, flushed by victory in a set of tennis, and then broached the idea – said I'd taken a fancy to the town, thought of stopping on a few weeks and making a start with my new book in the peace of the country, and suggested he might like me to give Phil a bit of coaching. George was a trifle sticky at first, but soon agreed to the idea and even went so far as to invite me to put up at his house. I refused politely and I think, to his relief. Not at any price would I stay in the Rattery household for a month. It's not that I feel any taboo against killing the man whose salt I've eaten; I just couldn't stick the sensation of being perpetually on the edge of some domestic squabble. Besides, I don't want to risk George's snooping about and finding this diary. My daily reading with Phil will give me all the foothold I need here.

After that had been fixed up, I watchd the tennis for a bit. George's partner in the garage, Harrison Carfax, was playing with Violet against George and Mrs Carfax. The latter is a big, dark-haired, gipsyish, come-hither sort of woman. I got the impression that she might be one of the reasons for George's return of good humour, I distinctly saw his fingers delaying on hers once when he handed her the tennis balls to serve, and she gave him one or two sultry looks all right. One can scarcely wonder; her husband's a dreary, dried-up little nondescript if ever I saw one.

Lena came and sat down beside me – we were rather apart from the rest. She looks amazingly attractive in tennis dress; it suits her supple movements, and she manages to put on a sort of synthetic but appealing schoolgirlishness to match it.

'You're looking very sweet,' I said.

'Go and tell that to the Carfax woman,' she said, but I could see she was pleased.

'Oh, I'll leave George to do that.'

'George? Don't be so absurd.' She was almost snappish about it. Then she recovered herself and said, 'I've hardly seen you since we've been here. You've been going about with a faraway look in your eyes, as though you'd lost your memory or got indigestion or something.'

'That's my artistic temperament coming out.'

'Well, you might snap out of it and give a girl a kiss now and then. At least.' She leant over and whispered in my ear. 'There's no need to wait till we get back to London, Pussy, you know.'

Nobody can say I'm not a single-minded murderer. I'd so concentrated on fixing things up with George that I'd forgotten about my attachment to Lena. I tried to explain to her why I was staying on here. I was afraid she would start to get temperamental – the fact that we were in full view of a dozen people would have stimulated rather than suppressed her. But, oddly enough, Lena took it quite quietly. Too quietly, in fact – I might have suspected something – there was a humorous, challenging lift at the corners of her mouth when I moved away to play a set of tennis, and halfway through it I noticed her deep in conversation with Violet. As we came off the court, I heard her saying to George (and obviously I was meant to hear it), 'George darling, how would you like your glamorous sister-in-law to stay on for a bit? We've finished making that film, so I thought I'd dig myself in here for a few weeks more of the simple country life. OK by you, chief?'

'This is all very sudden,' he said, giving her one of his calculating, slave market looks. 'I suppose, if Vi doesn't mind, we can put up with you. Why the change of heart?'

'Well, you see, I think I should pine away without my Pussy. But don't tell anyone.'

'Pussy?'

'Mr Felix Lane. Felix the Cat. Pussy. *Compris?*'

George gave a very loud, embarrassed, stupid laugh. 'Well I'm damned. Pussy! It does hit him off rather well. The way he pats the ball over the net. But really, Lena – ' He'd no idea I was listening. Perhaps it's just as well he didn't see my face then. I'll not forget that crack of his. But Lena – what does she think she's up to? Can it be possible that she thinks she's going to play me off against George? Or have I been making a damnable, inexcusable mistake about the girl all along?

5 August

Lessons with Phil in the morning, as usual. He's quite a bright youngster – heaven knows where he gets his brains from – but he wasn't in his best form this morning. From certain indications – his own wandering attention and a rather red-eyed look about Violet who passed me quickly as I came in – I guessed there must have been a dust-up in the Rattery household. In the middle of a Latin unseen Phil suddenly asked me if I was married. 'No. Why?' I said. I felt oddly ashamed, lying to Phil, though I lie like a trooper to the rest of the family without turning a hair.

'D'you think it's a good thing?' he asked, in a tight, severely controlled, precise little voice. His conversation is old for his years, like most only children's.

'Yes. I think so. It can be, anyway,' I said.

'Yes, I suppose so; for the right people. I shan't get married, ever. It makes people so miserable. I'd be afraid – '

'Love does make people miserable sometimes. It sounds all wrong, but it's quite true.'

'Oh, love – ' he said. He paused for a moment, then took a deep breath, and the words came out in a shocked rush, 'Dad hits Mummy sometimes.'

I didn't know what to say. I could see that he was desperately in need of some reassurance. Like any sensitive child, he's horribly torn by this squabbling between his parents – it's like living on the side of a volcano for him; no security. I was on the point of trying to comfort him; then, a revulsion from the whole business seized me; I didn't want to become involved, distracted. I said, a bit coldly, I'm afraid, that we'd better get on with the unseen. It was a wretched piece of cowardice really. I saw my betrayal of him reflected in Phil's face.

6 August

Had a look round the Rattery-Carfax garage this afternoon. Told George it might come in useful as material in a book – *nihil subhumanum a me alienum puto* is the detective novelist's motto though I didn't put it quite like that. Asked a number of idiotic questions which enabled George to patronise and me to discover that the garage keeps all spare parts of cars they're agents for. I didn't dare ask specifically about wings and bumpers – it might have made him suspicious that I was a policeman in disguise. I've found out already that he sometimes keeps his car there at night, though he's got a garage attached to his house.

Then we went out at the back. There's a patch of waste ground, with a godless rubbish dump on it, and the Severn at the far end. I wanted to have a look at this heap of old iron – not that I thought it likely that George would have been such a fool as to deposit his damaged wing there; so I delayed him with a little conversation.

'Pretty unsightly all this stuff is.'

'Well, what do you suggest we should do with it? Dig a neat hole and bury it, like the Anti-Litter League?'

George was quite up in the air. For such a self-satisfied creature, he's curiously touchy at times. Suddenly I decided to take a risk.

'Why don't you dump the stuff in the river? Don't you ever do that? Get it out of sight, anyway.'

There was a perceptible pause before he answered. I found myself trembling uncontrollably, so that I had to walk away from him towards the water's edge to prevent him seeing it.

'Good God, man, what an idea! I'd have the whole town council down on my head. In the river! That's a good one! I'll have to tell Carfax.' He was beside me now. 'Anyway, it'd be too shallow at the edge. Look.'

I was looking. I could see the bed of the river. But also I saw, twenty yards to my left, a derelict punt moored. Yes, George, it's too shallow at the edge to conceal anything, but you might easily have taken the punt into midstream and got rid of the tell-tale evidence there.

'I'd no idea the river was so broad here,' I said. 'I'd like to do a bit of sailing. I suppose I could hire a dinghy here?'

'I daresay,' he said indifferently. 'A bit slow for my taste, that game – sitting on one's fanny holding a piece of rope.'

'I'll have to take you out some day in a stiff breeze. You wouldn't call that "slow".'

I'd seen all I wanted to see. The old iron on the scrap heap was very old iron indeed. A dreadful eyesore. And I was pretty sure I'd seen a rat scuttling out of it when we were walking down; with a dump and the river, it must be heaven for them. Back in the garage, we came across Harrison Carfax. I happened to mention I'd like a bit of sailing, and he said his son kept a twelve-footer here which he was sure he'd lend me as he only used it at the weekends. It'll be a nice change for George, to get out on the river now and then. Might teach Phil to sail.

7 August

I nearly killed George Rattery this afternoon. Very, very nearly. I feel absolutely exhausted. No emotion. Just an aching emptiness where emotion ought to be – as if it was me, not him, who had been reprieved. No, not reprieve. A temporary stay of execution, that's all. It was so childishly simple, too – both my opportunity and his escape. Shall I ever get such an opportunity again? It's long after midnight already, and I've been going over and over and over what happened. Perhaps if I write it down, I'll be able to put it out of my head and get some sleep.

Five of us – Lena, Violet, Phil, George and myself – went for a drive this afternoon into the Cotswolds. We were to do a bit of sightseeing Bibury way, and then have a picnic tea. George showed me round Bibury as though he owned the village, while I tried to behave as if I hadn't been there a dozen times before. We leant over the bridge, staring at the trout, which are as fleshy and supercilious-looking as George himself.

Then we drove off high up on the hills. Lena was sitting at the back with Phil and me. She'd been acting very affectionate, and when we got out of the car she took my arm and walked very close to me. I don't know whether it was this that got George's goat. Something did, anyway, because, when we'd spread out the rugs just by the corner of a wood and Violet suggested we light a fire to keep the midges off, a really bloody scene began to boil up.

First, George sulked about having to fetch twigs. Lena started chaffing him, telling him that a little manual labour might reduce his figure. That didn't go down at all well. George, obviously simmering inside, picked on Phil, saying that as he was in the Boy Scout troop at his prep school, he'd better show them how to light a fire. The twigs were a bit damp, and poor Phil is no good at all with his hands. In any case, he'd no idea how to build a fire. George just stood over him, hectoring and scoffing at him, while the wretched lad fumbled with the sticks, wasted dozens of matches and blew his guts out trying to get the fire going. His face went redder and redder, and his hands began to tremble pitiably. George's display was sickening. After a good deal of this, Violet intervened – which was pouring oil, as they say, on the flames. George rounded on her, shouting that it was she who'd asked for a fire so what the hell did she mean by interfering, and anyway only futile little half-wits like Phil couldn't light a fire. This was too much for Phil – the senseless attack on his mother – he jumped up and said straight at George, 'Why don't you light it yourself then, if you're so good at it?'

The defiant little speech died away in a mutter – Phil hadn't quite the nerve to carry it right through. But George heard it all right. He gave Phil a box on the ears that sent him sprawling. The whole thing was horrible beyond words – the way George goaded the child into rebellion and then crushed him. I know I was furious with myself for not having the courage to interfere before this. I jumped to my feet; I believe I might have told George exactly what I thought of him (which would certainly have wrecked everything, including my future plans for George). However, Lena got in before me and said quite coolly, as if nothing had happened:

'You two go and have a look at the view. Tea'll be ready in five minutes. Go along, George, my sweet.' She gave him one of her most luscious and lingering glances, and he walked off with me like a lamb, or something like.

Yes, we went to look at the view. It was a splendid view. Almost the first thing I saw as we turned the corner of the wood, out of sight of the others, was a sheer drop of nearly a hundred feet, an old quarry. It takes a long time to describe, but it must have been all over in thirty seconds. I had moved away from George a little – there was an orchis I wanted to look at. When I got to it, I found myself on the edge of this quarry. There was the orchis, the sheer drop at my feet, the hills rolling round us, delicious with their rough grasses and clover and mustard, and there was George, his thick lips pouting beneath his moustache, poisoning the summer afternoon for Violet and poor little Phil. The man who had killed Martie. I seemed to see all this, and the rabbit hole on the cliff's edge, simultaneously. I knew exactly how I should destroy George.

I called out to him to come and have a look over here. He started to move towards me. I would call his attention to the stone crusher in the quarry beneath us. He would be on the very edge of the cliff. Then I would begin to walk on. But at my first step my foot would trip in the rabbit hole, I would fall heavily against George's legs, and he would go over the cliff. Its height and his weight would do the rest. It was a perfect murder. It didn't matter if anyone did happen to see us. I had no intention, in any case, of concealing the fact that I had tripped up and barged into George. But, since no one knew I had any motive for killing him, no one could doubt that it was an accident.

George was only five yards away now. 'Well, what is it?' he said, still strolling towards me. Then I made a fatal mistake – though I'd no way of knowing it was a mistake then. A sort of bravado seized me and I said to him – almost as though daring him to come on – 'There's a huge quarry here. A hell of a drop. Come and look.'

He stopped dead and said, 'Not for me, old man, thanks. I never could stand heights – no head for them. I get vertigo, or whatever it's called . . .'

So now I have to start all over again.

10 August

A party at the Ratterys' last night. Two little incidents, revealing things about George – if 'revealing' is the word for such a blatant character.

After dinner, Lena did one or two turns. Then we began to play a singularly erotic game called 'Sardines'. One person goes and hides, preferably in as confined a space as possible. Whoever finds him snuggles down beside him, and so on, till you get a cross between the Black Hole of Calcutta and a Babylonian orgy. Well, the first time we played, Rhoda Carfax was the 'he'. As it happened, I found her very quickly, in a cupboard full of brooms.

It was quite dark, and as I sat down beside her she whispered, 'Well, George, fancy you finding me so quickly. I must be magnetic.' I guessed from the ironic way she said it that she'd already told him where to look for her. Then she pulled my arm round her waist, put her head on my shoulder – and discovered that she'd made a terrible mistake. However, she carried it off very well and took no steps about removing my arm. Presently someone else came blundering down on the other side of Mrs Carfax. 'Hallo, it's Rhoda, isn't it?' he whispered. 'Yes.' 'So George found you first?' 'It's not George, it's Mr Lane.'

The chap who came in after me was James Carfax. It's interesting that he should have assumed I was George; he must be one of those complacent husbands.

George himself arrived third. I don't think he was too pleased to find company. At any rate, after one more turn of Sardines, he said we'd play something else (he's the kind of man who has to be bossing, even when it's only parlour games). So he started to organise an exceedingly rough and shrieking game, which involved kneeling in a circle and flinging a cushion at each other. He chose a very hard cushion, and made quite a rough-house, bellowing with laughter. At one point, he hurled the cushion deliberately with all his force into my face. I fell over sideways – it had got me in the eye and I was blinded for the moment. George gave one of his bellows of vacant laughter.

'Knocked him down like a fevver, it did!' he roared.

'You are an oaf,' said Lena. 'What's the idea knocking people's eyes out? The great big strong he-man, showing off.'

George clapped me on the shoulder with mock solicitude, saying, 'Poor old Pussy. Sorry, old man. No offence.'

I was furious, particularly at his using that idiotic nickname before all these people. I said, bogus hearty:

'That's all right, Rat, old boy. You don't know your own strength. That's all, isn't it?'

George was far from pleased. Teach him to keep his blundering, vulgar tongue to himself. I'm more and more inclined to think he's jealous about me and Lena.

I don't know. Perhaps it's that he's just baffled about it – can't make out what there is between us.

11 August

Lena asked me today why I didn't come and stay with the Ratterys for the rest of the month. I said I didn't think George would care for that very much.

'Oh, he doesn't mind.'

'How do you know?'

'I've asked him.' Then she looked at me seriously for a little and said, 'Darling, you don't have to worry. I'm through with George now.'

'You mean, there used to be something between you?'

'Yes, yes, yes,' she burst out. 'I was his lover. Now pack up and go home if you want to.'

She was nearly in tears. I had to try and comfort her. After a bit she said, 'You will come, then, won't you?'

I said, Yes, if George really didn't mind. I don't know if it's a stupid move on my part, but it's rather difficult to resist Lena. I'll have to keep my diary well hidden, but there's a great deal to be said for being on the spot. It's all very well to talk about accidents, but it's damned difficult when you try and work it out, to organise the right kind of 'accident' for George. I don't know enough, for instance, about cars to enable me to tamper with his. Any kind of mechanical accident is right out, as far as I'm concerned. Maybe living in his house will give me an inspiration. Accidents, they say, will happen even in the best-regulated families – and no one could call his family that. It will be nice, too, to be in the same house as Lena, though I hope she won't make me soft – there must be no room for love in my heart now – I am quite alone, and I must stay quite alone.

12 August

A nice afternoon on the river with young Carfax's dinghy. As I suspected last time I took her out – but there was not enough wind then to be certain – she carries a bit of lee helm and would be vicious to handle on a squally day. I really must take Phil out soon, he's obviously keen to come but I keep putting it off – I believe it's because I would have been teaching Martie to sail this month, if – All the more reason for taking Phil out; I cannot have too many reminders.

I've been wondering this evening how I am able to go on from day to day, seeing George, hating him in every fibre of my body so bitterly and inveterately that I am almost startled by the placid expression on my own face when I catch sight of it in a mirror. Hating him like this, body and soul, yet behaving towards him without any conscious effort at self-control or concealment and feeling no impatience now to get the thing done. It's not that I am afraid of the consequences; nor do I at all despair of discovering the right method. Yet it's true up to a point that I'm willing to procrastinate.

I believe the explanation is this: just as the lover often procrastinates, not through timidity but to prolong the sweet anticipation of love's fulfilment, so the man who hates wishes to savour his hatred, to gloat upon his unconscious victim, before he proceeds to the act by which his hatred will be consummated. This sounds far-fetched – so much so that I would not dare to confide it to anyone but my ghostly confessor, this diary. Yet I am convinced it is true. It may convict me of being a neurotic, abnormal creature – a thorough-going sadist – yet it answers so accurately my sensations when I am with George, I feel in my bones it must be the true explanation.

Doesn't it explain, too, the long 'indecision' of Hamlet? I wonder if any of the scholars suggested that it was due to his desire to prolong the anticipation of revenge, to eke out drop by drop the sweet and dangerous and never-cloying nectar of hatred? I don't think they have. It would be an agreeable piece of irony for me to write an essay on Hamlet, proposing this theory, when I've finished with George. By Jove, I've a damned good mind to do it! Hamlet was no hesitant, timid, veering neurotic. He was a man with a genius for hatred – one who brought it to a fine art. All the time he is supposed to have been vacillating, he was in reality sucking dry the body of his enemy; the final death of the King was no more than the flinging aside of an empty skin – the skin of a fruit sucked dry.

14 August

Talk about tragic irony! A most extraordinary conversation broke out at the dinner table last night. I don't know how it was started, or by whom, but it became a symposium on the Right to Kill. I think we began by discussing euthanasia. Should doctors, in incurable cases, 'strive officiously to keep alive'?

'Doctors!' exclaimed old Mrs Rattery, in her heavy, pig-lead sort of voice. 'Robbers, the whole lot of 'em. Charlatans. Wouldn't trust 'em an inch. Look at that India fella – what was his name? – cut up his wife and hid the pieces under a bridge.'

'Buck Ruxton, you mean, mater?' said George. 'Strange case, that.'

Mrs Rattery chuckled hoarsely. I fancied a glance of complicity passed between her and George. Violet blushed. It was a painful moment.

She said timidly, 'I do think, when people are incurably ill, they ought to be allowed to ask their doctors to put them out of their misery. Don't you think so, Mr Lane? After all, we do it to animals.'

'Doctors? Pah!' said old Mrs Rattery. 'Never had a day's illness in me life. Imagination, half of it – ' George guffawed a bit ' – and let me tell you, George, you'd be better off without all these tonics of yours. A great healthy brute like you paying a doctor to give him bottles of coloured water – through the nose too! I don't know what's come over your generation. A lot of hypochondriacs.'

'What's a hypochondriac?' asked Phil. We'd all forgotten he was there, I think. He'd only just been promoted to late dinner. I could see George had some crushing remark on the tip of his tongue, so I answered quickly:

'A person who likes to think he's ill, when he really isn't.'

Phil looked puzzled. He couldn't imagine anyone enjoying the idea of having a tummy ache, I expect. The conversation went on in this haphazard way for a bit. Neither George nor his mother listens to what anyone else says, they just pursue their own line of thought – if 'thought' is the word. I got rather irritated by this roughshod conversational method, and out of devilment said, blandly, to the table at large, 'But physical or mental incurables apart, what about the incurable social pest – the person who makes life miserable for everyone round about him? Don't you think one is justified in killing a person like that?'

There was an interesting moment of silence. Then several people began to speak at once.

'I do think you're all getting very morbid.' (Violet. Breathless, hostessy-y tones, with hysteria not far below the surface.)

'Oh, but think how many – I mean, where would one make a beginning?' (Lena, giving me a very long look indeed, almost as though seeing me for the first time – or was that my imagination?)

'Nonsense. Pernicious idea.' (Old Mrs Rattery, just plain shocked; perhaps the only straightforward reaction in the room.)

George didn't turn a hair. He obviously hadn't the least idea that my random arrow was featherd in him.

'What a bloodthirsty little chap your Felix is, eh Lena?' he said. It's typical of George's particular brand of moral cowardice that he never makes this sort of crack when he and I are alone together, and even in company he has to do it obliquely – shooting at me from behind Lena, so to speak.

Lena paid no attention to him. She was still gazing at me in that doubtful, speculative manner, her red mouth twisting up at one corner.

'But would you really, Felix?' she asked at last, soberly.

'Would I what?'

'Rub out a social pest – the sort of person you described?'

'Just like a woman!' George butted in. 'Always has to come down to particular cases.'

'Yes. I would. That kind of person has no right to live.' I added lightly, 'That's to say, I would if I could do it without running my neck into a noose.'

At this point, old Mrs Rattery charged into action. 'So you're a freethinker, Mr Lane? An atheist too, I daresay?'

I said soothingly, 'Oh no, ma'am. I have a very conventional mind. But do *you* consider there are any circumstances which justify murder – war apart, I mean?'

'In war it is a matter of honour. Killing, Mr Lane, is no murder where honour is at stake.' The old thing delivered herself of these excruciating antiquities in really rather an impressive way. With her heavy features and dominant nose she looked for a moment quite the Roman matron.

'Honour at stake? Your own honour, do you mean, or someone else's?' I asked.

'I think, perhaps, Violet,' boomed Mrs Rattery in her most Mussolini manner, 'we will leave the gentlemen over their wine. Phil, open the door. Don't stand there dreaming.'

George got confidential over the port. The relief of being rid of such a morbid, embarrassing topic of conversation, no doubt. 'Remarkable woman, the mater,' he said. 'Never forgets that her father was fifth cousin umpteen times removed to the Earl of Evershot. Don't think she's got used to the idea of me being in business, either. Needs must where the devil drives, though. She lost her money in the slump, poor old girl, you know – she'd be in the workhouse without me – you needn't let that go any further. Of course, titles mean nothing nowadays. I'm no snob, thank God. One's got to move with the times, I mean, eh? But there's something rather fine about the way the old girl clings to her pride. *Noblesse oblige*, and all that. Which reminds me, d'you know the one about the duke and the one-eyed housemaid?'

'No,' said I, fighting down the nausea . . .

15 August

Took Phil out sailing again this morning. A gusty wind, turning to rain later. The dinghy was a proper handful. Phil not very adroit with his hands, but learns quickly and has the nerve – the wild fascination by and surrender to danger – of the sensitive. Also, he told me how to kill his father.

Not consciously, of course. Out of the mouth of babes, etc. He had just taken the helm, and a particularly vicious gust nearly put the gunwale under. He luffed up, as I taught him to, then turned to me, laughing, his eyes quite brilliant with excitement.

'I say, this is jolly good fun, Felix, isn't it?'

'Yes. You did that very nicely. Your father ought to see you now. Look out! Keep your eyes over your shoulder. You can see the gusts coming, if you look to windward.'

Phil was obviously very pleased. George considers him – or pretends to consider him – an arrant coward. It's extraordinary the extent to which the character of children like Phil is conditioned by the need to justify themselves in the eyes of an unsympathetic parent, to prove the parent wrong.

'Oh yes,' he cried. 'D'you think – could we ask him to come out with us one day?' Then his face fell. 'No, I'd forgotten. He wouldn't come, I don't expect. He can't swim.'

'Can't swim?' I said. The phrase repeated itself over and over in my mind, shouting at me louder and louder from somewhere miles away and yet in the most secret core of my being – like the voices one hears as one is going under an anaesthetic – and the frenzied thumping of my heart was like that too, or like the revenging spirit battering a way out of its prison.

No more tonight. I must think it out carefully. Tomorrow I'll write down my plan. It will be simple and deadly. Already I can see it forming before my eyes.

16 August

Yes. I believe it's foolproof now. The only difficulty will be to get George out on the river, but a little judicious taunting ought to do the trick. And once he's aboard the dinghy his number's up.

I shall have to wait for another squally day, like yesterday. Assume a south-westerly wind, that's the prevailing wind here. We'll beat up the river half a mile or so, and then come round and run before the wind. That will be my moment. We'll be running with the boom on the port side. I'll wait for a squall, and then see to it that the boat gybes all standing. With the lee helm she carries she's bound to capsize. *And George can't swim.*

I thought first of upsetting her like this myself. But there are generally fishermen scattered along the banks of the river here, and one of them might happen to see the 'accident', might happen to know something about sailing, and awkward questions would be asked as to why an experienced sailor like myself allowed the boat to turn over. How much more convincing if George was holding the tiller at the crucial moment!

This is how I've worked it out. When we start to run, I'll hand over the tiller to George, looking after the main and jib sheets myself. As soon as I see a strong gust approaching, I'll tell George to put his helm up, that'll get the wind behind the leech of the mainsail, and the boom will swing right over with terrific violence. One's only hope of correcting a gybe all standing is to put the helm hard down then, but George won't know this, and I shan't have time to snatch the tiller away from him before the boat turns over. I must remember to pull up the centre-board when we start to run. This is quite the normal thing to do, and it will doubly ensure the boat's capsizing. George will be thrown clear, with luck, stunned by the boom. He shouldn't have a chance of getting back and gripping on to the hull. I'll have to work it so that I'm caught under the sail or tied up with one of the sheets or something, so that I can't extricate myself to rescue the poor dear fellow till it's too late. Must also see to it that we're not too near any of the fishermen on the banks when we turn over.

It will be a perfect murder, an absolute accident. The worst that can happen is that I may be censured by the coroner for allowing George to be sailing the boat in such a treacherous wind.

The coroner! My God, there's a snag there I'd overlooked. My real name will almost certainly have to come out at the inquest, and Lena will know I'm the father of the boy George ran over when she was in the car. Will she put two and two together, and begin to suspect that the sailing accident was not as genuine as it looked? I'll have to get round her somehow or other. Does she love me enough to hold her tongue? It's a dirty business, this part of it – using Lena like this. But why the hell should I care? Martie is what I must remember, the poor wavering little figure in the middle of the road, the burst bag of sweets. What do anyone's feelings matter compared with his death?

Drowning is very painful, they say, in the preliminary stages. Good. I'm glad. George's lungs bursting, the top of his head shrieking with pain, his hands scrabbling vainly to thrust the giant weight of water off his chest. I hope he remembers Martie then. Shall I swim near him and shout 'Martin Cairnes' in his ear? No, I think I can safely leave him to his own drowning thoughts; they will take sufficient vengeance for Martie.

17 August

I laid down my bait for George at lunch today. Carfax and his wife were there. The pitiful way Violet tried to pretend she did not notice the byplay between Rhoda Carfax and George – it sharpened my wits against him. I said that Phil looked like becoming a first-rate hand with a boat. In George's face there was a struggle between fatuous pride and ungracious scepticism. He said, rather grudgingly, he was glad to hear there was something the boy could do; stop him mooning about in the garden all the holidays; etc., etc.

'You ought to try your hand at it some day,' I said.

'Come out in your cockleshell? I value my own skin too much for that!' He laughed, a bit too strenuously.

'Oh, it's quite safe, if that's what you're worrying about. It's funny, though,' I went on, to the table at large, 'how many people are frightened of small boats, people who don't think twice about the chances of their getting run over every time they cross the street.'

George lowered his eyelids a little at that last crack of mine; it was the only sign he gave. Violet piped up:

'Oh, George isn't *frightened*, I'm sure. It's just a question of—'

It was the worst possible thing she could have said. George was obviously furious at the idea of his wife's taking up the cudgels for him. No doubt she was going on to say that it was just a question of George's not being able to swim; but he interrupted, mimicking her voice most disagreeably:

'No dear, George *isn't* frightened. Not frightened of baby boats, he isn't.'

'That's fine,' I said negligently. 'You'll come out one day, then? I'm sure you'll enjoy every minute of it.'

So that's that. I felt a breathless excitement. Everything else in the room seemed tenuous and remote – Lena chattering away to Carfax, Violet's vague flutterings, Rhoda laughing lazily into George's face, old Mrs Rattery picking at her fish with an air of disapproval, as though she'd found its pedigree missing, and darting a very sharp glance now and then from under her penthouse eyebrows at George and Rhoda. I had to sit very still, deliberately to relax my body that trembled like tense wire. I stared out of the window, till the grey house and the tree it framed were blurred and blended together into a kind of trembling, shifting, dappled pattern like river water under trees when the sun is shining.

I was jerked back out of this trance by a voice that seemed to come from a great distance. It was Rhoda Carfax, saying to me:

'And what do you do with yourself here all day, Mr Lane, when you're not instructing the young?'

I was pulling myself together to make some reply, when George broke in:

'Oh, he just sits upstairs, plotting his murder.'

In my thrillers I've often enough used the cliché about all the blood seeming to drain out of someone's heart. I'd never realised, though, how accurate it was. George's remark made me feel – and look, I expect – like white meat. I stared at him, for what seemed like hours, my mouth trembling out of control. It was not till Rhoda said, 'Oh, you're working on a new book, are you?' that I realised that George had been talking about fiction murder. Or was he? Is it possible that he can have discovered or suspected something? No, it's ridiculous to be afraid of that. My relief, at the moment, was so enormous that I became pugnacious and irritable, furious with George for giving me such a shock.

I said, 'Yes, I'm working out a very pretty murder – quite my masterpiece, I think.'

'He's certainly darned close about it,' said George. 'Locked doors, sealed lips, and all that. Of course, he *says* he's writing a thriller, but we've got no proof, have we? I think he ought to show us his manuscript, don't you, Rhoda? Just so we can be sure he's not a fugitive from justice, or a master criminal in disguise, or something.'

'I don't—'

'Yes, do read some of it out after lunch, Felix,' said Lena. 'We'll all sit round, and do some community screaming when the villain's dagger descends.'

It was appalling. The idea began to spread and rage like a heath fire. 'Please do.' 'Yes, you must.' 'Come on, Felix, be a sport.'

I said, trying to be firm but sounding, I'm afraid, like a flustered hen:

'No. I can't. I'm sorry. I hate anyone to see an unfinished manuscript of mine. I'm just funny that way.'

'Don't be a spoilsport, Felix. Tell you what – I'll read it out myself, if the blushing author is too coy. I'll read out the first chapter, and then we'll have a sweepstake on who the murderer is – a bob each in the pool. I suppose the murderer does come into the first chapter? I'll go upstairs and fetch it now.'

'You'll do nothing of the sort.' My voice cracked a little. 'I absolutely forbid it. I will not have people snooping about my manuscripts.' George's stupid grinning face infuriated me. I must have been glaring at him. 'You wouldn't like to have someone prying into your private correspondence, so lay off mine – too thick-headed to take a hint.'

George, of course, was delighted to have got me on the hop. 'Aha, so that's it! Private correspondence. Love letters. Hiding his love light under a bushel.' He roared with laughter at his witticism. 'You'd better look out, or Lena'll be getting jealous. She's a terror when roused, don't I know it.'

I made a desperate effort to get control of myself and speak in negligent tones. 'No. Not love letters, George. You mustn't give way to this one-track habit of mind.' Something made me go on, 'But I shouldn't read out my manuscript, George. Supposing I'd put you into the story – it'd be very embarrassing for you, wouldn't it?'

Carfax spoke up, unexpectedly, 'I don't expect he'd recognise himself. People don't, do they? Unless he was the hero, of course.'

A pleasantly acidulated remark. Carfax is such a neutral sort of figure – one didn't expect it of him. The point, needless to say, was much too fine for George's thick skin to feel any prick from it. We began to talk about the extent to which writers draw on real people for their fictitious characters, and the breeze passed over. But it was disagreeably chilly while it lasted. I hope to God I don't give myself away at all, losing my temper with George like that. I hope my hiding place for this diary is really safe. I doubt if lock and key would keep George out, should he feel really inquisitive about 'the manuscript'.

18 August

Can you imagine yourself, *hypocrite lecteur*, in the position of being able to do a murder with impunity? A murder which, whether the act – the manner of taking off – succeeds or through some incalculable mischance fails, must still beyond any shadow of suspicion appear to be an accident? Can you imagine yourself living day after day in the same house as your victim, a man whose existence – apart from your own knowledge of its special infamy – is a curse to everyone around him and an insult to its Creator? Can you imagine how easy it is to live with this detested creature – how soon familiarity with your victim breeds a contempt for him? He looks at you a little strangely, perhaps, sometimes: you seem to him distrait, and you return him a pleasant, absent-minded smile – absent-minded because at that very moment you are running over in your head, for the fiftieth time, the exact movements of wind, sail and tiller which will compass his destruction.

Imagine all this, if you can, and then try to conceive yourself baulked, baffled, held at check by one simple little thing. 'The still, small voice,' perhaps you are guessing, gentle reader. A generous thought, but incorrect. Believe me, I have no faintest qualm of conscience about removing George Rattery. If I had had no other reason, the way he is warping and bruising the life of that charming child, Phil, would be justification enough: he has killed one golden lad, I will not let him destroy another. No, it is not conscience that holds me back. Not even my own natural timidity. It's an even more elementary obstacle than these – nothing more nor less than the weather.

Here I am, and here I shall be for I don't know how many days, whistling for a wind like any ancient mariner. (I suppose whistling for a wind is sympathetic magic, as old as the first sailing ship; the same thing as when savages beat cymbals to bring down rain or enact fertility rites in their fields.) Not that it's quite true to say I'm whistling for a wind. There was wind today, but unfortunately too much of it – a near-gale, south-westerly. That's the trouble. I must have a day when there's enough breeze to turn over a badly handled boat, but not so much that it will appear wanton negligence to have taken out a novice in it. And how long shall I have to wait for just the right amount of wind? I can't stay on here for ever. Apart from anything else, Lena is getting restive. To tell the truth, I'm beginning to find her just the tiniest bit of a bore. It's abominable to say this, she's so sweet and loving, but she seems to have lost a lot of her verve lately; she's become a thought too girlish and clinging and intense for my present mood. Only this evening she said, 'Felix, can't we go away somewhere together. I'm tired of all these people. Won't you come away? Please.' She was oddly worked up about it. No wonder, it can't be much fun for her, seeing George every day, being reminded of that evening seven months ago when their car ran down a child in a lane. I had to fob her off with vague promises, of course. I don't feel too good about Lena, but I daren't break with her, even if I was willing to be caddish, because I must have her on my side when my real identity comes out at the inquest.

I wish she'd turn back into the tough, wise-cracking, high-tension girl she was when first I met her. It would be so much easier to betray that Lena – and sooner or later she's bound to feel that she's been betrayed, been used just as a clue to some problem of my own, even though she never realises what that problem was.

19 August

A curious sidelight on the Rattery household today. I was passing by the drawing-room door, which was half open. There was a sound of half-stifled sobbing from within. I meant to pass on – one gets accustomed to that sound in this house, when I heard George's mother saying, in a harsh, urgent, imperious undertone, 'Now then, Phil, stop blubbering. Remember you're a Rattery. You grandfather was killed fighting in South Africa – there was a ring of dead enemies round him – they cut him to pieces – they couldn't make him give in. Think of him. Aren't you ashamed to be blubbering when—?'

'But he shouldn't be – he – I can't bear it – '

'When you grow up, you'll understand these things. Your father may be a little hot-tempered, but there can be only one master in a house.'

'I don't care what you say. He's a bully. He's no right to teat Mummy like – it's so unfair. I—'

'Stop that, child! Stop it this instant! How dare you criticise your father?'

'Well, *you* do. I heard you telling him yesterday that the way he was carrying on with that woman was a scandal and you'd—'

'Phil, that's enough. Don't dare to mention that to me or anyone else again.' Mrs Rattery's voice was like the edge of a rusty, jagged blade. Than it grew sweet and patient, a horrible change, and she said, 'Promise me, child, you'll forget whatever you heard yesterday. You're much too young to trouble your head with grown-up matters like this. Promise.'

'I can't promise to *forget* it.'

'Don't quibble, child. You understand very well what I meant.'

'Oh, all right. I promise.'

'That's better. Now then, you see your grandfather's sword hanging up there on the wall? Fetch it down, please.'

'But – '

'Do as I tell you . . . That's right. Now give it to me. I want you to do something for your old granny. I want you to go down on your knees and hold that sword in front of you and swear on it that, whatever happens, you'll uphold the honour of the Ratterys and never be ashamed of the name you bear. Whatever happens. You understand?'

This was too much for me. George and that old harridan will drive the child insane, between the pair of them. I strode into the room, saying:

'Hello, Phil, what *are* you doing with that frightful weapon? For heaven's sake don't drop it, or it'll cut your toes off. Oh, I didn't see you, Mrs Rattery. I'm afraid I must take Phil away now. It's time we started our lessons.'

Phil blinked at me stupidly, like a sleepwalker just awoken. Then he glanced nervously at his grandmother.

'Come along, Phil,' I said.

He shivered, and suddenly scurried out of the room in front of me. Old Mrs Rattery was sitting there, the sword across her knees, lumpish and stone still, an Epstein figure. I felt her eyes on my back as I went out. I coud not have turned round and faced them, to save my life. I wish to God I could drown her as well as George. Then there'd be some hope for Phil.

20 August

It is surprising how entirely reconciled I am to the idea that, within a few days (weather permitting), I shall commit a murder. I feel quite unemotional about it – nothing more than the faint twinges of uneasiness which any normal person might feel before a visit to the dentist. I suppose, when one is on the verge of an undertaking like this, which has been in full view for a long time, one's sensibility is bound to have become dulled. It's interesting. I say to myself, 'I am shortly about to become a murderer' – and it strikes my ear as naturally and dispassionately as if I were to say, 'I am shortly about to become a father.'

Talking of murderers, I had a great jaw with Carfax this morning, when I took my car into their garage to get the oil changed. He seems really a very decent sort. I can't imagine how he puts up with the unspeakable George as partner. He's a great detective-story fan, and plied me with questions about the technique of murders in fiction. We discussed the science of fingerprints, and the comparative merits of cyanide, strychnine and arsenic from the fiction murderer's point of view. I'm afraid I was pretty shaky on the latter. I must do a course of poisons when I return to my writer's trade (it's odd how calmly I assume that I shall settle down again to my profession when this annoying little George interlude is over. It's as though Wellington were to have gone back to a box of tin soldiers after winning Waterloo.)

After we'd chatted for quite a bit, I wandered along towards the rear of the garage. A rather bizarre scene met my eyes. George, his huge back turned to me and quite blocking up the window, was standing in the attitude of a man firing from a beleaguered house. There was a 'phut'. I went up to George. He *was* shooting – with an air rifle. 'That's got another of the bastards,' he said as I came up beside him. 'Oh, it's you. I'm just having a pot at the rats on the dump out there. We've tried everything – traps, poison, rat hunts – but we can't keep 'em down. The little bastards came in and chewed up a new tyre last night.'

'That's a nice little rifle.'

'Yup. Gave it to Phil last birthday. Said he could have a penny for every rat he shoots. He got a brace yesterday, I believe. Look here, like a go? Let's have half a dollar on it. Whichever of us gets most rats in half a dozen shots.'

The diverting spectacle then ensued of a murderer and his prospective victim, standing amicably side by side, taking alternate shots at a rat-infested scrap heap. I commend this scene to my colleagues in the thriller racket; it would work up very nicely into the opening chapter of a Dickson Carr; Gladys Mitchell would deal with it pleasantly, too, or Anthony Berkeley.

George won the half-crown. Each of us got three rats, but George swore I'd only winged my last one. I didn't bother to argue about it; what's half a crown between friends, after all?

The wind has dropped a bit today, but it is still good for a few first-rate squalls. I could do worse than kill George tomorrow. He generally takes the afternoon off on Saturday, and there's no point in my putting it off. It's an agreeable piece of irony that my connection with George will have both begun and ended with an accident.

21 August

Yes, today. George is coming out in the dinghy this afternoon. It is the end of my long journey and the beginning of his. My voice sounded quite ordinary when I asked him at breakfast to come out sailing. My hand holding the pencil now is trembling. There are white clouds forming across the sky; the leaves are playing with the sunlight boisterously. Everything should go off pat.

End of Felix Lane's Diary

Part Two

Set Piece on a River

George Rattery came back into the dining room, where the others were sitting over their coffee. He spoke to the bearded, round-faced man who was holding a lump of sugar in his spoon and watching it crumble and subside beneath the surface of the hot liquid.

'Look here, Felix, I've got to attend to a couple of things. Will you go and get the boat ready? I'll meet you at the landing stage in quarter of an hour's time.'

'Very well. There's no hurry.'

Lena Lawson said, 'Have you made your will, George?'

'That's just what I was going to do, but I was too polite to put it like that.'

'You will be careful of him, won't you, Felix?' said Violet Rattery.

'Don't fuss, Vi. I can look after myself. I'm not quite a babe in arms, you know.'

'Anyone would think,' said Felix Lane mildly, 'that George and I were about to cross the Atlantic in a canoe. No, George will live to be hanged yet – as long as he does exactly what I tell him and doesn't mutiny in mid-stream.'

George looked sulky for a moment. His lips pouted beneath his heavy moustache. He did not relish the idea of being ordered about by anyone.

'That's all right,' he said. 'I'll be a good little boy. I've no intention of getting drowned, I assure you. Never did like water, except to pour whisky into. Run along and put on your yachting cap, Felix. I'll be with you in quarter of an hour.'

They all rose and left the dining room. Ten minutes later, Felix Lane was hauling the dinghy round to the outside of the landing stage. With the meticulous deliberation of the expert, he lifted up the floorboards, baled out the water, and replaced them; shipped the rudder; fixed the jib and hauled on the halliard to see that it was running free, before he left the sail lying in the bows and turned to the mainsail. He bolted the boom on to the mast, hooked one end of the halliard to the strop on the yard and, standing to windward, hauled up the sail. It thrashed and flacked in the gusty wind. Smiling abstractedly, he lowered it again, then shipped the sculls and rowlocks, lowered the centre-board, fiddled for a moment with the jib sheets, and lighting a cigarette sat down to wait for George Rattery.

Everything had been done with a leisurely, meticulous certainty. It would be fatal for anything to go wrong before the moment he was waiting for. The water clucked and sidled past the landing stage. Looking upstream, he could see the bridge and the patch of water in front of the garage dump where George must have sunk the damning evidence of the accident. Remembering that day nearly eight months ago, whose horror now fully arose from the drift of intervening days beneath which it had at times been almost submerged, his mouth tightened and the cigarette in his fingers began to tremble. He was beyond right or wrong now; they were words as empty and ineffectual as the tin can and the ice-cream carton now floating past him on the current. He had built a structure of false pretences around his real purpose; now it had begun to move, it was too late to jump out. He would be carried on towards the inevitable end as surely as that debris out there was borne by the current. To the inevitable end, one way or the other. For a moment he contemplated the possibility of the failure of his plan. He was quite fatalistic about it – like a soldier in the firing line, he could not look further ahead than the present hour; beyond that, all was unreal, drowned by the keyed-up staccato note of the moment's excitement, the drums thudding in his heart, the wind intermittently drumming in his ears.

His reverie was broken by the clatter of feet on the landing stage. George was looking down at him, a mountain of a man, his hands on his hips.

'God! do I have to get into this? Oh well, come on, do your worst.'

'No, not there. Sit on the centre thwart and keep on the windward side.'

'Can't I even sit where I want to? I always thought this was a mug's game.'

'It's safer where I tell you – balances the boat better.'

'Safer? Oh yes. OK, teacher, push off.'

Felix Lane hoisted the jib, then the mainsail. He sat down in the stern and with two nimble movements drew the port-side jib-sheet tight and secured it by a slippery hitch; then, as he hauled on the mainsheet, the boat felt the wind and began to slide away from the landing stage. They were sailing free, the wind on the starboard beam blowing unimpeded across the water-meadows. His feet braced against the centre-board case, his hands gripping the gunwale, George Rattery watched the mill slide past. He had never seen it from this side before. Picturesque old place, he thought, but they must be running at a loss. The bubbles chucked and boiled in their wake, the water slapped hurriedly against the bows. It was peaceful, sliding along like this, watching the houses glide smoothly past as if on a moving band. George's feeling of apprehension began to diminish. It amused him to see the way Felix was incessantly jockeying with the rope in his hand and the tiller, constantly glancing over his right shoulder, pretending it was all very difficult.

He said, 'Always looked upon sailing as a bit of a mystery. Can't see there's much in it, though.'

'Oh, it *looks* easy enough. But wait till we – ' Felix started again. 'You care to try your hand when we come out on the broad reach up there?'

'A greenhorn like me?' George laughed jovially. 'Aren't you afraid I'd upset the boat?'

'You'd be all right, provided you did exactly what I told you. Look, "helm up" is this way, "helm down" the other way. Always put your helm down when you feel the boat heeling over; it brings you up into the wind, see, and spills the wind from your sails. Not too hard, though, or you'll find yourself in stays—'

'In stays! My Gawd – just like an elderly pansy!'

'And when you're in stays, the boat loses way and you're at the mercy of any gust that strikes you broadside as you fall away from the wind again.'

George grinned. His teeth were large and white and he looked for a moment like a continental caricature of a British statesman – a look of hungry, humourless complacence.

'Well, it all seems easy as pie to me. Can't imagine what all the fuss is about.'

Felix felt a sudden wave of exasperation. He wanted to smack this jeering, self-satisfied hulk of a man in the face. Whenever Felix reached a certain pitch of irritability, his reaction was – not directly to attack its cause – but to take risks, if he was driving a car or sailing, which went to the very edge of recklessness and scared the second party out of his wits. Now glancing over his shoulder, noting a gust scurrying towards them over the water, he drew in the mainsheet. The dinghy heeled hard over as if a hand as big as a cloud were pushing against the mast. He thrust the helm hard down. A spatter of water came over the lee gunwale, as the dinghy swerved round into the wind and stood upright, shaking off the gust like a dog shaking water from its back. A startled oath had broken from George when he felt the first mad plunge and tilt of the boat. Now, Felix observed with ferocious pleasure, the big man was looking distinctly green and eyeing him with an uneasiness that had not even begun to turn into bravado.

'Look here, Lane,' George began, 'I'd better – '

But Felix, smiling at him innocently, his temporary irritation gone, innocently delighted by the pleasure of running his manoeuvre so fine, said:

'Oh, that's nothing. No need to get excited about it. We'll be doing that all the time when we get out into the main reach and start tacking.'

'In that case, I'll get out and walk.' George gave a short, uneasy laugh. The little tick, he thought, he's trying to frighten me, I mustn't give any signs of wind-up – I haven't got the wind-up, anyway, who the hell says I have? 'No need to get excited'? Huh.

After a few minutes' more sailing, they came to the lock. The garden on the right bank, in front of the lock-keeper's house, was spilling over with flowers – dahlias, roses, hollyhocks, red linum – solid in their ranks and tossed by the exciting wind, an army in a brilliant diversity of uniforms. The lock-keeper ambled out, smoking his short clay pipe, and leant backwards, his arms outstretched against the great timber balk that opened the gates.

'Morning, Mr Rattery. Don't often see you this way. Nice day for boating.'

They handled the dinghy into the lock. The sluices were opened, the water began to roar out, and the boat sank lower and lower till the masthead showed only a foot above the lock and they were prisoned between its green-slimed walls. Felix Lane tried to control his mounting impatience. Out there, half a mile beyond that wooden gate, lay the last lap; he wanted to get there quickly, to get it over, to prove that his calculations had been correct. In theory, it looked foolproof; but when it came to the point? Supposing, for instance, that George could really swim after all? The water thumped and bellowed through the sluices, like a herd of wild cattle thrusting their way through a gate; but for Felix it was a slow, meagre trickle – no more than the sand running out of an hourglass. Now the water in the lock must be level with the stream outside but George, blast him, was still yammering away to the lock-keeper, protracting the agony of Felix – almost, it seemed, as if he wished to postpone his own.

Felix thought, God – how much longer? We'll be here all day at this rate; the wind may drop before we get out into the reach. He looked up covertly at the sky. The clouds were still marching overhead, marching up from the horizon and sweeping away to the other end of the sky. he found himself minutely observing George: the black hair that sprounted on the back of his hands, the mole on his forearm, the tilt of his right elbow as he held a cigarette in front of his lips. At that moment, George had no more meaning for him emotionally than a dead body with which certain specific things had to be done. Felix's keyed-up excitement had carried him beyond even the feeling of hatred for this man; there was no room in him for anything but the excitement, the sensation of a wildly spinning periphery and in the centre of it a deep-sleeping, unaccountable peace.

The roar of water had died away to a sucking chuckle. The gates began to open, showing a gradually widening vista of river and sky.

'You'll catch a nice bit of breeze round the bend there,' the lock-keeper shouted as the boat began to slide away.

George Rattery shouted back. 'We caught a hell of a puff on the way here. Mr Lane did his best to tip me out.'

'Mr Lane's all right, sir. Handles a boat very pretty. You're safe enough with him.'

'Well, it's nice to know that,' said George, glancing carelessly at Felix.

The boat slid indolently along, meek as milk; it was not easy to imagine the temperamental, vicious, hard-mouthed horse she would become when she felt the full lash of the wind. Here, she was sheltered by the high bank on the starboard beam. George lit another cigarette, cursing petulantly under his breath when the first match went out.

He said, 'Pretty slow, this, isn't it?'

Felix didn't trouble to reply. So George, too, feels that the boat is moving too slowly, does he? Excitement again flared out in him and dropped like flags on a gusty day. The willows on the bank were trailing and streaming their hair in the wind, but here it only bathed his forehead gently. He thought of Tessa, and

Martie, and without apprehension of the doubtful future. The willows, flickering their ash-blonde leaves, reminded him of Lena, but she seemed very far away frm this boat that carried two men towards a crisis in whose creation her part had already been played.

Now they were approaching the bend of the river. George from time to time had glanced at his companion and made as if to speak; but there was something in Felix's intense absorption which penetrated even George's insensitiveness and kept him silent. Felix had a strange unusual authority about him while he was sailing this boat. George recognised it with a vague feeling of petulance, but the conflicting emotions in his mind were soon scattered by the stress of the south-westerly wind which met them as they rounded the bend into the half-mile reach. The river in front of them was dark and troubled, its surface running with cats' paws all the time and often more deeply scratched by the nails of an angrier squall. The wind blowing straight down this reach fought against the current, rising abrupt waves that jolted and slapped against the blunt bows of the dinghy. Felix, sitting right up on the boat's side, his feet pressed hard against the edge of the opposite side-bench, was sailing her close-hauled on the starboard tack. The dinghy, with her vicious habit of falling away from the wind, plunged and kicked like an unbroken horse beneath him as he fought with main-sheet and tiller to keep her head into the gusts. Glancing continually over his shoulder, he measured the force and direction of each gust that came clawing its way over the water towards them. In a pause, he thought sardonically what a pity it would be if one of these squalls turned them over before the moment he was awaiting. For the present, all his energies were concentrated on preserving the life of this man whom for so many days he had been sedulously hunting down.

Now he put up his tiller to go about. As her head struggled up into the wind, he let go the starboard jib-sheet. The wind took hold of the jib and shook it ferociously from side to side, like a dog shaking an unwieldy piece of rag. There was a wild flurry of noise and movement: the stern, skidding round, made the water seethe and little waves went knocking at the bank six feet away. As she drew away slowly on the port tack, a gust flung her over sideways, but Felix already had the helm hard down and forced her to bore into the wind, and she stood up presently and with a weary shake of the mainsail paid off on the new tack. George, leaning out desperately to windward, had felt the panicky toppling of the boat and seen the water hissing by, level with the lee gunwale. He clenched his teeth, determined not to betray his own fear again to the little, bearded man who was whistling between his teeth as he wrestled with the wind, who was master for the movement, whose neck he could break any moment like a twig.

Felix, indeed, was so absorbed in the controlling of this unruly boat that he scarcely gave George a thought. He was vaguely aware of the delicious power he exercised over this cheap, complacent bully; he was enjoying the man's ill-concealed fear, but only at present as a minor, accidental part of the familiar struggle against wind and wave. Another part of his mind was recording the black and white inn standing back on the far bank; the derelict, broken-backed barge that lay in front of it beside the slipway; the fishermen contemplating their floats in a mystic trance unbroken by the twistings and turnings of the dinghy that wove its criss-cross way from bank to bank. I could drown George now, if I wanted to, he thought, and I don't believe one of these fishermen would notice.

At that moment a blare of sound reached them; looking back, Felix saw nosing round the corner two motor barges, running abreast, each towing a couple of lighters behind it. He measured the distance carefully with his eye. They were a couple of hundred yards behind him, and would catch him up on his third tack from now. As they passed, he could do short tacks between the bank and the nearer string of barges, but there was a danger of being temporarily blanketed by their hulls and thus laid at the mercy of the next gust, the danger of their wash throwing him off his course, the danger of the rigid hawser that stretched between them. The alternative was to turn and run past them before the wind, and bring her round again after they had passed. His calculations were interrupted by George, who cleared his throat and said:

'What do we do now? They're getting pretty close, aren't they?'

'Oh, there'll be plenty of room.' Felix added mischievously, 'Power vessels have to give way to sailing vessels, you know.'

'Give way? Huh! Can't see them giving way. Damn it, though, do they think they own the blasted river – coming along two abreast? It's a scandal. I'll take their numbers and make a complaint to the owners.'

George was obviously working up for an attack of nerves which he would soon be quite unable to repress. And indeed the great motor barges bearing down on them, moustaches of foam waving up on either side of their bows, were formidable enough. But Felix calmly put about on another tack, and began crossing the river a bare seventy yards ahead of them. George was now mopping his face, shifting furtively nearer to Felix, glaring at him with the whites of his eyes showing larger. Suddenly he burst out shouting.

'What are you going to do? Look out, I tell you! You can't – ' but whatever he was going to say was snapped short and drowned by a great bellow from the siren of one of the barges, which seemed to echo the rising hysteria in George's own voice. Seeing George's ludicrously working face, it occurred to Felix in a sudden flash that now would be the perfect opportunity for staging an impromptu accident. George's panic, even as he despised it, was also goading him towards this. But he repelled the temptation to alter his original plan; that plan, he knew, was the best

– to make assurance doubly sure. Let him stick to the set piece, and venture on no improvisations. But there would be no harm in giving George another fright.

The barges were now twenty yards away, hemming the dinghy into the bank. Felix had little room to manoeuvre in. He put about, and the course of the dinghy began to converge with that of the nearer barge. He was dimly aware of George gripping his leg and shouting in his ear, 'If you run us into that barge, you bloody fool, I'll bloody well hang on to you.' Felix put his helm up and paid out the main-sheet, so that she spun about, her boom flying out to port, the great minotaur-browed stem of the barge sweeping past with ten feet to spare. As they were carried downwind past her side, George in an uncontrollable fury, staggered to his feet, and waved his fists and shouted imprecations at the impassive man in the deck-house. A youth sitting further aft stared at his gesticulations indifferently. Then the barge's wash caught the dinghy, and George lost his balance, collapsing on to the floorboards.

'I shouldn't stand up again,' said Felix Lane mildly. 'Next time you mightn't fall into the boat.'

'Damn this—! Damn their eyes! I'll—'

'Oh, take a grip on yourself. We were never in the least danger.' Felix went on conversationally. 'The same thing happened the other day when I was out with Phil. *He* didn't lose his nerve.'

The following barge swept past, a long, low, iron craft with INFLAMMABLE written along its deck cover.

It certainly looked as if Felix was out to inflame his companion. As he hauled the dinghy round into the wind again on the port tack, and bounced across the swelling wake of the barges, he remarked coldly and distinctly, 'I've never seen a grown-up person make such an exhibition of himself.'

It must have been a long time since anyone had addressed George like that. He stiffened, stared incredulously at Felix as though wondering if he could believe his own ears; then glowered at him dangerously. But after a few moments some new thought struck him, for he turned away, shrugging his shoulders and smiled a secret, sly smile to himself. Of the two, it was now Felix Lane who seemed to be growing more and more nervous, fiddling unnecessarily with the gear and casting uncertain glances towards his companion; while George, shifting his great bulk from side to side of the boat as she went about on new tacks, began to whistle and make occasional facetious remarks to Felix.

'I'm beginning quite to enjoy myself,' he said.

'Good. Care to take a turn with the tiller now?' Felix's voice was dry, tense, almost a gasp. So much hung on the answer to that question. But George did not seem to notice anything amiss.

'When you like,' he replied carelessly.

A shadow, an expression that might have been translated as ambiguity or consternation or dark irony, came and went on Felix's face. When he spoke, his voice was little more than a whisper, yet there was a challenging note in it which could not be concealed.

'Right you are. We'll just go up a little bit farther, and then we'll turn round and you can steer.'

Putting off, he thought to himself; infirm of purpose, putting off the crisis, your last chance, it must be, if it were done when 't were done then 't were well it were done quickly, but that was different, a very different kettle of fish, that fisherman there I wonder what he uses for bait, my rod is baited too, a rod in pickle for George Rattery.

The positions were now reversed. Felix was in a state of pitiable nerves, fidgeting no longer, but his whole body rigid with misery; George had regained his jocular tongue, his self-confident, supercilious, brutal attitude; or so it would have seemed to one of those ubiquitous, omniscient observers of Thomas Hardy, if such a one had been a third party in this bizarre voyage. Felix noted that the place he had marked out for action – a clump of elms away on the right bank – was now astern. Setting his teeth, still unconsciously watching for the approach of gusts on the port bow, he brought the dinghy round in a broad sweep. The swirled water chuckled at him sardonically. He could not meet George's eyes as he said, in an abrupt, breathless voice:

'Here you are. Take the tiller. Keep the main-sheet right out, like it is now. I'll just go forward and raise the centre-board – she runs better like that, less resistance to the water.'

Even as he spoke, he received a queer impression that the wind had dropped, that everything had hushed into silence, the better to hear his crucial words and await their outcome. Nature seemed to be holding its breath, and in the hush his own voice sounded like a loud challenge cried from the top of a watchtower in a desert. Then he began to perceive that this shocking silence was not of wind and water, but emanated like a chill mist from George himself. The centre-board, he thought, I said I was going forward to raise the centre-board. But still he remained sitting in the stern-sheets, as though nailed there by George's eyes, which he could feel boring into him. He forced himself to look up and meet them. George's whole body seemed to have swollen and horribly advanced, like a creature of nightmare. It was just that George had quietly moved aft and was sitting close to him, of course. In George's eyes there was an expression of crafty, naked triumph. George licked his gross lips, and said sweetly, 'Very well, little man. Budge up and I'll take the tiller.' His voice dropped to an edged whisper. 'But I shouldn't try any of those funny tricks you've been planning.'

'Tricks?' said Felix dully. 'What do you mean?'

George's voice rose in a shattering gust of rage. 'You know damn' well what I mean, you filthy murderous little tick!' he roared. The, quietly again, he said, 'I posted your precious diary to my solicitors today – that's the little job I had to do after lunch when I sent you off to get the boat ready. They've got instructions to open it in the event of my death and take the necessary action. So it'll really turn out more unfortunate for you if you let me drown this trip, won't it? Won't it?'

Felix Lane kept his face averted. He swallowed hard and tried to speak, but no words would come out. The knuckles of his hand were dead white on the tiller.

'Lost your lying little tongue, have you?' George went on. 'And your claws, too. Yes, I think we've drawn Pussy's claws for him all right. Thought you were so damned superior, didn't you? So much cleverer than all the rest of us. Well, you've been just a bit too clever.'

'Do you have to be so melodramatic about it?' Felix muttered.

'If you start being rude, little man, I'll break your jaw for you. In fact, I've a good mind to break it anyway,' said George dangerously.

'And sail the boat home yourself?'

George stared truculently at him. Then he grinned. 'Yes, that's quite an idea. I think I will sail the boat home myself. I can always break your jaw when we get back to terra firma, what?'

He pushed Felix aside, and took the tiller. The boat surged and swooped downwind, the banks fled past. Felix, still holding the main-sheet and automatically watching the leech of the sail for the dangerous lifting that would mean the beginning of a gybe, seemed sunk in apathy.

'Well, hadn't you better start something soon? We're halfway to the lock already. Or have you decided not to drown me after all?' Felix lifted one shoulder in a little gesture of resignation, of defeat. George sneered, 'No? I thought so. Lost your nerve, eh? Want to save your rotten little neck. I thought you wouldn't have the guts to go through with it now and take the consequences. I banked on that. Quite the psychologist, aren't I? . . . Well, if you won't talk, I will.'

And he proceeded to explain, amongst other things, how Felix's remarks one day at lunch had made him curious about this 'detective novel' he was writing, so he had gone up to his guest's room one afternoon when he was out, and found where it was hidden, and read it. He had felt vague suspicions about Felix before that, he said, and the diary proved them well founded.

'So now,' he concluded, 'we've got you in a cleft stick. From now on, you'll have to behave, Pussy; you'll have to watch your step very, very carefully.'

'You can't do anything,' said Felix sullenly.

'Oh, can't I just? I don't know exactly about the legal position, but that diary of yours would land you precious near a charge of attempted murder.'

Whenever George mentioned the word 'diary', he checked, then spat it out fiercely, as though the thing had stuck in his throat. He had evidently not appreciated the analysis of his character which it contained. Felix's dull silence seemed to infuriate him: he began cursing his companion again, not full-bloodedly as before, but in querulous, shocked, incredulous terms, almost as though he was complaining about a neighbour's radio which kept him awake at night.

As George whipped himself up into another frenzy of righteous indignation, Felix cut across it with, 'Well, what do you propose to do about it?'

'I've a darned good mind to hand over your diary to the police. That's what I *ought* to do. But of course it would be very upsetting for Lena and – er – everybody. It's just possible that I might decide to sell the diary back to you. You're quite well off, aren't you? Care to make an offer for it? – a generous offer, it'll have to be.'

'Don't be silly,' remarked Felix unexpectedly. George's head jerked. He stared at the little man unbelievingly.

'Wha – what's that? What the devil d'you mean by—?'

'I said don't be silly. You know perfectly well that you won't hand over my diary to the police—'

George gave him a wary, calculating look. Slumped in the stern, his arm rigid on the thwart, Felix was gazing up at the mainsail intently. George followed the direction of his gaze, persuaded for a moment that some surprise was going to be sprung at him out of the curved and bellying sail.

Felix went on, ' – for the very good reason that you don't want the police to haul you in on a charge of manslaughter.'

George blinked his eyes. His heavy face became suffused with blood. Incredibly, in the heat of his triumph over this dangerous little adversary, in the tumult of relief he had been feeling now that physical danger was past, in the gloating expectation of all he could do with the purchase money of the diary, he had been quite overlooking its contents – the perilous knowledge which Felix possessed. His fingers twitched; they ached to be at his companion's neck, delving into his eyes, gouging and breaking this rotten little twister who seemed to have extricated himself from an impossible position, who had beaten him to the punch.

'You can't prove anything about that,' he said truculently.

Felix's voice was indifferent. 'You killed Martie, you killed my son. I've no intention of buying the diary back from you. I don't think blackmailers ought to be encouraged. Hand it over to the police, if you like. They give quite long sentences for manslaughter, you know. You can't bluff it out. And even if *you* could, Lena would soon crack up. No, it's a stalemate, my friend.'

The veins stood out on George's temples. His clenched fists began to rise. Felix said quickly, 'I shouldn't try anything on, or there might be a genuine accident. A little self-control would do you no harm.'

George Rattery burst out into a torrent of abuse, which startled one of the riverside fishermen out of his trance. Chap must have been stung by a wasp, he thought, bad year for wasps, this is. One of the county team got stung the other day while he was fielding, they say. The little chap don't seem to be worrying much. Wonder what pleasure he gets sailing a little boat up and down the river – give me a cosy motor launch every time, with a case of beer in the cabin.

' – you'll get out of my house and stay out,' George was shouting. 'If I ever see you again after today, you runt, I'll bash you into a jelly. I'll—'

'But my luggage – ?' said Felix meekly. 'I'll have to come back and pack.'

'You'll not cross my threshold, do you hear? Lena can pack up for you.' A crafty expression slid over George's face. 'Lena. I wonder what she'll say when she hears you made up to her just to get at me.'

'Leave her out of it.' Felix smiled sourly to himself, annoyed at being infected by George's melodramatics. He felt exhausted, bruised all over. Thank God, they'd reach the lock in a minute and he could put George ashore there. He put down the tiller and hauled in the mainsheet as they reached the bend. The boom swung over to starboard; the boat swerved and plunged. He thrust the helm hard up and she came back on to her course. The part of him that did this was real, all the rest a dream. Over the port bow he could see the flowers serried and shining in the lock-keeper's garden. He felt melancholy and alone. Lena. He did not dare to think of the future. That had now been taken out of his hands.

'Yes,' George was saying. 'I'll see that Lena knows what a treacherous swine you are. That'll finish things between you two.'

'Don't tell her too soon,' said Felix wearily, 'or she may refuse to pack my things for me. Then you'd have to do it yourself, and that'd be terrible, wouldn't it? Escaped victim packs foiled murderer's bag.'

'How you can sit there and joke about it beats me. Don't you realise—'

'All right, all right. We've both been just a bit too clever. Let's leave it at that. You killed Martie, and I've not quite managed to kill you, so I suppose you win on points.'

'Oh, for God's sake shut up, you cold-blooded freak! I can't stand your face any longer. Let me out of this damned boat.'

'All right. Here's the lock. This is where you get off. Shift up, I've got to lower the mainsail. You can send my things over to the Angler's Arms. Do you want me to write in your visitors' book, by the way?'

George opened his mouth to let out the rage which suddenly boiled up in him again but Felix, pointing to the lock-keeper who was approaching, said, 'Not before the servants, George.'

'Had a good sail, gentlemen?' asked the lock-keeper. 'Oh, you getting out here, Mr Rattery?'

But George Rattery had already clambered out of the boat and thrust past the man, and was walking rapidly away without a word through the neat and coloured garden, his huge body looming ruthlessly over the flowers like a tank, walking straight across the beds in a blind fury and crushing the red flax under his feet.

The lock-keeper stared after him open-mouthed. The clay pipe dropped from between his lips and was shattered on the stone quay. 'Here! Hi, sir!' he called out at last in an injured, uncertan voice; 'mind my flowers, sir!' But George paid no heed. Felix watched his broad back retreating towards the town, and the swathe his feet had cut through the astonished, bright-eyed flowers. It was the last he saw of George Rattery.

Part Three

The Body of this Death

1

Nigel Strangeways was seated in an armchair in the flat to which he and Georgia had moved after their marriage, two years ago. Outside the window lay the precise and classical dignity of one of the few seventeenth-century London squares not yet delivered over to unnecessary luxury shops and portentous blocks of flats for the mistresses of millionaires. On Nigel's knee was a huge vermilion cushion, and on the cushion an open book. At his side stood the exceedingly complex and expensive reading-stand which Georgia had given him for his last birthday; at the moment Georgia was out in the Park, so he could revert to his old habit of reading in comfort off his cushion-lectern.

Soon, however, he tipped book and cushion over on to the floor. He felt too tired to take it in. The peculiar case of the Admiral's butterfly collection, which he had just brought to a successful if rather embarrassing conclusion, had left him exhausted and depressed. He yawned, got up, teetered around the room for a bit, pulled a face at the wooden idol on the mantelpiece which Georgia had brought back from Africa, then picked some sheets of foolscap and a pencil off the desk, and slumped back into the chair again.

Georgia, coming into the room twenty minutes later, found him absorbed in composition.

'What are you writing?' she asked.

'I'm composing a general knowledge paper. *Favete linguis.*'

'Does that mean I'm to sit quiet till you've finished? Or do you want me to come and breathe over your shoulder?'

'The former course would be preferable. I'm having a tête-à-tête with my unconscious. Very soothing.'

'Do you mind if I smoke?'

'Please. Make yourself quite at home.'

After five minutes, Nigel handed over a sheet of foolscap. 'I wonder how many of those questions you can answer,' he said.

Georgia took the sheet and read out loud what was written on it.

'(1) How many fine words does it take to butter no parsnips?
(2) Who or what was "the dry wet-nurse of lions"?
(3) In what sense were the Nine Worthies?
(4) What do you know about Mr Bangelstein? What do you not know about Bion and Borysthenite?
(5) Have you ever written a letter to the press on the subject of bursting bullrushes? Why?
(6) Who is Sylvia?
(7) How many stitches in time save ten?

(8) What is the third person plural of the pluperfect tensor of *Eivστεϊν*?
(9) What was Julius Caesar's middle name?
(10) What can't you have with one fish ball?
(11) Give the names of the first two men to fight a duel with blunderbusses in balloons.
(12) Give reasons why the following have not fought duels with blunderbusses in balloons: Liddell and Scott; Sodor and Man; Cato the Younger and Cato the Elder; You and Me.
(13) Distinguish between the Minister of Agriculture and Fisheries.
(14) How many lives has a cat o' nine tails?
(15) Where are the boys of the old brigade? Illustrate your answer with a rough sketch map.
(16) Should auld acquaintance be forgot?
(17) "Poems are made by fools like me." Refute this statement, if you like.
(18) Do you believe in fairies?
(19) What celebrated sportsmen made the following remarks?
 (a) "I'd cut that playboy in ribbons again."
 (b) "*Qualis artifex pereo.*"
 (c) "Come into the garden, Maud."
 (d) "I've never been so insulted in my life."
 (e) "My lips are sealed."
(20) Distinguish between Sooterkin and Puss-in-Boots.
(21) Would you prefer Cosmo-therapy or Disestablishment?

(22) Into how many languages has Bottom been translated?'

Georgia wrinkled up her nose at Nigel over the sheet of foolscap.

'It must be a terrible thing to have received the benefit of a classical education,' she said sombrely.

'Yes.'

'You do need a holiday, don't you?'

'Yes.'

'We might pop out to Tibet for a few months.'

'I would prefer Hove. I don't like yaks' milk, or foreign parts, or llamas.'

'I don't see how you can say you dislike lamas when you've never met one.'

'I should dislike them even more if I met one. They harbour vermin and their coats are worn by pansies.'

'Oh, but you must be talking about llamas. I mean lamas.'

'That's what I meant too. Llamas.'

The telephone bell rang. Georgia moved over to answer it. Nigel watched her movements. Her body was agile and light as a cat's; it never failed to delight him. You had only to be in the same room with her to feel physically refreshed, and the sad, pensive little monkey-face contrasted so oddly with the barbaric grace of her body which she clothed always in flamboyant reds and yellows and greens.

'Georgia Strangeways speaking ... Oh, it's you, Michael, how are you? How's Oxford? ... Yes, he's here ... A job for him? No, Michael, he can't ... No, he's tired out – a very difficult case ... No, really, his mind has given way slightly – he's just asked me to distinguish between Sooterkin and Puss-in-Boots, and ... yes, I know the allusion is highly improper, but we're going off for a holiday somewhere, so ... A matter of life and death? My dear Michael, what queer phrases you do pick up. Oh, all right, he's going to speak to you himself.'

Georgia relinquished the receiver. Nigel carried on a long conversation. When it was over he took Georgia under the arms and swung her round and round and round in the air.

'I suppose all this ebullience means that somebody's murdered somebody, and you are going to poke your nose into it,' she said when he had put her down in a chair.

'Yes,' said Nigel enthusiastically. 'A very queer set-up indeed. Friend of Michael's – chap called Frank Cairnes – he's apparently the Felix Lane who writes detective novels. He set out to kill some chap, and failed, and now the chap really has been killed – strychnine. This Cairnes wants me to go and prove it wasn't him.'

'I don't believe a word of it. It's a hoax. Look, if you really insist, I'll come to Hove with you. You're not fit to take on another job now.'

'I must. Michael says Cairnes is a decent chap, and he's in a frightfully tough spot. Besides, Gloucestershire will be nice for a change.'

'He can't be a decent chap if he set out to murder someone. Leave him alone. Forget it.'

'Well, there were extenuating circumstances. This chap had run down Cairnes' kid in a car and killed him. The police couldn't trace him, so Cairnes got after him himself, and – '

'It's fantastic. Things like that don't happen. This Cairnes must be mad. What's he come out with the whole story for, if the man was killed by somebody else?'

'He wrote a diary, Michael said. I'll tell you about it in the train. Severnbridge. Where's the ABC?'

Georgia gave him a long, pensive look, nibbling her under lip. Then she turned away, opened a drawer in the desk, and began flicking through the pages of the ABC.

2

Nigel's first impression of the slightly built, bearded man who came forward to meet them in the lounge of the Angler's Arms was that here was a person singularly unperturbed by the disastrous position into which he had got himself. He shook them briskly by the hand, glancing at them and away with a faint, deprecating smile, a suggestion of apology in the slight lift of his eyebrows, as though he was tacitly asking their pardon for dragging them all this way on so trivial an errand. They talked for a bit.

'It's awfully good of you to have come down,' Felix said presently. 'The position is really—'

'Look here, let's wait to talk it over till after dinner. My wife is a bit done up by the journey. I'll just take her upstairs.'

Georgia, whose prodigiously resilient frame had before now surmounted the ordeal of many long expeditions through desert and jungle – she was, indeed, one of the three most famous women explorers of her day – did not bat an eyelid at this outrageous lie of Nigel's. Only when they were alone in their bedroom did she turn to him, grinning, and say, 'So I'm "done up", am I? Coming from a gentleman on the verge of physical and mental collapse, that was good. Why all this solicitude for the frail little woman?'

Nigel took her face, vivid under the bright silk handkerchief she wore over her head, between his hands; he rubbed her ears gently and kissed her.

'We don't want to give Cairnes the impression that you're a tough. A womanly woman you must be, my sweet, a nice, soft, yielding creature in whom he can confide.'

'The great Strangeways on the job already!' she mocked. 'What a disgustingly opportunist mind you have. But I don't see why I should be dragged into this.'

'What did you think of him?' Nigel asked.

'A deep one, I should say. Highly civilised. Highly strung. Lives too much alone – the way he looks past you when he's talking to you, as though he was more used to talking to himself. A person of delicate taste and spinsterish habit. Likes to imagine himself self-sufficient, able to get on without society, but in fact very sensitive both to the *vox populi* and the still, small voice. He's nervous as a jumping bean at the moment, of course, so it's difficult to judge.'

'Nervous, you thought? He struck me as remarkably self-possessed.'

'Oh, my dear, no, no, no. He's holding himself down by the scruff of the neck. Didn't you notice his eyes whenever the conversation dropped and there was nothing to distract his mind? Why, they just brimmed over with panic. I remember seeing a chap looking like that one evening when we wandered too far from the camp, up under the Mountains of the Moon, and got lost for an hour in the scrub.'

'If Robert Young wore a beard he'd look rather like Cairnes. I hope he didn't commit this murder after all, he seems quite an agreeable little chipmunk. Are you sure you wouldn't like to lie down for a bit before dinner?'

'No, blast you. And let me tell you, I'm not going to put the tip of my little finger into this case of yours. I know your methods, and I don't like them.'

'I'm prepared to lay five to three that you'll be in the thick of it before two days: you have the sort of sensational mind which—'

'Taken.'

After dinner, as they had arranged, Nigel went up to Felix's room. Felix studied his guest carefully as he poured out the coffee and handed him the cigarettes. He saw a tall, angular young man in the early thirties, his clothes and his tow-coloured hair untidy and giving him the appearance of having just woken up from uneasy slumber on a seat in a railway waiting room. His face was pale and a little flabby, but its curiously immature features were contradicted by the intelligence of the light-blue eyes, which gazed at him with disturbing fixity and gave the impression of reserving their judgement on every subject under the sun. There was something about Nigel Strangeways' manner, too – polite, solicitous, almost protective – which struck Felix for a moment as unaccountably sinister; it might have been the attitude of a scientist towards the subject of an experiment, he thought, interested and solicitous, but beneath that inhumanly objective. Nigel was the rare kind of man who would not have the slightest compunction about proving himself wrong.

Felix was a little startled to realise how much he already seemed to have found out about his guest. He realised that the perilous nature of his present position must have sharpened all his faculties. He said, with a sidelong half smile:

'Who shall deliver me from the body of this death?'

'St Paul, if I remember rightly. You'd better tell me all about it.'

So Felix told him the essentials of the story, as he had set it down in his diary: the death of Martie, his own growing preoccupation with the idea of revenge, the combination of reasoning and lucky accident by which he had arrived at George Rattery, the plan to drown George in the dinghy and the way the tables had been turned upon him at the last moment. At this point Nigel, who had been sitting quiet, staring down at the toes of his shoes, interrupted.

'Why did he leave it so late to spring upon you the fact that he'd found out all about you?'

'I can't really be sure,' said Felix after a pause. 'Partly cat-and-mouse fun on his part, I dare say; he was an obvious sadist type. Partly, perhaps, that he wanted to make quite sure I was going to go through with it – I mean, he couldn't have wanted a showdown, because he must have known it would lay him open to the charge of manslaughter over Martie. I don't know, though: actually he tried to blackmail me in the boat – said he'd sell the diary back to me; he seemed thoroughly taken aback when I pointed out to him that he'd never dare to hand the diary over to the police.'

'Mm. What happened next?'

'Well, I came straight back here, to the Angler's Arms. George was to have sent my luggage over. He refused to have me back for a moment in his home, not unnaturally. This all happened yesterday, by the way. About half-past ten Lena rang up to say that George had died. It gave me a hell of a turn, as you can imagine. He had been taken ill after dinner. Lena described the symptoms; it sounded to me exactly like strychnine. I went straight over to the Ratterys' house; the doctor was still there and he confirmed it. I was properly caught. There was my diary, in the hands of his solicitors, to be opened in the event of his death. It was going to tell the police that I had set out to murder George, and there was George murdered; an open-and-shut case for them.'

The rigid posture of Felix's body and the staring anxiety in his eyes belied his steady, almost indifferent tones.

'I damned nearly went and chucked myself in the river,' he said. 'It seemed so utterly hopeless. Then I remembered Michael Evans telling me you'd got him out of a similar jam, so I phoned him up and asked him to put me in touch with you. And there we are.'

'You've not told the police about this diary yet?'

'No no. I was waiting till—'

'That must be done at once. I'd better do it myself.'

'Yes. Please, if you would. I'd rather—'

'And this must be understood between us.' Nigel gazed speculatively and impersonally into Felix's eyes. 'From what you've told me, I should say it's most improbable that you killed George Rattery, and I'll do all I can to prove that you didn't. But, of course, if by any chance you did, and my investigations convince me of it, I shall not attempt to conceal it.'

'That seems reasonable enough,' said Felix with a tentative smile. 'I've written so much about amateur detctives, it'll be interesting to see how one really goes to work. Oh God, this is awful,' he went on in a different voice, 'I must have been mad these last six months. Little Martie. I keep on wondering whether I would really have tipped George into the river and let him drown, if he hadn't – '

'Never mind. You didn't – that's the point. No use crying over spilt milk.'

Nigel's cool, astringent, but not unfriendly tones were more effective than sympathy in pulling Felix together.

'You're right,' he said. 'Not that one ought to feel any qualms even if one had murdered George. He was a most unmitigated swine all round.'

'By the way,' asked Nigel, 'how do you know it wasn't suicide?'

Felix looked startled. 'Suicide? I'd never thought – I mean, I've thought about George for so long in the – er – context of murder, it never occurred to me it might have been suicide. No, it couldn't have been. He was far too insensitive and complacent a creature to – besides, why should he?'

'Who would you say might have killed him then? Any local candidates?'

'My dear Strangeways,' said Felix uneasily, 'you really can't ask the chief suspect to start slinging dirt at all and sundry.'

'The Queensberry rules don't apply here. You can't go all chivalrous on me – there's too much at stake.'

'In that case, I should say that anyone who had anything to do with George was potentially his murderer. He bullied his wife and son, Phil, unspeakably. He was also a womaniser. The only person he didn't bully and couldn't corrupt was his mother, and she's a very grim old harridan indeed. Do you want me to tell you all about these people?'

'No. Not yet, at least. I'd rather get my own impressions about them first. Well, I don't think there's anything more to be done tonight. Let's go along and talk to my wife.'

'Oh, look here, there's one thing. This kid Phil: he's a very decent kid, only twelve years old. We must get him out of that house, if we can. He's a thoroughly nervous subject, and this business might tip him over the edge. I don't like to ask Violet myself, considering what she's very soon going to find out about me. I was wondering could your wife perhaps – '

'I expect we can arrange something about that. I'll have a talk to Mrs Rattery about it tomorrow.'

3

When Nigel arrived at the Ratterys' house next morning, he found a policeman leaning over the gate and gazing phlegmatically across the street at a flustered driver who was trying to extricate his car from the almost empty car park opposite.

'Good morning,' said Nigel. 'Is this – ?'

'It's pathetic. Just pathetic, isn't it, sir?' said the policeman unexpectedly. It took Nigel a few seconds to realise that the constable was speaking, not of the recent events in this house, but of the erratic manoeuvres of the motorist. Severnbridge was already living up to its reputation for honest, yeoman stolidity. The constable jerked his thumb towards the car park. 'He's been at it for five minutes,' he said. 'Pathetic, I call it.'

Nigel agreed that the situation contained elements of pathos. Then he asked could he come in, as he had business with Mrs Rattery.

'Mrs Rattery?'

'Yes. This is her house, isn't it?'

'Ah, that is so. Terrible tragedy, isn't it, sir? Prominent figure in our town. Why, only last Thursday he was passing the time of day with me and—'

'Yes, a terrible tragedy, as you say. That's really what I want to see Mrs Rattery about.'

'Friend of the family?' asked the constable, still leaning massively across the gate.

'Well, not exactly, but—'

'One of these reporters. I guessed it. You'll have to cool your heels a bit longer, sonnie,' said the constable, with an abrupt change of front. 'Inspector Blount's orders. That's what I'm here—'

'Inspector Blount? Oh, he's an old friend of mine.'

'That's what they all say, son.' The constable's voice was tolerant but lugubrious.

'Tell him Nigel Strangeways – no, take him this card. I'll lay you seven to one he sees me at once.'

'I'm not a betting man. Not regular, that is. A mug's game, and I don't care who hears me say it. Mind you, I've had my little flutter on the Derby; but what I say – '

After five minutes more of this passive resistance, the constable agreed to take Nigel's card to Inspector Blount. They've been prompt enough about calling in the Yard, thought Nigel as he waited, fancy running into Blount again. With mixed feelings he recalled his last encounter with that bland-faced, granite-hearted Scot; Nigel had been Perseus then to Georgia's Andromeda, and Blount had been dangerously near playing the role of the sea monster; it was at Chatcombe, too, that the legendary airman, Fergus O'Brien, had set Nigel the knottiest problem of his career.

When a somewhat less talkative constable showed Nigel into the house, Blount was sitting – as Nigel best remembered him – behind a desk, giving a perfect imitation of a bank manager about to interview a client on the subject of his overdraft. The bald head, the gold-rimmed pince-nez, the smooth face, the discreet dark suit spelt affluence, tact, respectability. He looked quite absurdly unlike the remorseless hunter of criminals that Nigel only too well knew him to be. Fortunately he had a sense of humour – the extra-dry-sherry, not the Burns Night type.

'Well, this is an unexpected pleasure, Mr Strangeways,' he said, rising and extending a pontifical hand. 'And your lady wife, is she very well?'

'Yes, thanks. She came down with me, as a matter of fact. Quite a gathering of the clans. Or should I say, a gathering of the vultures?'

Inspector Blount permitted himself the driest, frostiest twinkle of the eye. 'Vultures? You're not going to tell me, Mr Strangeways, that you've got yourself mixed up with crime again?'

'I'm afraid so.'

'Well now, isn't that a – well now indeed! And you're going to spring some surprise on me, I can see it written all over you.'

Nigel played for time. He was never above a nice piece of exhibitionism, but, when he had a good curtain line, he liked to lead up to it.

'So this is a crime?' he said. 'Murder, I mean, not one of your two-a-penny suicides.'

'Suicides,' remarked Blount a trifle sententiously, 'do not generally swallow the bottle as well as the poison.'

'You mean, the vehicle, or whatever you call it, has disappeared? You'd better tell me all about it, if you will. I don't know a thing about Rattery's death so far, except that a chap who's been living here, Felix Lane – his real name's Frank Cairnes, as I expect you know, but everyone's so used to calling him "Felix" that we'd better call him Felix Cairnes in future – anyway, this chap intended to murder George Rattery, but, according to him, it didn't come off, so somebody else must have stepped into the breach.'

Inspector Blount received this bombshell with an aplomb worthy of the Old Guard. He removed his pince-nez with great deliberation, blew on the glasses, polished them, and replaced them on his nose. Then he said:

'Felix Cairnes? Ye-es, ye-es. The wee man with the beard. He writes these detective novels, doesn't he? Now that's very interesting.'

He glanced at Nigel with mild indulgence.

'Shall we toss for first innings?' asked Nigel.

'Are you – e-eh – in any sense acting for this Mr Cairnes?' Inspector Blount was treading delicately, but very firmly.

'Yes. Until he is proved guilty, of course.'

'Uh-huh. I see. And you are convinced he's innocent. I think you had better put your cards on the table first.'

So Nigel told him the gist of Felix's confession. When he arrived at Felix's plan to drown George

Rattery, Blount for once failed to conceal perfectly his excitement.

'The dead man's solicitors rang us up just now. They said they had something in their possession which would interest us. That wil be this diary you mention, I've no doubt. Very damaging for your – e-eh – client, Mr Strangeways.'

'You can't tell that till you've read it. I'm not at all sure that it won't save him.'

'Eh well, they're sending it by special messenger, so we'll know soon enough.'

'I won't argue it yet. You tell me a story now.'

Inspector Blount picked up a ruler from the desk, and sighted along it with one eye screwed up. Then he suddenly sat up straight, speaking with remarkable incisiveness.

'George Rattery was poisoned by strychnine. Can't enlarge upon that till after the autopsy – be finished by midday. He, Mrs Rattery, Lena Lawson, old Mrs Rattery, his mother, and his son Philip – a wee boy – had dinner together. They all ate the same food. The deceased and his mother took whisky with their food, the rest water. None of the others suffered any ill effects. They left the dinner table about quarter-past eight, the women and the wee boy first, the deceased following them in a minute's time. They all repaired to the drawing room with the exception of Master Philip. George Rattery was seized with severe pains between ten and fifteen minutes later. The women folk, poor souls, were helpless. They gave him a mustard emetic, but that only aggravated the seizure; the symptoms, of course, are very horrifying. Their own medical man, whom they rang up first, was out to a road accident, and by the time they had got hold of another, it was too late. Dr Clarkson arrived a little before ten – he'd been out on a maternity case – and applied the usual chloroform treatment, but Rattery was too far gone then. He died five or ten minutes later. I'll not bother you with the details. I've assured myself, however, that the poison could not have been introduced through any of the food or drink taken at dinner. The symptoms of strychnine poisoning, moreover, rarely take longer than an hour to supervene. The company sat down to dinner at quarter-past seven, therefore Rattery could not likely have taken the poison before dinner. There remains the interval of one minute between the time the others left the dining room and the time Rattery rejoined them in the drawing room.'

'Coffee? Port? No, of course it couldn't have been in the port. Nobody gulps that down and strychnine's got such a bitter taste, anyone'd spit it out at once unless he was expecting a bitter taste.'

'Just so. And the family did not take coffee on Saturday night – the parlourmaid had broken the percolator.'

'It sounds to me like suicide, then.'

Inspector Blount's face betrayed a slight impatience. 'My dear Mr Strangeways,' he said, 'a suicide does not take poison and then walk into the drawing room – into the bosom of his family – so that they can all watch the poison taking effect. In the second place, Colesby could find no trace of *how* he took it.'

'Had the dinner things been washed up?'

'The glass and silver. Not all the crockery, though. Mind you, Colesby – he's the local chap – may have missed something. I didn't get down here till this morning myself, but – '

'You know that Cairnes did not return to this house after he left it in the early afternon?'

'Indeed? Have you proof of that?'

'Well, no,' said Nigel, taken rather aback. 'At the moment, I haven't. He told me that, after the showdown in the dinghy, Rattery refused to let him come back here, even to pack his things. It can be verified, anyway.'

'Maybe,' said Blount cautiously. He drummed his fingers on the desk. 'I think – ye-es, I think we might take another peek at the dining room.'

4

It was a dark, heavy room, congested with pieces of Victorian walnut-wood furniture – table, chairs and a huge sideboard – which had obviously been designed for a much bigger room and gave off a kind of aura of overeating and stodgy conversation. This meaty, congested motif was continued in the heavy, maroon plush curtains, the faded but still repellent dark-red wallpaper, and the oil paintings on the wall, which represented respectively a fox gorging itself on a semi-eviscerated hare (very realistic), a miraculous draught of fishes – lobsters, crabs, eels, cod and salmon – laid out on a marble slab, and an ancestor of sorts who had evidently died of apoplexy or a surfeit of rich food.

'Gluttony recollected in tranquillity,' murmured Nigel, looking round instinctively for a bottle of soda mints. Inspector Blount was standing over the sideboard, meditatively rubbing his finger on its jaundice-yellow surface.

'Take a look here, Mr Strangeways,' he said. He was pointing at a sticky ring – the kind that might have been left by a medicine bottle whose contents had dribbled down to its base. Blount licked his finger.

'Well now,' he said. 'I wonder – '

With great deliberation, he took out a white silk pocket handkerchief, wiped his finger, and pressed the bell push. Presently a woman appeared – the parlourmaid, no doubt – very starched and disapproving in stiff cuffs and high, old-fashioned white cap.

'You rang, sir?' she asked.

'Yes. Tell me now, Annie – '

'Merritt.' Her thin, pursed lips expressed her disapproval of policemen who ventured to address parlourmaids by their Christian names.

'Merritt? Tell me then, Miss Merritt, what made this ring here?'

Without appearing to raise her eyes, which she kept downcast and discreet, like a nun, the woman said:

'The master's – the late master's tonic.'

'Oh ye-es. Uh-huh. And where has the bottle gone to?'

'I couldn't say, sir.'

Further questioning elicited a statement that Merritt had last seen the bottle after lunch on Saturday; she had not noticed if it was there when she cleared away after dinner.

'Did he take it out of a glass or a spoon?'

'A tablespoon, sir.'

'And after dinner on Saturday, did you wash up this particular spoon with the others?'

Merritt bridled slightly. 'I do not *wash up*,' she said, with frigid emphasis. 'I clear away.'

'Did you clear away the spoon with which your master took his tonic?' said Blount patiently.

'French without Tears,' Nigel giggled.

'I did, sir.'

'And it was washed up?'

'Yes, sir.'

'That's a pity. Now let me see – e-eh – would you ask your mistress to step this way.'

'Mrs Rattery senior is indisposed, sir.'

'I meant – oh, well, perhaps it'd be better – yes, ask Miss Lawson if she can spare me a few minutes.'

'It's easy to see who's mistress in this house,' remarked Nigel when the parlourmaid had gone out.

'Very interesting. This substance tastes to me like a tonic I once had, that contained nux vomica.'

'Nux vomica?' Nigel whistled. 'So that would account for his not noticing the bitter taste. And he stayed behind a minute after the others left the dining room. You seem to have got somewhere.'

Blount looked at him slyly. 'Still keen on the suicide theory, Mr Strangeways?'

'It doesn't look too good, if this bottle was really the vehicle of the poison. But how very odd of the murderer to get rid of the bottle. Spoilt his chance of making it look like suicide.'

'Murderers do very odd things, you'll not be denying.'

'However, it seems to let out Felix Cairnes. That is to say, if—'

Nigel stopped short, hearing a step outside the door. The girl who entered was unexpected yet somehow not out of place in the sombre room, like a sunray slanting into a prison cell. Her ash-blonde hair, the white linen suit she wore, and her vivid make-up were a defiance to everything this room meant – both in life and in death. Even if Felix had not told him, Nigel would have known she was an actress by the slight pause she made inside the door, the studied naturalness with which she took the seat Inspector Blount offered her. Blount introduced Nigel and himself, and expressed his sympathy for Miss Lawson and her sister. Lena received this with a rather perfunctory inclination of her head; she was evidently as eager as the Inspector to get down to brass tacks. Eager, and yet apprehensive of the results, thought Nigel, noticing the way her fingers were twidding a button of her coat, the exhibited candour in her eyes.

Blount was asking questions gently, moving from one aspect of the case to another, like a doctor palpating the body of a patient, waiting for the twinge that reveals the seat of the trouble. Yes, Miss Lawson had been in the room when the first convulsion seized her brother-in-law. No, Phil had not been there, luckily, he must have gone straight upstairs after dinner. What had she herself done from the time they left the dining room? Well, she was with the others till George's seizure began. Then his mother sent her out to fetch some mustard and water – yes, she particularly remembered it was his mother who had suggested this – and afterwards she'd been busy on the phone trying to get a doctor. No, George had not said anything in between the spasms of pain to suggest what had happened – he had lain quite still, and once or twice seemed to have fallen asleep.

'And during the attacks?'

Lena's lashes swept down over her eyes, but not quickly enough to hide the start of fear in them.

'Oh, he was groaning terribly, complaining of the pain. It was awful. He was on the floor. He curved up, like a hoop – I ran over a cat once in a car, and it – oh, don't please don't, I can't bear it!'

She hid her face in her hands and began to sob. Blount patted her shoulder in a fatherly way but, when she had recovered, he insisted gently:

'And during these attacks, he didn't say – didn't mention anyone's name, for instance?'

'I – I wasn't in the room most of the time.'

'Come now, Miss Lawson. You must realise there's no point in concealing something that doubtless two other people beside you heard. What a man may have said in extremity of pain is not going to convict anyone without a great deal more evidence.'

'Well, then,' the girl flung at him angrily, 'he said something about Felix – Mr Lane. He said, "Lane. Tried it on before" – something like that. And he cursed him horribly. It doesn't mean anything. He hated Felix. He was bewildered – beside himself with pain. You can't—'

'Don't upset yourself, Miss Lawson. Mr Strangeways here will be able to reassure you about that, I hope.' Inspector Blount smoothed his jaw, and said confidentially, 'Do you know, by any chance, what reason Mr Rattery could have had for suicide? Money troubles? Illness? He was taking a tonic, I am told.'

Lena stared at him, frozen rigid, her eyes like the insensate glare of a tragedy mask. For a second or two she could not speak. Then she said hurriedly:

'Suicide? You startled me for a moment, I mean, we'd all thought he must have eaten some bad food or something. Yes, it must have been suicide, I suppose, though I can't imagine why – '

Nigel felt somehow that suicide was not the operative word in causing the girl so openly to panic. His intuition was shortly to be justified.

'This tonic that he took, now,' Blount said, 'it contained nux vomica, I believe?'

'I wouldn't know about that.'

'No. Did he take his usual tablespoonful after lunch?'

The girl knitted her brows. 'I don't remember for certain. He always did, so I suppose if he hadn't after lunch, I'd have noticed it.'

'Quite right. Ye-es. A very subtle observation, if you'll allow me to say so,' Blount congratulated her. He took off his pince-nez, and played with them indecisively. 'You see, Miss Lawson, I'm wondering about the bottle. It's disappeared. It's vairy awkward, you see, because we've an idea – just an idea, mind you – that this bottle may be – e-eh – connected with his death. Nux vomica is a poison, you see, of the strychnine group, and Mr Rattery might have added a wee bit more of the poison to his dose, if he'd wanted to make away with himself. But if that was the way of it, he'd no be like to make away with the bottle too.' Blount's suppressed excitement resurrected his almost extinct Glasgow accent, so that the last word sounded like 'the boul tu'. This time Lena had either regained control over her expression or had nothing to give away. She spoke hesitantly.

'You mean, if this bottle had been found on the sideboard after George's death, it would have proved it was suicide?'

'No, not quite that, Miss Lawson,' said Blount benignly. Then his lips lost their kindness, he leant forward and spoke with cold deliberation. 'I mean that the absence of this bottle makes it look like murder.'

'A-ah,' sighed the girl. A sigh of relief, almost, as though the suspense of waiting for this dreadful word was now ended, and she knew there was nothing worse left for her to face.

'You are not surprised?' asked Blount sharply, a little piqued by the girl's calmness.

'What ought I to do? Burst into tears on your shoulder? Start chewing the legs of the table?'

Nigel caught Blount's embarrassed eye and gave him a saucy look. He enjoyed seeing Blount discomfited.

'Just one thing, Miss Lawson,' said Nigel. 'It sounds a rather alarming question, but I expect Felix has told you I've come down here on his behalf. I'm not trying to get at you. But did you ever suspect that Felix intended all along to murder George Rattery?'

'No! No! It's a lie! He didn't!' Lena's hands went up in front of her face, as though she was trying to push Nigel's question away from her. The panic was replaced by a kind of puzzlement on her expressive features. 'All along?' she said slowly. 'How do you mean, "all along"?'

'Well, since you met him, before he came down here,' said Nigel, equally puzzled.

'No, of course he didn't,' the girl replied with obvious sincerity. Then she bit her lip. 'But he didn't,' she cried, 'he never killed George. I know he didn't.'

'You were in George Rattery's car when he ran over and killed a small boy, Martin Cairnes, last January,' said Inspector Blount, not unsympathetically.

'Oh God,' Lena whispered, 'so you've found that out at last.' She gazed at them candidly. 'It wasn't my fault. I tried to make him stop and – but he wouldn't. I've dreamt about that for months. It was ghastly. But I don't understand. What – ?'

'I think we can let Miss Lawson go now, don't you, Blount?' interposed Nigel quickly. The Inspector smoothed his chin.

'Ye-es. Maybe you're right. Just one thing more. Had Mr Rattery any enemies, would you say?'

'He might. He was the sort who'd make them, I think. But I don't know of any.'

After the girl had gone out, Blount said, 'That was very suggestive. She knows something about the missing bottle, I'll swear. And she's afraid that this Mr Cairnes did the job, but she hasn't yet connected up Felix Lane with the father of the boy George Rattery killed. A pretty lassie. Pity she won't tell the truth. Eh well, we'll find it out before long. What made you ask her whether she suspected Felix of intending to murder Rattery? I thought it was a wee bit early to be letting that cat out of the bag.'

Nigel flicked his cigarette out of the window. 'The point was this. If Felix did *not* kill Rattery, we're up against a most outrageous coincidence – that on the very day he planned and failed to murder him, somebody else planned and succeeded.'

'A most outrageous coincidence, as you admit,' said Blount sceptically.

'No. Wait a minute. I'm not prepared to dismiss the coincidence as impossible. If a sufficient number of monkeys played with typewriters for a sufficient number of centuries, they'd have turned out all the sonnets of Shakespeare: that's a coincidence, but it's also scientifically true. But if George's poisoning was not a coincidence, and if Felix wasn't responsible, it follows logically that some third person must have known of Felix's intentions – either through reading the diary himself or through being taken into George's confidence.'

'Ah. Now I see what you're driving at,' said Blount, his eyes gleaming behind his spectacles.

'Assume a third person, who had this special knowledge *and wanted George to be killed*. When Felix's attempt failed, this third person took up the running himself and conveyed the poison to George, probably through that tonic. He could be pretty sure of the suspicion falling on Felix, on account of the diary. But he had to act immediately, since he could not expect Felix to stay on in Severnbridge for more than a night after the failure of the dinghy scheme. Lena was the obvious person to ask first, since she'd be the obvious person for George to have confided in over the diary – he and she both having been mixed up in the manslaughter of Martin Cairnes which it revealed. But I think she was quite sincere just now, when she gave the impression that she hadn't connected up Felix Lane with the boy, Martin. Therefore she doesn't know of the diary. Therefore we can eliminate her from our list of suspects, unless the attempted murder and the real one were sheer coincidence.'

'But, if Lawson didn't know about the diary, why is she so evidently afraid that Cairnes poisoned Rattery, or afraid of our suspecting it, at any rate?'

'I don't think we can discover that till we know more about this household. You noticed how puzzled she was when I asked her had she suspected Felix of intending to kill George *all along*? Genuinely puzzled. That looks as if she knew nothing about the diary, but knew of some other motive for Felix's killing George – some enmity that had arisen after the two men met.'

'Yes. That seems reasonable. I'll need to ask each member of the household whether they had any suspicions about Felix – Felix Lane, I'd better say – and watch the reactions. If someone's tried to use him as a blind, it'll come out in the wash.'

'That's the idea. Look here, the boy Phil – d'you mind if we have him over at the hotel for a few days? My wife'll look after him. This isn't a very healthy environment for the tender mind, just at the present.'

'No. That'll be all right. I'll have to ask the wee boy a few questions some time, but they'll keep.'

'Right. I'll go and ask Mrs Rattery about it.'

5

Violet Rattery was sitting at a bureau writing, when Nigel was shown in. Lena was there too. Nigel introduced himself and explained his errand. 'Of course, if you've made arrangements of your own – but he and Mr Lane get on very well, I believe, and my wife would be delighted to do anything she can.'

'Yes. I see. Thank you. It's very good – ' said Violet vaguely. She turned with a helpless gesture towards Lena, who was standing facing the flood of sunlight that poured through the window.

'What do you think, Sis? Would it be all right?'

'Of course. Why not? Phil oughtn't sto stay here any longer,' said Lena carelessly, still gazing down into the street below.

'Yes. I know. I was just wondering what Ethel would—'

Lena swung round, her red mouth alive and contemptuous. 'My dear Vi,' she exclaimed, 'it's time you started thinking for yourself. Whose child is Phil, anyway? Anyone'd think you were a slavey, the way you let George's mother order you about – the interfering old bitch. She and George have made life hell for you – no, there's no good frowning at me – and it's time you told her where she gets off. If you haven't enough spirit left to stand up for your own child, you might as well take a dose of poison too.'

Violet's indecisive, over-powdered face quivered. Nigel thought she was going to break down. He saw the struggle in her between her long habit of subjugation and the real woman that Lena's words had deliberately aimed to provoke. After a little, her bloodless lips tightened, a light appeared in the faded eyes, and she said – with a small, unconscious tilt of the chin, 'Very well. I'll do it, I'm very grateful to you, Mr Strangeways.'

As though in answer to this unspoken challenge, the door opened. Without knocking, an old woman, swathed in black, entered. The sunlight pouring through the window seemed to stop dead at her feet, as if she had killed it dead.

'I heard voices,' the woman said gruffly.

'Yes. We were talking,' said Lena. Her pertness was disregarded absolutely. The old woman stood there a moment, her large body blocking the door. Then she stumped over to the window, suddenly less dignified now that her movement betrayed the too short leg beneath that formidable trunk and pulled down the blind. The sunlight fought against her, thought Nigel; in this gloom her mastery is regained.

'I am surprised at you, Violet,' she said. 'Your husband lying dead in the next room, and you cannot even pay him the respect of keeping the blinds drawn.'

'But, Mother—'

'I let the blind up,' interrupted Lena. 'Things are quite bad enough without our having to sit in the dark.'

'Be quiet!'

'I'll do nothing of the sort. If you care to go on bullying Violet, as you and George have done for the last fifteen years, that's not my business. You're not mistress in this house, let me tell you, and I'm not taking anything from you. Do what you like in your own room, but don't interfere with other people's, you obscene old cockroach!'

Light versus Darkness, Ormuzd and Ahriman, thought Nigel as he watched the girl, her supple shoulders thrust forward, her throat curving up like a scimitar, confront the old woman who stood like a pillar of darkness in the middle of the room. True, this representative of Light has reverted to type, but, even if she is vulgar, she's not unhealthy, not unclean, she doesn't infect the room with a stink of camphor and stale proprieties and rotting power, like that appalling creature in black. However, I suppose I'd better intervene. Nigel said pleasantly:

'Mrs Rattery, I have just been sugesting to your daughter-in-law that we – my wife and I – would be very pleased to take Phil off her hands for a few days, till things are cleared up.'

'Who is this young man?' asked the old lady, her imperial manner scarcely shaken by Lena's assault. Explanations followed. 'The Ratterys have never run away. I forbid it. Phil must stay,' she said.

Lena opened her mouth to speak, but Nigel with a gesture restrained her. Violet must speak now or be for ever silent. She looked imploringly at her sister, making an ineffectual gesture with her hand, then her drooping shoulders straightened, an expression which was indeed one of sheer heroism transfigured the dim features, and she said:

'I've decided that Phil shall go to the Strangeways. It would be unfair to keep him here – he's too young.'

Old Mrs Rattery's acceptance of defeat was more formidable than any display of violence. She stood immobile for a moment, looking steadily at Violet, then she stumped over to the door.

'I see there is a conspiracy against me,' she said in her leaden-echo voice. 'I am very ill satisfied by your behaviour, Violet. I have long ceased to expect anything but fishwife's manners from your sister, but I had thought you at least were cleansed by now of the taint of the gutter from which George picked you up.'

The door closed decisively. Lena made an improper gesture towards it. Violet half collapsed into the chair from which she had risen. A smell of camphor hung in the air. Nigel looked down his nose, automatically fixing the scene upon his memory. He was far too self-critical to conceal from himself that for a moment he had been really alarmed by the old woman. God, what a household! he thought. What an environment for a sensitive child – father and mother constantly bickering, and that bogy-woman of an old matriarch no doubt trying to turn him against his mother all the time and gain possession of his mind. In the middle of his reflections, he became aware of having heard footsteps overhead – the waddling, stumping gait of Mrs Rattery.

'Where's Phil?' he asked sharply.

'In his room, I expect,' said Violet. 'Straight above this one. Are you going to – ?'

But Nigel was already out of the door. He ran silently upstairs. Someone was talking in the room on his right – a dull, weighted voice he recognised only too well, but now with a note of pleading beneath its blunted tones.

'You don't want to go away, to leave me, do you, Phil? Your grandfather wouldn't have run away; he wasn't a coward. You are the only man in the house, remember, now your poor father's dead.'

'Go away! Go away! I hate you.' There was a feeble, panicky defiance in the voice. It might have been that of a small child rebuking some large animal which had come too near it, thought Nigel. With a considerable effort he restrained himself from going in.

'You're overwrought, Phil, or you wouldn't talk to your poor old grannie like that. Listen, child. Don't you think you ought to stay with your mother now she's all alone? She's going to have a very difficult time. You see, your father was poisoned. Poisoned. You understand?'

Mrs Rattery's voice, which had become ingratiating, with a heavy, atrocious sweetness like chloroform, paused. There was a whimper from the room – the sound of a child fighting against an anaesthetic. Nigel heard footsteps behind him.

'Your mother will want all our help. You see, the police may find out how she quarrelled with your father last week, and what she said, and that might make them think she'd—'

'This is too much,' muttered Nigel, his hand on the doorknob. But Violet whirled past him like a fury into the room. Old Mrs Rattery was kneeling in front of Phil, her fingers biting into his thin arms. Violet plucked at her shoulder, trying to pull her away from the boy, but she might as well have tried to move a basalt rock. With a swift movement she knocked away the old woman's arm and stood between her and Phil.

'You beast! How could you – how dare you treat him like this! It's all right, Phil. Don't cry. I won't let her come near you again. You're quite safe now.'

The boy stared at his mother – a dazed, incredulous stare. Nigel noticed how bare the room was; no carpet, a cheap iron bed, a kitchen table. No doubt this was his father's idea of 'hardening' the boy. On the table a stamp album lay open. The two pages were grimy with finger-marks and there were tear stains on them too. Nigel came nearer to losing his temper than he'd been for a long time, but he knew he could not afford to alienate old Mrs Rattery just yet. She was still on her knees.

'Will you be so good as to help me up, Mr Strangeways,' she said. In that impossible position she maintained a kind of dignity. What a woman, thought Nigel, as he helped her to her feet. This is going to be exceedingly interesting.

6

Five hours later, Nigel was talking to Inspector Blount. Phil Rattery had been conveyed safely to the Angler's Arms, where he was now finishing a large tea and discussing Polar exploration with Georgia.

'It was strychnine all right,' said Blount.

'But where did it come from? You can't just stroll into a chemist's and buy the stuff.'

'No. You can buy vermin-killers, though. Several of them contain considerable percentages of strychnia. Not that I think our friend needed to buy it.'

'You interest me strangely. You mean, no doubt, that the murderer is the brother of an official rat-killer, or maybe the sister. "Anything like the sound of a rat makes my heart go pit-a-pat." Browning.'

'Not just that. But Colesby was making some routine inquiries round at Rattery's garage. It's by the river and infested with rats. He happened to notice a couple of tins of vermin-killer in the office. Anyone – any member of the family, that is – could easily have come in and helped themselves.'

Nigel digested this. 'Did he ask whether Felix Cairnes had been seen in the garage lately?'

'Yes. He was there once or twice,' said Blount, a little reluctantly.

'But not on the day of the murder?'

'He was not *seen* there on the day of the murder.'

'You know, you mustn't let Cairnes become an *idée fixe* with you. Preserve the open mind.'

'It's not so easy preserving an open mind when a man is murdered and another man writes it out in black and white that he is going to murder him,' said Blount, tapping the cover of a foolscap-size notebook that lay on the desk before him.

'As I see it, Cairnes can be written off.'

'And how do you make that out?'

'There's no earthly reason to doubt his statement that he meant to kill Rattery by drowning. When this attempt failed, he went straight back to the Angler's Arms. I've been making enquiries there. The waiter remembers giving him tea in the lounge at five o'clock – that was about four minutes after he left the dinghy at the landing stage. After tea, he sat out on the hotel lawn till six thirty, reading. I've witnesses to that. At six thirty he went into the bar and was drinking there till dinner. He could not have gone back to the Ratterys' house during that period, could he?'

'We'll have to go into this alibi,' said Blount cautiously.

'You can put it through the mangle if you like, it won't get you anywhere. If he put the poison into

Rattery's medicine he must have done it between the time Rattery took a dose out of it after lunch and the time he himself set out for the river. You may find that he had the *opportunity* to do it then. But why in hell should he? He had no reason to imagine that the dinghy accident was going to fail, but even if he had determined on a second string to his bow, he wouldn't choose poison – the dinghy business shows he's got plenty of brains – he'd have arranged something to look like an accident too, not this blatant business of rat-killer and a disappearing bottle.'

'The bottle. Ye-es.'

'Exactly. The bottle. Removing the bottle at once made the thing look like murder; and, whatever you may think of Felix Cairnes, you can't believe he'd be such a halfwit as to draw attention like that to a murder he'd committed. In any case, I think it'll be fairly easy to prove that he didn't come near the house till some time after Rattery died.'

'I know he didn't,' said Blount unexpectedly. 'I've been into that already. Immediately after Rattery's death, Dr Clarkson telephoned the police; the house was guarded from ten fifteen onwards. We've witnesses for Cairnes' whereabouts from dinner till ten fifteen – and his whereabouts wasn't hereabouts,' added Blount with a prim quirk at the corners of his mouth.

'Well then,' said Nigel helplessly, 'if Cairnes couldn't have done the murder, what – ?'

'I didn't say that. I said he couldn't have removed the medicine bottle. Your arguments have been very interesting,' Blount continued, in the manner of a tutor about to demolish a pupil's essay, 'very interesting indeed, only they're based on a fallacy. You're presupposing that one and the same person must have poisoned the bottle and later removed it. But suppose Cairnes filled it up with the poison after lunch, to take effect at dinner should the river accident fail; suppose he never intended to remove it afterwards, but meant to give the impression that Rattery had committed suicide; supposing some third party comes along after Rattery has been taken ill – some third party who already knows or suspects that Cairnes was out for Rattery's blood; this third party might want to protect Cairnes, might connect the bottle with the poisoning, and – in a desperate, unreasoning attempt to shield him – get rid of the bottle.'

'I see,' said Nigel after a long pause. 'You mean, Lena Lawson. But why – ?'

'Oh, she's in love with Cairnes.'

'God bless my soul, how do you know that?'

'My psychological insight,' said the Inspector, with heavy-handed mockery of Nigel's strongest point. 'Also, I asked the servants. They were more or less officially engaged, I gather.'

'Well,' said Nigel, his head reeling under these shrewd and unexpected blows, 'it seems that I've still got some work to do here. I was afraid my part in this case was going to be too easy.'

'And there's one other little point – just so that you won't get overconfident. No doubt you'll call it a – e-eh – an outrageous coincidence. But your client mentions strychnine in this diary of his. I've not had time to read much of it yet, but just cast your eye over this.'

Blount held out the foolscap notebook, marking a place with his finger. Nigel read, 'I'd promised myself the satisfaction of his agony – he does not deserve a quick death. I'd like to burn him slowly, inch by inch, or watch ants honeycomb his living flesh, or there's strychnine, that bends a man's body into a rigid hoop – by God, I'd like to bowl him down the slope into Hell . . .'

Nigel was silent for a few moments. Then he began to pace up and down with his ostrich strides.

'It won't do, Blount,' he broke out, more serious than he had yet been. 'Don't you see? – this equally well supports my own theory that some third person had access to this diary and used his knowledge to kill Rattery in such a way as to throw suspicion on Cairnes. But leave that. Does it seem humanly credible to you that anyone – let alone Cairnes, who is a decent ordinary chap apart from the irreparable injury Rattery did him – that anyone could be so insanely cold-blooded and calculating as to prepare a second murder like this in the event of his first attempt missing fire? It doesn't ring true. You know it doesn't.'

'When the mind is cracked – I don't mean any pun – you cannot expect its actions to ring true,' said Blount, no less seriously.

'The unbalanced man who intends to commit a murder always errs on the side of overconfidence, not lack of confidence. You'll agree with that?'

'As a general principle, yes.'

'Well then, you're asking me to believe that Cairnes, who had worked out an almost perfect murder plan, had so little confidence in it and himself that he prepared a supplementary one as well. It won't wash.'

'You go your ways, and I'll go mine. I've no wish to arrest the wrong man, any more than you'd have.'

'Good. Can I have this diary to read some time?'

'I'll just look through it myself first. I'll send it up tonight.'

7

It was a warm evening. The last rays of the sun left an apricot tinge, a mellow bloom on the lawn that sloped gently down from the Angler's Arms to the waterside. One of those preternaturally still evenings on which, as Georgia remarked, you could hear a cow chewing its cud three fields away. In one corner of the bar-parlour a group of anglers was collected – desiccated, scrawny men, who ran to shabby tweeds and doleful moustaches. One of them was illustrating, with liberal gestures, a real or imagined catch. If indeed any rumour of violence had penetrated into the dull, aqueous world in which these men lived and moved and had their being, it must clearly have been snubbed as an impertinent intrusion. Nor did they pay the least attention to the group who sat round another table in the parlour, drinking gin and ginger beer.

' "A fishing-rod," ' quoted Nigel, in a by no means inaudible voice, ' "is a stick with a hook at one end and a fool at the other." '

'Shut up, Nigel,' whispered Georgia. 'I will not be a party to any rough house. Those men are dangerous. They might gaff us.'

Lena, sitting next to Felix on a high-backed bench and leaning against him, stirred impatiently.

'Let's go out in the garden, Felix,' she said. The invitation was obviously meant for him alone, but he replied, 'All right. Drink up, you two, and we'll all go and play clock-golf or something.'

Lena bit her lip, and got up rather brusquely. Georgia shot Nigel a swift glance which he interpreted, correctly, as meaning – we'd better all go out, no use being arch with those two, but why doesn't he want to be alone with her?

Why indeed? thought Nigel. If Blount is right, and Lena suspects Felix of having murdered Rattery, one could understand her being a bit shy of his company – afraid of hearing her suspicions confirmed by his own lips. But in fact it is just the other way round.

He is avoiding her. At dinner, even, one got the impression that he was keeping her at arm's length. There was a sort of sharp edge on his conversation, particularly when he addressed her, that seemed to warn – come any nearer and you'll cut yourself. It's all very complicated but Felix is a complex character, I'm beginning to realise. I think it's time for putting a few cards on the table – see how they react to some plain speaking.

So, when they had finished a round of clock-golf, and were sitting on deckchairs with the river glimmering more darkly before them, Nigel began talking about the case.

'The incriminating document is now in the hands of the police, you'll be relieved to hear. Blount's bringing it up tonight.'

'Oh. Well, it's a good thing for them to know the worst, I expect,' said Felix lightly. There was a strange mixture of shyness and complacency in his expression. He went on, 'I suppose I might as well shave my beard off, now that all disguise is useless. I never liked the thing – never did like hairs in my food – finicky, no doubt.'

Georgia played with her fingers. Felix's facetiousness jarred upon her: she was not sure yet whether she liked him.

Lena said, 'May a girl ask what you're talking about? What is this "incriminating document", anyway?'

'Felix's diary. You know,' said Nigel quickly.

'Diary? But why? – I don't understand.' Lena glanced helplessly towards Felix, but he avoided her eyes. She sounded entirely mystified. Of course she's an actress, thought Nigel, and she *may* be putting it all on, but I'd be prepared to lay a modest bet that this is the first she's heard of the diary. He continued to probe.

'Look here, Felix, there's no point our going on at cross-purposes. Doesn't Miss Lawson know about your diary – and everything? Oughtn't you to – ?'

Nigel did not know what would be the result of this angling in troubled waters. The one thing he could least have expected was what actually happened. Felix sat up in his deckchair, fixed Lena with a gaze in which familiarity, cynicism, bravado, and a certain cool brutality of contempt – whether for her or for himself – seemed to be mingled, and told her the whole story of Martie, of his own search for George, of the diary which he had kept hidden under a loose floorboard in his room at the Ratterys', and the attempted murder on the river.

'So now you know the sort of person I am,' he said finally. 'I did everything except kill George.'

His voice had been quite level and objective. But Nigel could see that his whole body was trembling, jerking almost, as though he had been bathing too long in ice-cold water. The silence when he ended was interminable. The river clucked and chuckled against its banks, a moorhen came out with its hysterical cry, the radio in the hotel was repeating unemotionally the Japanese claim that their bombing of open towns in China was pure self-defence. But, between the little group on the lawn, silence was stretched like an exposed nerve. Lena's hands gripped the wood of her chair; she had sat like this all the time Felix was talking, motionless except for her lips which opened now and then as though to guess what Felix would say next, or to help him to say it. Now at last her rigid pose relaxed, her wide mouth trembled, her whole body seemed to grow small and lost as she cried, 'Felix! Why didn't you tell me all this before? Oh, why didn't you?'

She gazed full into his face, which was still tense and unyielding. Nigel and Georgia might have been miles away. Felix said nothing, determined – it seemed – to withhold himself absolutely from her. She got to her feet, beginning to cry, and hurried towards the hotel. Felix made no move to follow her . . .

'All this secret diplomacy of yours has me guessing,' said Georgia when they were in their room an hour later. 'Did you mean to precipitate that harrowing scene?'

'I'm sorry about it. I certainly didn't expect it to turn out just like that. Still, it pretty well proves that Lena didn't kill Rattery. I'm certain she didn't know about the diary, and that she's really in love with Felix. So there were two obstacles to her poisoning George and letting Felix take the rap for it. Of course, if it was coincidence,' he went on, half to himself, 'that would account for the way she said "Why didn't you tell me all this before?" I wonder – '

'Nonsense,' said Georgia briskly. 'I like that girl. She's got spirit. Poison isn't a woman's weapon, as they glibly say, it's a coward's weapon. Lena's got too much guts to use it. If she wanted to kill Rattery, she'd have blown his head off, stabbed him, something like that. She'd never kill except at white heat. Take it from me.'

'I daresay you're right. Now tell me something else. Why is Felix treating her so harshly? Why didn't he tell her about the diary as soon as Rattery was murdered? And why on earth did he come out with the story in front of you and me?'

Georgia shook her dark hair back from her forehead. She looked like an intelligent, rather worried monkey.

'Safety in numbers,' she said. 'He'd been putting off confessing to her, because his confession would show that he'd only used her – at first, anyway – as an unconscious accessory to the murder he intended to commit. He's a sensitive creature, which means that he must have realised how genuinely she's in love with him, and must have shrunk from wounding her feelings by letting her realise that he's only been using her. I should say he has that particular kind of moral cowardice which hates above all things giving offence, not so much because of the damage to the other person's feelings as out of a desire to protect his own. He would hate embarrassing emotional scenes. That's why he seized the chance of telling Lena the whole story in front of us. Our presence safeguarded him from its immediate consequences – from tears, reproaches, explanations, reassurances, and all the rest of it.'

'You think he's not in love with her?'

'I'm not sure. He seems to be trying to persuade her, or himself, that he isn't. I wish I didn't rather like him,' Georgia added inconsequentially.

'Why?'

'Have you noticed how extraordinarily good he is with Phil? He's really devoted to the boy, I believe, and Phil looks up to him as a sort of Great White Father. If it weren't for that – '

' – you could suspect Felix of the worst with an easy conscience,' Nigel interrupted.

'I wish you wouldn't take the words out of my mouth when they were never in it,' she complained, 'like a conjurer with a gold watch.'

'You funny thing. You are sweet and I love you and that's almost the first time you're told me a cracking lie.'

'No.'

'Well, not quite the first then.'

'It wasn't one.'

'All right, it wasn't one. How would it be if I were to scratch the back of your head for a bit?'

'It'd be lovely. That is, if you haven't any more urgent business to attend to.'

'There's the diary. I must read that through tonight. I'll shade the light, and read it when you're in bed. By the way, I must arrange for you to meet old Mrs

Rattery some time. She's a hundred per cent Grand Guignol type. I should be much happier if I could find some motive for her having poisoned George.'

'Matricide I've heard of. But filicide must be rather rare surely.'

Nigel muttered:

> ' "O I fear ye are poisoned, Lord Randal, my son!
> O I fear ye are poisoned, my handsome young man!" –
> "O yes! I am poisoned; mother, make my bed soon,
> For I'm sick at heart, and I fain would lie down." '

'But it was Lord Randal's young woman who did that to him, I thought,' Georgia said.

'So *he* thought,' said Nigel, with sinister emphasis.

8

'I wish I could lay my hands on that bottle,' said Inspector Blount next morning, as he and Nigel were setting out towards the garage. 'If it was one of the household who concealed it, it can't be far away. None of them was out of sight of the others for more than a few minutes, after Rattery was taken ill.'

'What about Miss Lawson? She said she was at the telephone quite a lot of the time. Have you verified that?'

'I have. I've worked out a chart of the movements of every member of the household from after dinner till the time the local police were called in and they were under observation, and checked each statement against that of the others. There were times when any of them could have nipped into the dining room and removed the bottle, but no one could have had time to take it far away. Colesby's chaps have searched the house, the garden and the neighbourhood within a radius of a few hundred yards. No bottle.'

'But surely – didn't Rattery take this tonic regularly? What about his empties?'

'They'd been taken away by a rag-and-bone man in the middle of last week.'

'You seem to have bitten off quite a sizeable segment,' remarked Nigel cheerfully.

'Uh-huh.' Blunt removed his homburg, mopped his glistening bald head, and replaced the hat in a severely upright position.

'You'd save yourself a lot of trouble if you asked Lena point-blank where she put the ruddy bottle.'

'You know I never bully witnesses,' said Blount.

'I wonder you're not struck dead by lightning for that. A more barefaced lie—'

'Did you read that diary yet?'

'Yes. Several useful pointers there, didn't you think?'

'Well, ye-es, perhaps. I gathered Rattery was not too popular in the family circle, and he seems to have been playing fast and loose with the wife of this man, Carfax, we're just going to see. But, mind you, Cairnes may have stressed all that in his diary just to divert suspicion on to somebody else.'

'I don't think "stressed" is the word. He only mentioned it *en passant*.'

'Oh, he's a clever wee man. He wouldn't pile it on too thick.'

'Well, his observations can be verified easily enough. In fact, we've got enough evidence already that Rattery was an infernal bully in his own house. He and that appalling mother of his seem to have reduced everyone but Lena Lawson to pulp.'

'I grant you that. But are you suggesting he was poisoned by his wife or one of the servants?'

'I'm not suggesting anything,' said Nigel a little irritably, 'except that Felix put down no more than the bare truth about the Ratterys in his diary.'

They walked the rest of the way to the garage in silence. The streets of Severnbridge dozed in the midday sunshine. If its inhabitants, gossiping at the mouths of its picturesque, historical and squalid alleys, were aware that the prosperous businessman who trotted past them was in reality New Scotland Yard's most formidable Chief Inspector, they concealed their curiosity with remarkable ease. Even when Nigel Strangeways began to sign, mezzo forte, the 'Ballad of Chevy Chase', it caused no sensation – except in the bosom of Inspector Blount, who quickened his step and began to wear a rather hunted look. Severnbridge, unlike Inspector Blount, was quite inured to discordant voices raised in song along its main thoroughfare, though not usually at so early an hour. The charabanc loads of trippers from Birmingham had seen to that, kicking up every summer weekend a shindy that Sevenbridge had not experienced since the Wars of the Roses.

'I wish you'd stop making that fearful noise,' said Blount desperately at last.

'Surely you cannot refer to my rendering of the greatest ballad – '

'I can.'

'Oh. Well, never mind. There are only fifty-eight more stanzas.'

'My God!' exclaimed Blount, a man exceedingly sparing of profanity. Nigel resumed:

> 'Then the wild thoro' the woodies went
> On every sidè shear;
> Grayhounds thoro' the grevès glent
> For to kill their deer.'

'Ah, here we are,' said Blount, scurrying into the garage. Two mechanics were sparring with each other, lighted cigarettes in their mouths, under a notice which proclaimed that Smoking was Strictly Forbidden. Blount enquired for the boss, and he and Nigel were shown into the office. While the Inspector made a little preliminary conversation, Nigel was studying Carfax; a small man, neatly dressed, quite nondescript in general appearance, his smooth, tanned face had that suggestion of subdued playfulness and open good humour which one sees on the faces of professional cricketers. He is a man with energy without ambition, thought Nigel – the kind that is happy to be a nonentity, is popular but has a deep fund of reserve, is mad-keen on some hobby, may very well be an unacknowledged expert in some unlikely branch of knowledge, makes an excellent husband and father. One would not for a moment connect him with violent passions. But that sort is deceptive, very deceptive. The 'Little Man', when roused, has the cool furious courage of the mongoose; the Little Man's home is, traditionally, his castle – in defence of it he will show the most startling tenacity and initiative. This Rhoda, now. I wonder . . .

'You see,' Inspector Blount was saying, 'we've made inquiries at all chemists in the district, and it is now – e-eh – established that no member of the deceased's household has made purchases of strychnia in any form. Of course, whoever did it may have gone further afield. We shall continue to make inquiries on those lines, but provisionally we must assume that the murderer took some of the vermin-killer you keep here.'

'Murderer? You have excluded the possibility of suicide or accident, then?' asked Carfax.

'Do you know any reason why your partner should have committed suicide?'

'No. Oh no. I just wondered.'

'There were no financial difficulties, for instance?'

'No, the garage is doing reasonably well. In any case, I'd stand to lose a great deal more than Rattery if it failed. I put up the whole of the purchase price, you know, when we took it over.'

'Indeed? Just so.'

Staring rather foolishly at the end of his cigarette, Nigel asked suddenly, 'Did you *like* Rattery?'

Inspector Blount made a deprecatory movement with his hand, as though dissociating himself from so unorthodox a question. Carfax seemed less perturbed.

'You're wondering why I came in with him?' he said. 'As a matter of fact he saved my life during the war, and when I came across him again – oh, about seven years ago – he was, well, in difficulties. His mother had lost her money and – well, you see, the least I could do was to help him out.'

Without replying directly to Nigel's question, Carfax had made it quite clear that his association with Rattery had been the repayment of a debt and not friendship. Blount got into his stride again. It was the usual routine question, of course, but he had to ask Mr Carfax about his movements on Saturday afternoon last.

Carfax, a subdued derisive twinkle in his eye, said, 'Yes, of course. Routine enquiry. Well, about quarter to three I went over to the Ratterys' house.'

Nigel's cigarette dropped out of his mouth. He bent down hastily and picked it up. Blount went on, as suavely as though this was not the first he'd heard of any such visit.

'Just a private call?'

'Yes. I went to see old Mrs Rattery.'

'Dear me,' said Blount mildly, 'I didn't know of this. The servants – we questioned them – didn't say anything about your visiting the house that afternoon.'

Carfax's eyes were bright, unwinking, non-committal as a lizard's. He said:

'No. They wouldn't. I went straight up to Mrs Rattery's room – she had asked me to do so when she made the appointment.'

'Appointment? It was – e-eh – in the nature of a business discussion you had with her then?'

'Yes,' said Carfax, a trifle more grimly.

'Was it relevant at all to the case I am handling?'

'No. Some might think it was, though.'

'It is for me to decide that, Mr Carfax. You would do much better to be quite—'

'Oh, I know, I know,' said Carfax impatiently. 'The trouble is, it involves a third person.' He pondered for a moment, then said, 'Look here, this won't go past you two, will it? – if you find it's nothing to do with—'

Nigel cut in, 'Don't worry. It's all down in Felix Lane's diary, anyway.' He watched Carfax closely. The man was thoroughly puzzled – or else was giving a masterly imitation of a man thoroughly puzzled.

'Felix Lane's diary? But what does he know – ?'

Ignoring a rather sultry glance from Blount, Nigel went on, 'Lane noticed that Rattery – how shall I put it? – was an admirer of your wife's.' Nigel spoke in a subtly offensive manner, hoping to get Carfax angered and off his guard. Carfax, however, was equal to the thrust.

'I see you have the advantage of me,' he said. 'Very well. I'll make it as brief as I can. I'll tell you the plain facts, and I only hope you won't draw the wrong conclusions from them. George Rattery had been making advances to my wife for some time. She was amused, intrigued, gratified by it – any woman might be, you know; George was a handsome brute, in his way. She may even have carried on a harmless flirtation with him. I did not remonstrate with her. If one is afraid to trust one's own wife, one has no right to be married at all. That's my view, at any rate.'

Good heavens, thought Nigel. Either this man is a blind but rather admirable Quixote, or else he's one of the subtlest, most plausible deceivers I've come across, or there's the possibility, of course, that Felix deliberately over-coloured the relationship between Rattery and Rhoda Carfax in his diary.

Carfax went on, twisting his signet ring, his eyes screwed up as though against a too dazzling light, 'Recently George's attentions had been getting a bit too outrageous. Last year, by the way, he seemed to have lost interest altogether – he was carrying on then with his sister-in-law, at least that's what people said.' Carfax's mouth was twisted into an expression of apologetic distaste. 'Sorry about all this gossip. Apparently he and Lena Lawson had some sort of a row in January, and it was after this that George – er – redoubled his attentions to my wife. I still did not interfere. If Rhoda really preferred him to me – in the long run, I mean, there was no use my making scenes about it. Unfortunately at this point George's mother stepped in. That's what she wanted to talk to me about on Saturday afternoon. She pretty well accused me of Rhoda being George's mistress, and asked me what I intended to do about it. I said I intended to do nothing at the moment, but, if Rhoda came and asked me to divorce her, of course I should do so. The old lady – she's really rather an old horror, I'm afraid I've never been able to stomach her – then started a fantastic scene. Made it clear that she thought me a complacent cuckold, abused Rhoda, said she had led George on – which I thought pretty steep, and all the rest of it. Finally she more or less commanded me to put a stop to things. It would be very much the best thing, for all parties, if Rhoda was dragged back into the family pen and the whole affair hushed up; she, for her part, would see to it that George behaved himself in the future. It was, in effect, an ultimatum, and I don't like ultimatums – ultimata, should I say? – especially from domineering old women. I repeated, more firmly, that if George liked to try and seduce my wife, it was his own lookout, and if she really wanted to live with him, I would agree to divorce her. Mrs Rattery then spoke at some length on public scandal, family honour and suchlike topics. She made me sick. I just walked out of her room in the middle of a sentence and out of the house.'

Carfax had been speaking more and more to Nigel, who nodded sympathetically as he made his points. Blount felt excluded, and somewhat out of his depth. This put a sceptical edge on his voice when he said, 'That's a very interesting story, Mr Carfax. Uh-huh. But you'll have to admit that your conduct was a wee bit – e-eh – unconventional.'

'Oh, I daresay,' said Carfax indifferently.

'And you walked straight out of the house, you say?'

There was a challenging emphasis on the word 'straight'. Blount's eyes glittered coldly behind his pince-nez.

'If you mean, did I make a detour on the way, for the purpose of putting strychnine into Rattery's medicine, the answer is in the negative.'

Blount pounced. 'How did you know that was the way the poison was conveyed?'

Carfax regrettably failed to crumple up before this assault. 'Gossip. Servants will talk, you know. Rattery's parlourmaid told our cook that the police were all up in the air about a bottle of tonic having disappeared, so I put two and two together. One doesn't have to be a Chief Inspector, you know, to be able to do a simple sum like that,' Carfax added, with a touch of rather likeable malice.

Blount said, ponderously official, 'We shall have to go into your statement, Mr Carfax.'

'It would save you some trouble perhaps,' rejoined the surprising Mr Carfax, 'if I pointed out two things. No doubt they have occurred to you already. First, even if you don't quite understand the attitude I've taken up about Rattery and my wife, you can't imagine I'm lying about it; old Mrs Rattery will confirm that part of my – er – statement. Secondly, you may be thinking that it was just a blind – this attitude of mine – to conceal my real feelings, to conceal my intention of finishing this affair between George and Rhoda. But do please realise that I'd no need to do anything so drastic as murdering George. It was I who financed the garage and, if I'd wanted to choke George off, I could simply have told him he must lay off Rhoda or be thrown out of the partnership. His money or his love life, in fact.'

Having thus with consummate neatness spiked Blount's whole battery of guns, Carfax sat back, gazing at him good-humouredly. Blount tried to counter-attack, but was met all along the line with the same cool candour and colder logic. Carfax almost seemed to be enjoying himself. The only new piece of evidence Blount could extract was that Carfax had an apparently unshakable alibi for the time of leaving the Ratterys' house up to the time of the murder.

When the two had left the garage, Nigel said, 'Well, well, well. The redoubtable Inspector Blount meets his match. Carfax played us off the field.'

'He's a cool customer,' growled Blount. 'Everything pat – just a wee bit too pat, maybe. You'll have noticed, too, in Mr Cairnes' diary, he mentions that Carfax pumped him about poisons one day he was down at the garage. We shall see.'

'So your thoughts are straying from Felix Cairnes, are they?'

'I'm keeping an open mind, Mr Strangeways.'

9

While Blount was receiving a temporary quietus from Carfax, Georgia and Lena were sitting beside the tennis lawn at the Ratterys'. Georgia had come down to see if she could be of any use to Violet Rattery, but Violet, in the last day or two, had developed amazingly in confidence and authority. She seemed quite equal to any demands the situation might make upon her, and the jurisdiction of old Mrs Rattery was now confined to the four walls of her own room. As Lena remarked, 'I suppose I oughtn't to say it, but George's death has made a new woman of Vi. She's become what our English mistress used to call "such a serene person". What a God-awful expression! But Vi – really, one would never suppose to look at her that she'd been a doormat for fifteen years – yes George, no George, oh George please don't – and now George's been poisoned and who knows the police mayn't have got their eye on the widow.'

'Oh, surely that's not very—'

'Why not? We're all of us bound to be under suspicion – all of us who were in the house. And Felix has apparently been doing his best to get himself hung, though I don't believe he'd have gone through with – you know, what he was telling us about last night.' Lena paused, and went on in a lower voice, 'I wish I could understand what – oh, to hell with it! How's Phil today?'

'When I left him, he and Felix were reading Virgil. He seemed quite cheerful. I don't know about children, though; he's awfully nervy at times, and then he suddenly shuts up like an oyster for no apparent reason.'

'Reading Virgil. It's just beyond me. I give up.'

'Well, I suppose it's a good idea to try and take his mind off this business.'

Lena did not answer. Georgia stared up at the clouds that rolled overhead. Her thoughts were broken at last by a scrunching noise beside her. She looked down quickly; Lena's hand, supple and sunburnt, was tearing up grass by the roots, viciously tearing it up and sprinkling the handfuls on the lawn.

'Oh, it's you,' said Georgia. 'I thought for a minute a cow had got in.'

'You'd start eating grass if you had to go through – it's sending me haywire!' Lena turned upon Georgia, with one of those impulsive movements of her shoulders that seemed to create a dramatic situation out of thin air. Her eyes blazed. 'What's wrong with me? Just tell me, what is wrong with me? Is it BO, or is it what her closest friends wouldn't tell her?'

'There's nothing wrong with you. How do you mean?'

'Well, why does everyone avoid me, then?' Lena was whipping herself up into hysteria. 'Felix, I mean. And Phil. Phil and I used to get on rather well, and now he disappears round corners to get out of my way. But I don't care a damn about him. It's Felix. What did I have to fall in love with the man for? Me – in love – I ask you? Several million males to choose from, in this country alone, and I fall for the one chap who didn't want me – except as a card of introduction to the late lamented. No, that's not true. I swear Felix loved me. You can't pretend that sort of thing – women may, but men can't. Oh God, we were so happy. Even when I began to wonder what Felix was after – well, I didn't really, I wanted to be blind.'

Lena's face, a little stupid and conventional-pretty in repose, became beautiful when her feelings made her forget poise, make-up, and the careful 'grooming' of her film training. She gripped Georgia's hands – an impulsive, extraordinary appealing gesture – and went on urgently.

'Last night – you noticed now he wouldn't come out into the garden when I asked him, alone. Well, afterwards I thought that must have been because of this diary, because he was afraid of my knowing that he'd been playing a double game with me at first. But then he told us about the diary, he knew that secret wasn't between us any longer. But when I rang him up this morning, and said I didn't mind about it and loved him and wanted to be with him and help him – oh, he was just calm, polite, quite the gentleman, said it would be best for us not to meet more than necessary. I just don't understand. It's killing me, Georgia. I used to think I had my pride, but here I go trailing after this chap on my knees, like a blasted pilgrim or something.'

'I'm sorry, my dear. It must be absolutely foul for you. But pride – I shouldn't worry about that – it's the white elephant of the emotions, very imposing and expensive, and the sooner one can get rid of it, the better.'

'Oh, I'm not worrying about *it*. It's Felix I'm worrying about. I don't care if he killed George or not, but I wish he didn't have to kill me too. D'you think – I mean, are they going to arrest him? It's so awful, to think they may arrest him any minute and then I'd perhaps never see him again, and every minute we're not together now is being wasted.'

Lena began to cry. Georgia waited till she recovered, then said gently, 'I don't believe he did it, nor does Nigel. We'll get him out of it, between us. But we must have all the truth, if we're to save him. He may have some very good reason for not wanting to see you just now, or it may be some misguided chivalrousness – he doesn't want to get you mixed up, perhaps, in this case. But you mustn't hide anything, keep anything back – that'd be misguided chivalry too.'

Lena gripped her hands together in her lap. Staring straight in front of her, she said, 'It's so difficult. You see, it involves someone else beside me. Aren't you liable to be chucked into prison if you conceal evidence?'

'Well, if you are what they call an accessory after the act. But it's worth risking, isn't it? You mean, about this medicine bottle that's disappeared?'

'Look, will you promise to tell no one but your husband, and ask him to talk to me about it before he passes it on?'

'Yes.'

'All right. I'll tell you. I've kept it to myself because, you see, the other person involved is Phil – and I'm rather fond of him.'

Lena Lawson began to tell her story. It started with a conversation at dinner in the Ratterys' house. They were talking about the right to kill, and Felix said he believed one was justified in getting rid of social pests – people who made life a hell for everyone around them. She hadn't taken it seriously at the time, but, when George was taken ill and spoke Felix's name, she remembered it again. She had had to go into the dining room, and there she noticed the bottle of tonic on the table. George was groaning and writhing in the next room, and somehow she immediately connected this in her mind with the bottle and with Felix's words. It was quite irrational, but she was convinced for a moment that Felix had poisoned George. The one thought in her mind was to get rid of the bottle. It never occurred to her that, by doing so, she was removing the only possible evidence for George's death being suicide. Instinctively, she had moved to the window, with the idea of throwing the bottle into the shrubbery. It was then that she saw Phil staring in at her, his nose pressed against the pane. At the same moment, she heard old Mrs Rattery calling to her out of the drawing room. She opened the window, gave Phil the bottle, and told him to hide it somewhere. There was no time for explanations. She didn't know, even now, where he had put it; he seemed to be avoiding her whenever she tried to speak to him alone.

'Well, you can scarcely wonder, can you?' said Georgia.

'Scarcely – ?'

'You ask Phil to hide a bottle – he sees you in a very agitated state. Then he hears that his father has been poisoned and the police are looking for this bottle. What conclusions could you expect him to draw?'

Lena stared at her wildly. Then she broke out, half laughing, half sobbing, 'Oh God! That's just too rich! Phil thinks *I* did it? I – oh, that's too much – !'

Georgia was on her feet and bending over the girl in one swift movement. She took her shoulders and shook her without mercy, till Lena's bright hair was tumbling in a wave over one eye and the wild, idiot laughter ceased. Looking up over Lena's head, now held fast to her breast, and feeling the convulsive trembling of her body, Georgia saw a face gazing down at them from an upper window – the face of an old woman – harsh, sombre, patrician in feature, the mouth set squarely in an expression that might have been merely a rebuke at the wild laughter playing around this hushed house, or might have been the cold, appeased triumph of a vengeful god, a stone image on whose knees the blood sacrifice has been laid.

10

Georgia related this conversation to Nigel when he returned to the hotel before lunch.

'That explains it,' he said. 'I felt pretty sure it was Lena who had got rid of the bottle, but I couldn't think why she should keep dark about it after she realised that its disappearance wouldn't make things any easier for Felix. I suppose it couldn't have been suicide after all. Well, we'll have to talk to young Phil.'

'I'm glad we've got him away from that house. I saw Mrs Rattery senior this morning. She was looking down at us from an upper window, like Jezebel – at least, not very like Jezebel, more like a ju-ju I came across in Borneo once, sitting all by itself in the middle of a forest with a great deal of dried blood on its knees. A very interesting find.'

'Very, I'm sure,' said Nigel, shuddering slightly. 'You know, I'm beginning to get ideas about that old lady. If she wasn't such an obvious choice – just the sort of frightfully high red herring that any detective writer might draw across the trail – Oh well. If this was a book, I'd put my money on that chap Carfax. He's as smooth and transparent as glass; I kept wondering if he wasn't doing some sort of mirror-trick on us.'

'The great Gaboriau said, didn't he? – "always suspect that which seems probable, and begin by believing what appears incredible".'

'If he said that, the great Gaboriau must have been a halfwit. I've never heard such a cheap, fantastic paradox.'

'But why not? Murder *is* fantastic, except when it's governed by strict rules like those of the blood feud. There's no use taking up a realistic approach to it; no murderer is a realist – he wouldn't commit murder if he was. Your own success at your profession is due to the fact that you're semi-unhinged a great part of the time.'

'Your tribute, though spontaneous, is uncalled for. By the way, did you see Violet Rattery this morning?'

'Only for a minute or two.'

'I'm just wondering what it was she said to George when they had a scene last week. George's mother was slinging dark hints when we rescued Phil from her yesterday morning. I think this is where the womanly touch will come in again.'

Georgia grimaced. 'For how long do you propose to use me as an agent provocateur, may I ask?'

'Provocateuse. You are, my sweet, amazingly provocative, in spite of your hard-bitten exterior. I can't imagine why.'

'Woman's place is in the kitchen. From now on I stay there. I've had enough of your insidious stuff. If you want to plant vipers in people's bosoms, go and plant yourself there for a change.'

'Is this mutiny?'

'Yes. Why?'

'Oh, I just wanted to know. Well, the kitchen is downstairs, first left, second right . . .'

After lunch, Nigel took Phil Rattery out into the garden. The boy was polite enough, but in one of his distrait moods, as Nigel made conversation. His pallor, the pathetic thinness of his legs and arms, the occasional wincing look in his eyes kept Nigel shying away from the subject he wished to talk about. Yet the boy's composure, his air of delicate secrecy – like a cat's – challenged him.

He said at last more abruptly than he meant, 'About this bottle. You know – the bottle of tonic, Phil. Where did you hide it?'

Phil looked straight into his eyes, with an almost aggressive expression of innocence. 'But I didn't hide the bottle, sir.'

Nigel was on the point of accepting this at its face value when he remembered a dictum of his schoolmaster friend, Michael Evans. 'A really accomplished and intelligent boy always stares a master full in the eyes when he's indulging in any important piece of duplicity.' Nigel hardened his heart.

'But Lena says she gave it to you to hide.'

'She says that? But – then, you mean it wasn't her who – ' Phil swallowed hard – 'who poisoned my father?'

'No, of course it wasn't.' The boy's dreadful, strained gravity made Nigel feel he wanted to get his hands on whoever was responsible for it. He had to keep looking at the boy to remind himself that Phil was a tortured, bewildered child, not the adult that so often seemed to be speaking out of his mouth. 'Of course, it wasn't. I admire you for wanting to protect her, but there's no need for that now any longer.'

'But if she didn't do it, why did she ask me to hide the bottle?' asked Phil, his brow painfully creased.

'I shouldn't worry about that,' said Nigel incautiously.

'I can't help it. I'm not a kid, you know. I think you ought to tell me why.'

Nigel could see the boy's quick, inexperienced mind already wrestling with the problem. He decided to tell him the truth. It was a decision that was going to have very strange consequences, but Nigel could not have anticipated them.

'It's rather a mix-up,' he said. 'Lena was trying to protect somebody else, as a matter of fact.'

'Who?'

'Felix.'

Phil's luminous face darkened, as though a shadow passed over a pure, ash-pale mere. 'He who shall teach the child to doubt,' Nigel repeated uneasily to himself, 'The rotting grave shall ne'er get out.' Phil had turned to him, was gripping his sleeve.

'It's not true, is it? I know it's not true!'

'No. I don't think Felix did it.'

'But do the police?'

'Well, the police have to suspect everybody at first, you know. And Felix has been a bit foolish.'

'You won't let them do anything to him, will you? Promise me.' The innocent, physical candour of Phil's appeal made him seem for a moment strangely girlish.

'We'll look after him,' said Nigel. 'Don't you worry. The first thing is to get hold of that bottle.'

'It's on the roof.'

'On the roof?'

'Yes, I'll show you. Come along.' All impatience now, Phil dragged Nigel out of his chair and, half-running, kept a pace ahead of him all the way down to the Ratterys' house. Nigel was out of breath by the time he had been hustled up two flights of stairs and a ladder and was looking out of an attic window on to the gabled roof. Phil pointed.

'It's in the gutter, just down there. I'll climb down and fetch it.'

'You'll do nothing of the sort. I don't want you to break your neck. We'll fetch a ladder and lean it up against the wall of the house.'

'It's all right, sir, honestly it is. I've often climbed about on the roof. It's easy as pie if you take your shoes off, and I've got a rope.'

'D'you mean to say you climbed down there and put the bottle in the gutter on Saturday night? In the dark?'

'Well, it wasn't quite dark. I thought of letting the bottle slide down on a piece of string. But then I'd have to let go of the string and it might have dangled down the wall below the gutter and someone might have spotted it, you see.'

Phil was already tying round his waist a coil of rope which he had taken from an old leather Gladstone bag in the attic.

'It's certainly a jolly good hiding place,' said Nigel. 'Whatever made you think of it?'

'We lost a ball there once. Dad and I were playing cricket with a tennis ball on the lawn, and he hit it on the roof and it got stuck in the gutter. So Dad climbed out of the window here and fished it up. Mum was in an awful stew. She thought he was going to fall off. But he's – he was a jolly good climber. He used to use this rope in the Alps.'

Something rapped hard on Nigel's mind, knocking for admittance, but the door was locked and for the moment he had mislaid the key. It would come to him presently; he had an extraordinarily comprehensive memory, in which even the most apparently irrelevant details of a case were neatly filed away. It had never failed him. At present he was too much distracted by the sight of Phil sliding down into the recess base of a chimney, crawling up the other gable and disappearing over the top of it.

I hope the rope's sound. Damn it all, he's quite safe with it tied round his waist, but has he tied it securely? What a long time he's taking. He's such a queer kid – I wouldn't put it past him to untie the rope and chuck himself off the roof, if he got an idea into his head that –

There was a cry, an intolerable silence, and then – not the thudding fall that Nigel awaited with all his nerves wincing – but a faint, tinkling smash. His relief was so enormous that, when Phil's face and hands appeared over the gable, coated with grime, he shouted at him irritably, 'You *are* a little fool! What the devil's the idea of dropping it? We ought to have used a ladder, only you were so darned keen on showing off.'

Phil grinned apologetically through the grime. 'I'm awfully sorry, sir. The bottle had got slimy outside, somehow, it slipped out of my hand, just when I was – '

'Yes. All right. It can't be helped. I'd better go and pick up the fragments. By the way, was the bottle empty?'

'No, about half full.'

'Save us! Are there any dogs or cats about?' Nigel was about to hurry downstairs; when a plaintive voice from Phil arrested him. The knots of the rope round his waist and the chimney had pulled so tight that he could not undo them. Nigel had to waste a precious minute or two scrambling out of the attic window and unfastening Phil. By the time he had got out of the house on to the lawn, he was fuming with impatience – and more than a little worried too. The thought of half a dozen doses of strychnine splashed all over the grass was not exactly reassuring.

However, he had no need to worry. As he ran round the corner of the house, he was confronted by the spectacle of Blount on his knees, his homburg still perched at the same angle of severe rectitude, dabbing at the grass with his handkerchief. There was already a neat pile of broken glass upon the path beside him. He looked up and said reproachfully:

'You nearly hit me with that bottle. I don't know what you were playing at – the pair of you, but – '

Nigel heard a gasp behind him. Then Phil flew past him, like a little puff of hot wind, and leapt upon Blount, kicking and scratching in a furious attempt to snatch the sodden handkerchief out of his hands. The boy's eyes were black with fury; his whole face and body seemed transfigured into a malicious imp's. Blount's hat was knocked sideways, his pince-nez dangled jerking on their cord. His face, however, did not betray excess of emotion as he pinioned the boy's arms and thrust him not ungently towards Nigel.

'Better take him inside and see he washes his hands. I doubt he may have got some of this stuff on them. You take on someone your own size next time, Master Phil. And I'd like a word with you, Mr Strangeways, when you've finished with him. You might ask his mother to look after him for a bit.'

Phil allowed himself to be led away into the house. His gait was utterly dispirited. His mouth and the corners of his eyes twitched – a twitching like that of a dog having a bad dream. Nigel could find nothing to say. He felt that something besides the bottle had been shattered and the pieces would take a great deal of putting together.

11

When Nigel came out of the house again, he found Blount handing over the stained handkerchief and the broken glass to a constable. The liquid had been mopped up and wrung out from handkerchief and cloth into a basin.

'Lucky the ground's hard,' said Blount abstractedly, 'or it'd have sunk in and that'd have meant digging up the turf. This is the stuff all right, all right.' He advanced the tip of his tongue with extreme caution towards the handkerchief. 'Bitter. Can still taste it. I'm grateful to you for finding it, but there was no need to drop it on my head. More haste, less speed, Mr Strangeways. What did the wee boy try to savage me for, by the way?'

'Oh, he's a bit upset.'

'So I noticed,' said Blount dryly.

'I'm sorry about the bottle. Phil said he'd hidden it in the gutter up there, and I rather foolishly allowed him to climb down and get it. He was roped to a chimney. It slipped out of his hands – the bottle, I mean, not the chimney.'

'Oh dear me no, it didn't.' With irritating deliberation Blount dusted the knees of his trousers, adjusted his pince-nez, and led Nigel on to the spot where the bottle had fallen. 'You see, if he'd just dropped it, it'd have landed on the flower bed here. But it landed farther out, just on the edge of the lawn. He must have thrown it. Now, if you can spare a moment, we'll sit down over yonder where we'll be out of earshot of the house, and you can tell me all about it.'

Nigel told him of Lena's confession to Georgia and Phil's climb on Saturday night. 'Phil's a remarkably quick-witted child, in some ways. He must have got the idea into his head that the bottle would incriminate Felix – and, as Georgia says, he looks up to Felix like a god. But he'd already told me he knew where the bottle was, so the only thing he could do then to help Felix was to destroy it – chuck it off the roof and delay me with untying the knots of the rope and hope by the time I'd got downstairs the stuff would all have sunk into the earth. It was logical and clever within the limits of his mental capacity. Like many solitary children, he's capable of the most passionate hero-worship and at the same time of deep distrust for strangers. He obviously could not have believed me when I assured him that the discovery of the bottle would not necessarily hurt Felix. He may even believe that Felix poisoned his father. But it's Felix he was trying to protect. That's why he went for you when he saw that his plan had failed.'

'Ye-es. That's a possible explanation, I daresay. Eh well, he's a plucky wee lad. Fancy him scrambling about on that gable! Rope or no rope, I'd not like it. But I never had a head for heights. It's vertigo – '

'*Vertigo!*' Nigel exclaimed, his eyes suddenly blazing. 'I knew I'd remember before long! By Jove, we're on to something at last!'

'What?'

'George Rattery was subject to vertigo, and he wasn't subject to it. He was afraid of the edge of a quarry, but he wasn't afraid of the Alps.'

'If that's meant to be a riddle – '

'Not a riddle. The answer to one. Or the beginning of an answer. Now stop chattering and let Uncle Nigel indulge in what passes with him for thought. You remember Felix Cairnes wrote in his diary how he'd come upon a quarry in the Cotswolds and was all set to stage an accident, only George Rattery refused to come near the edge because, he said, he was subject to vertigo?'

'Yes, I remember that all right.'

'Well, just now when I was up in the attic with Phil, I asked him how he came to think of such a hiding place for the bottle. He said that his father had once hit a ball up on the roof and it had stuck in the gutter, and his father had climbed out to fetch it. What's more, he said his father was an Alpine climber. So what?'

Blount's affable mouth was set in a thin line, his eyes gleamed. 'It means that Felix Cairnes for some reason told a lie in that diary.'

'But why should he?'

'That is a question I shall very shortly ask him.'

'But whatever possible motive could he have had? The diary was not meant for anyone's eyes but his own. Why in the name of the Grand Cham of Tartary should he want to tell a lie to himself?'

'E-eh, but come now, Mr Strangeways, you must admit it was a lie – this statement that Rattery suffered from vertigo.'

'Oh yes, I admit that. What I don't admit is that Felix told it.'

'But, hang it all, he *did* – it's down in black and white. What alternative have you?'

'*I suggest that it was George Rattery who told the lie.*'

Blount gaped. He resembled momentarily a respectable bank manager who had just been told that Montague Norman had been caught tampering with a balance sheet.

'Easy now, easy now, Mr Strangeways – you're not seriously asking me to swallow that?'

'I am indeed, Chief Inspector Blount. I've maintained all along that Rattery had become suspicious of Felix, that he communicated his suspicions to some third person, and that it was this person who actually killed Rattery – sheltering himself behind the would-be murderer. Now, suppose that Rattery was vaguely suspicious of Felix that day they went out for a picnic. He may very well have known about the quarry beforehand – people tend to return to the same places for picnics when they've lived in the district for some time. Felix, standing by the edge of the quarry, calls out to George to come over and have a look at something. George senses some agitation in his voice, or sees it in his appearance. The spark of suspicion is fanned into a blaze. Suppose Felix really means to push me over into the quarry, he thinks. Or, alternatively, he didn't know there was a quarry there till Felix, as he admits in his diary, rather incautiously announced the fact. In either case, George could not confront him immediately with his suspicions. He had no *proof* of anything yet. His game was to give the impression of being the unconscious murderee until he had real proof of Felix being a would-be murderer. At the same time, he didn't dare to go nearer the edge of the quarry. He had to make some excuse for not going nearer, which would not put Felix on his guard. On the spur of the moment he says, "Sorry. Nothing doing. I've no head for heights. Vertigo" – the very excuse an experienced climber would naturally think of first.'

After a long silence, Blount said, 'Well, I'm not denying that's a plausible theory. But it's all a cobweb; it's finely spun, but it won't hold water.'

'Cobwebs aren't meant to hold water,' replied Nigel acrimoniously. 'They're meant to hold flies, as you'd know if you took a rest occasionally from examining bloodstains and the interior of beer mugs, and indulged in a little nature study.'

'And what fly, may I ask, has this cobweb of yours caught?' asked Blount, his eyes twinkling sceptically.

'My whole case for the defence of Felix Cairnes is based on the theory that a third person knew of his plans – or at least of his general intention. That person may have discovered them independently, but it's not very likely. After all, Felix presumably hid his diary pretty carefully. But suppose George communicated his suspicions, perhaps from the start, to this third person – who would you say he'd be most likely to confide in?'

'There's no charge for guessing, is there?'

'I'm not asking you to guess. I'm asking you to use the machine behind that bulging brow of yours.'

'Well, he'd not confide in his wife – he despised her too much, from what one knows. Nor in Lena, if Carfax is right in saying that she and George had parted brass-rags. He might have told Carfax, I suppose. No, I'd say his mother was the most likely person – he and she were pretty thick.'

'You've forgotten one person,' said Nigel impishly.

'Who? You don't mean the wee—?'

'No. Rhoda Carfax? She and George were—'

'Mrs Carfax? Now you're pulling my leg. Why should she want to kill Rattery? Anyway, her husband says she never came near the garage, so she'd not have taken the rat-killer.'

' "Her husband says" – that's worth nothing.'

'I've got evidence to corroborate that. Of course, she might have slipped in at night and abstracted some of the poison. But e-eh, as it happens, she's got an alibi for Saturday afternoon. She couldn't have put the poison into the medicine bottle.'

'Sometimes I think you've got the makings of a quite good detective. So you *did* have your eye on Rhoda, after all.'

'Oh, but that was merely part of the routine investigation,' said Blount, rather shocked.

'Well, that's all right. I didn't mean Rhoda. As you say, old Mrs Rattery is the likeliest person.'

'I don't say that,' replied Blount dogmatically. 'There's Felix Cairnes. All I said was—'

'All right. Your protest has been noted and will receive our attention. But let's stick to Ethel Rattery for the time being. You've read Cairnes' diary. Did you pick up any possible motive for her there?'

Inspector Blount settled himself more comfortably in his chair. He pulled out a pipe, which he did not light but polished meditatively on his smooth cheek.

'The old lady is very hot on the honour of the family, isn't she? According to Cairnes' diary, she said "Killing's no murder where honour is at stake," or something to that effect. And furthermore, Cairnes claims to have overheard her telling the wee boy that he must not be ashamed of his family, *whatever happens*. But that's very slight evidence to go on, you'll have to admit.'

'Yes, in itself. But not when it's linked up with the fact that she had the opportunity – she and Violet were alone in the house on Saturday afternoon till George came back from the river, and with what we know – *and she knew* – about George and Rhoda.'

'How do you work it out?'

'We know she asked Carfax along that afternoon to make an appeal to him to restrain Rhoda and hush up the scandal. She got very angry when Carfax said he was determined to divorce Rhoda if she wished for a divorce. Now, supposing that was the old lady's last appeal, suppose she had already decided in her own mind that, if it failed, she would kill George rather than allow the scandal of his affair and possible divorce to smirch the good old family escutcheon. She had pleaded with George to give up playing around with Rhoda; she has pleaded with Carfax to take a strong line. Both appeals failed. So she falls back on strychnine. How d'you care for that?'

'I'll admit the possibility entered my mind. But there are two fearful drawbacks.'

'To wit – ?'

'First, do mothers poison their sons to protect the family honour? It's very fanciful. I don't like it.'

'As a general rule, mothers don't. But Ethel Rattery is a real old Roman matron of the toughest school. And she's not exactly right in the head, either. You can't expect normal behaviour from her. We know that she's a thorough-going autocrat, and that she's crazy about family honour, and being a Victorian she looks upon sexual scandal as the arch-disgrace. Combine those three, and you get a potential murderess. What's your second objection?'

'Your theory is that George confided his suspicions about Felix Cairnes to his mother. You say that the murderer knew about the dinghy plan, and the poison was only a second line of attack if Felix's attempt failed. Now, if Mrs Rattery only intended to poison her son in the event of her appeal to Carfax falling flat, she would surely have made this appeal earlier. As it was, her appeal might have succeeded, but George would have been drowning at the very moment she was making it. That doesn't fit.'

'You're confusing two alternative theories of mine. I suggest that Mrs Rattery, as well as George, knew of the dinghy plan described in Felix's diary. But I'm suggesting, too, that they discussed it together and George told his mother that he was going through with his role of victim in order to obtain absolute confirmation of Felix's intent, but that at the crucial moment he would turn the tables on Felix by telling him that his diary was in the hands of a solicitor. In fact, George had no intention of letting himself be drowned, *and his mother knew it*. But she had every intention of using the poison on him, if her appeal to Carfax failed.'

'Yes. Of course. That is certainly possible. Uh-huh. E-eh well, it's a queer case, this. Mrs Rattery, Violet

Rattery, Carfax and Cairnes – they all had opportunity and motive to murder George Rattery. Miss Lawson, too. She had opportunity, but it's difficult to see what her motive could have been. It's strange the way none of them have alibis. I'd feel happier with a nice, juicy alibi to get my teeth into.'

'What about Rhoda Carfax's then?'

'It's too hot. She was at Cheltenham from ten thirty a.m. to six p.m. playing in a tennis tournament. After that she went to the Plough with friends for dinner, and didn't get back here till after nine o'clock. Of course, we're still testing all the links, but so far there's not the slightest evidence that she could have slipped back here any time in the afternoon. It was not a large tournament, you see, and when she wasn't playing, she was umpiring or talking to her acquaintances.'

'Mm. That seems to let her out. Well, where do we go from here?'

'I have to interview old Mrs Rattery again. I was going to do it when you dropped that bottle on my head.'

'May I sit in on this?'

'Very well. But let *me* do the talking, please.'

12

It was the first time Nigel had had leisure to study George's mother dispassionately. The other morning in Violet's boudoir, so much mud had been stirred up that calm reflection had been impossible. Now, standing in the middle of her room and extending to him an arm from which the voluminous black draperies fell curving away, Ethel Rattery might have been a model posed for a statue of the Angel of Death. Her harsh, large features, beneath their expression of set and conventional mourning, seemed to hold neither grief nor compunction, pity nor fear. She was more like the statue than the model for it. Somewhere deep within her, thought Nigel, there is a stone core of lifelessness, an anti-life principle. He briefly noticed, as her hand touched his, a big black mole on her forearm with long hairs sprouting from it. It was a disagreeable sight, yet for that moment it seemed the one human thing about her. Then, with a bobbing inclination of her head to Blount, she walked to a chair and sat down. At once the illusion vanished; she was no longer the Angel of Death, no longer the pillar of black salt, but an ungainly old woman whose stumpy, waddling legs were grotesquely too small for the body they carried. Nigel's wandering thoughts were brought up with a jerk, however, by Mrs Rattery's first words. Sitting bolt upright in the high-backed chair her hands disposed palm upward on her huge lap, she said to Blount, 'I have decided, Inspector, that this sad affair was an accident. It is the best thing for all parties concerned that this should be so. An accident. We shall, therefore, not require your services any longer. How soon can you make it convenient to withdraw your men from my house?'

Blount was a man, both by temperament and experience, not easily startled and even more seldom did he allow his features to express any surprise he might be feeling. But now, for a moment, he frankly gaped at the old lady. Nigel took out a cigarette, and hastily put it back in his case again. Mad, quite mad, crazy, he thought. Blount regained command over his tongue.

'What makes you think it was an accident, ma'am?' he asked politely.

'My son had no enemies. The Ratterys do not commit suicide. Accident is the only explanation, therefore.'

'Are you suggesting, ma'am, that your son *accidentally* put a quantity of vermin-killer into his own bottle of medicine and then drank it? Doesn't it strike you as rather – e-eh – improbable? How do you suppose he would come to do such an extraordinary thing?'

'I am not a policeman, Inspector,' the old lady replied with monstrous aplomb. 'It is your business, I conceive, to discover the details of the accident. I am asking you to do so as quickly as possible. You will realise that it is excessively inconvenient for me to have my house full of constables.'

Georgia simply won't believe this when I tell her, thought Nigel, it ought to be wildly funny, this dialogue, but somehow it isn't. Blount was saying, with dangerous mildness, 'And what makes you so eager, ma'am, to convince me – and yourself – that it was an accident?'

'I naturally wish to protect the reputation of my family.'

'You are more concerned with reputation than with justice?' asked Blount, not unimpressively.

'That is a most impertinent observation.'

'Some might consider it an impertinence on your part to dictate to the police how they should handle this case.'

Nigel scarcely forbore to cheer. Here was the dour covenanter's spirit coming out in Blount. Nolo Ratterari. The old lady flushed slightly at this unexpected opposition. She gazed down at the wedding ring which had grown into her fleshy finger, and said:

'You were speaking of justice, Inspector?'

'If I told you that we can prove your son was murdered, would you not wish the murderer to be brought to book?'

'Murdered? You can prove it?' said Mrs Rattery in her dull, leaden voice. Then the voice suddenly became molten lead as she came out with one word, 'Who?'

'That, as yet, we have not found out. With your help we may be able to arrive at the right answer.'

Blount began to take her through the events of Saturday evening again. Nigel's wandering attention was caught by a photograph on a kidney-shaped table to his right. It was in a florid gold frame, flanked by medals, a bowl full of immortelles in front and two tall vases behind it stuffed with roses that were badly arranged and beginning to shed their petals. It was not these relics which interested Nigel, however, but the face of the man in the photograph: a young man, in military uniform, Mrs Rattery's husband, no doubt. The fluffy moustache and the long side-whiskers did not conceal the features – delicate, indecisive, oversensitive, more like those of a Nineties' poet than of a soldier – and their extraordinary resemblance to Phil Rattery's. Well, Nigel silently addressed the photograph, if I'd been you and offered the choice of a bullet in South Africa or a lifetime with Ethel Rattery, I should have chosen the speedier death too. But what queer eyes you have. Insanity, they say, often skips a generation; what with you and Ethel, there's no wonder that Phil is so highly strung. Poor kid. I think I'd like to go a bit deeper into the history of this family.

Inspector Blount was saying:

'On Saturday afternoon you had an interview with Mr Carfax?'

The old woman's face seemed to darken. Nigel looked up involuntarily, expecting to see a cloud across the sun, but all the blinds in the room were drawn down.

'That is so,' she said, 'but it can be of no interest to you.'

'That is for me to judge,' said Blount implacably. 'Do you refuse to tell me the substance of this interview?'

'Absolutely.'

'Do you deny that you asked Mr Carfax to put a stop to the association between his wife and your son, that you accused him of conniving at this association, and that – when he said he proposed to divorce his wife if she wished it – you abused him in – e-eh – somewhat unmeasured terms?'

During this recital, Mrs Rattery's florid face grew purple and began to work. Nigel thought she would burst into tears, but it was in a voice of shocked indignation that she exclaimed, 'The man's no better than a pimp, and I told him so. The scandal was bad enough, but deliberately to encourage it – '

'Why didn't you speak to your son, if you felt so strongly about it?'

'I had spoken to him. But he was very strong-willed – he takes that from my side of the family, I'm afraid,' she said with a kind of sly complacence.

'Did you get the impression that Mr Carfax was concealing any enmity to your son on account of this affair?'

'Why no—' Mrs Rattery broke off short. The sly look came into her eyes again. 'At least, I didn't notice anything. But of course I was very agitated. It's certainly very strange – the attitude he affected to take up.'

Old poison-tongue, thought Nigel.

'After this interview, I understand that Mr Carfax went straight out of the house.' Just as when he had talked to Carfax, Blount put the same faint emphasis on 'straight'.

Almost a leading question. Naughty, thought Nigel.

Mrs Rattery said, 'Yes, I suppose so. No, now that I come to think of it, he couldn't have gone straight out. I happened to be at the window here, and it was a minute or two after he left me before I saw him walking up the drive.'

'Your son told you about Felix Lane's diary, of course?' Blount had employed the old trick of popping a vital question when the victim's attention is concentrated in another direction. His tactic had no visible effect, unless there could be something suspicious about the stony hauteur with which Mrs Rattery received it.

'Mr Lane's diary? I fear I do not follow you.'

'But surely your son told you he had discovered that Mr Lane planned to make an attempt upon his life?'

'Do not snap at me, Inspector, please. I am not accustomed to being snapped at. As for this fairy story – '

'It is the truth, ma'am.'

'In that case, had you not better conclude this interview, which I find excessively distasteful, and arrest Mr Lane?'

'One thing at a time, ma'am,' said Blount with equal frigidity. 'Did you ever notice any hostility between your son and Mr Lane? Were you at all puzzled as to Mr Lane's position in the household?'

'I knew perfectly well that he was here on account of that abominable creature, Lena. It's a matter I do not much care to discuss.'

You thought the friction between George and Felix was on account of Lena, Nigel interpreted to himself. He said out loud, staring down his nose, 'Just what *did* Violet say when she was quarrelling with her husband last week?'

'Really, Mr Strangeways! Is every little domestic incident to be dragged up like this? I consider it most undignified and unnecessary.'

'Incident? Unnecessary? If you think it so trivial, why did you say to Phil the other morning, "Your mother will want all our help. You see, the police may find out how she quarrelled with your father last week, and what she said, and that might make them think – "? Make them think what?'

'You had better ask my daughter-in-law about that.' The old lady would not commit herself further. After a few more questions, Blount rose to go.

Absent-mindedly Nigel strolled over to the kidney-shaped table and, running his finger along the top of the photograph there, said, 'This is your husband, I suppose, Mrs Rattery? He fell in South Africa, didn't he? What action was it?'

The effect of this harmless remark was electrifying. Mrs Rattery was on her feet and coming with a horrible insect kind of rapidity – as though she had fifty legs, not two – across the room. In a waft of camphor, she thrust her body between Nigel and the photograph.

'Take your hands off, young man! Will you never be done poking and prying about my house?' Breathing hard, her fists clenched, she listened to Nigel's apologies. Then she turned to Blount. 'The bell is beside you, Inspector. Will you kindly ring, and the maid will show you out.'

'I think I can find my own way, ma'am, thank you.'

Nigel followed him downstairs and out into the garden. Blount puffed out his lips and mopped his brow. 'Phew, that's a thrawn old body. She gives me a fair scunner, I don't mind telling you.'

'Never mind. You faced her with the utmost intrepidity. Dare to be a Daniel. And now what?'

'We're no further. No further at all. She wanted us to call it an accident. Then she fell in – a bit too obviously, I thought – with my suggestion that Carfax might have done it. She took the bait about Carfax going straight out of the house – we'll have to find out which of them is wrong about that, but likely there'll be some quite innocent explanation. On the other hand, she wouldn't be drawn into any talk about Felix Cairnes or Violet Rattery. She genuinely didn't know about Cairnes' diary – at least that was my impression; and that's a bit of a slap in the eye for your theory. She's daft about the family prestige, but we knew that before. Her insinuations against Carfax may very well have been prompted purely by her dislike for him. No. If she murdered George, she didn't tell us anything about it just now. We're back where we started. And that's with Felix Cairnes, whether you like it or not.'

'Nevertheless, there's one thing that will bear looking into.'

'You mean this quarrel between George and his wife?'

'No. I have a feeling you'll find there's nothing to that. Violet may have made some hysterical threat or other, but a woman who has bowed under her husband's rod for fifteen years doesn't suddenly up and murder him. It's simply not in character. No, I'm referring to what old Watson would have described as "the Singular Episode of the Old Lady and the Photograph".'

13

Nigel left Blount, who wished to interview Violet Rattery, and returned to the hotel. Georgia and Felix Cairnes were having tea in the garden when he arrived.

'Where's Phil?' asked Felix at once.

'Down at the house. His mother'll bring him up later, I expect. There've been some goings-on.' Nigel gave an account of Phil's exploits on the roof and his attempt to destroy the evidence of the bottle. While he was talking, Felix grew more and more fidgety, and at last could contain himself no longer.

'Damn it all,' he exclaimed, 'can't you keep Phil out of this. It's absolutely sickening – a boy like that being chivvied about. I don't mean you. But this man Blount, he can't understand what damage it may do to a highly strung child.'

Nigel had not realised before how Felix Cairnes' nerves were on edge. He had seen him strolling around the garden, reading with Phil, talking to Georgia about politics; a quiet, amiable man whose natural reserve alternated with sudden confidences and flicks of sardonic humour. An uncomfortable man to live with, perhaps, but likeable even in his prickliest, most unapproachable moods. Nigel was reminded by this outburst of Felix's how heavily the cloud of suspicion must be weighing upon him.

He said gently, 'Blount's all right. He's quite human, at least, fairly. I'm afraid it was my fault that Phil had to go through this. It's extraordinarily difficult at times to remember how young he is. One starts treating him as a contemporary, almost. And he pretty well dragged me on to that roof.'

There was an easy silence. Georgia took a cigarette out of the box of fifty which she always carried about with her. The bees hummed amongst the dahlias in the round bed opposite. In the distance they could hear a prolonged, mournful hoot from a barge warning the lock-keeper of its approach.

'The last I saw of George Rattery,' said Felix, half to himself, 'he was walking through the lock garden over there, trampling on the flowers. He was in a very bad temper. He'd trample on anything that got in his way.'

'Something ought to be done about people like that,' said Georgia sympathetically.

'Something *was* done about him.' Felix's mouth set in a grim line.

'How are things going, Nigel?' asked Georgia. The pallor of her husband's face, the puckered frown on the brow over which a lock of hair hung childishly, the childish, obstinate jut of his underlip – all moved her unbearably. He was tired out, he should never have taken this case. She wished Blount, the Ratterys, Lena, Felix, even Phil, at the bottom of the sea. But she kept her voice cool and impersonal. Nigel did not like being mothered, and there was Felix Cairnes, who had lost his wife and then his only son – Georgia felt she could not allow him to hear in her voice the kind of affection which was not for him any longer.

'Going? Not too well. This seems to be one of those nasty, straightforward cases, where no one has an alibi and everyone could have done it. Still, we'll sort it, as Blount would say. By the way, Felix, do you realise that George Rattery was not subject to vertigo at all?'

Felix Cairnes blinked. His head cocked to one side, like the head of a thrush considering some movement it has seen out of the corner of its eye.

'Not subject to vertigo? But who said he was? Oh Lord, I'd forgotten. Yes. That quarry business. But why did he say so, then? I don't understand. Are you sure?'

'Quite sure. You see the implication?'

'The implication is, I suppose, that I told a naughty lie in my diary,' said Felix, gazing at Nigel with a kind of wary, timorous candour.

'There's another possibility – that George already suspected your intentions, or began to suspect them then, and said he had no head for heights so as to keep out of your reach without letting you suspect that he suspected you.'

Felix turned to Georgia. 'This must be all very cryptic to you. The reference is to an occasion when I tried to push George over the edge of a quarry, but at the last moment he failed to come up to scratch. Pity, it would have saved us all a lot of trouble.'

His levity jarred on Georgia. But poor chap, she thought, his nerves are raw, he can't help it. She remembered too vividly how she herself had once stood in the same predicament, and Nigel had got her out of it. Nigel would save Felix, too, if anyone could. She glanced at her husband; he was staring down his nose in the rather boiled manner that meant his brain was working at extra pressure. Darling Nigel, she said to herself, darling, darling Nigel.

'Do you know anything about old Mrs Rattery's husband?' Nigel asked Felix.

'No. Except he was a soldier. Killed in the South African War. A merciful release from Ethel Rattery, I should say.'

'Quite. I wonder where I could find out about him. I haven't got any acquaintance in retired military circles. I say, what about that friend of yours? – you mentioned him early in your diary – Chippenham, Shrivellem, Shrivenham – that's it, General Shrivenham.'

'That's like, "Oh, you come from Australia? Have you met a friend of mine called Brown over there?" ' jeered Felix. 'I shouldn't think for a moment that Shrivenham would know anything about Cyril Rattery.'

'Still it might be worth trying.'

'But why? I don't see what's the point?'

'I've a queer feeling that it'd be worth going into the history of the Rattery family. I'd like to know why old Mrs R. got all seized up when I asked her a harmless question about her husband this afternoon.'

'The nose you have for skeletons in family cupboards is really too indecent,' said Georgia. 'I might have married a blackmailer.'

'Look here,' said Felix thoughtfully, 'if you want to get information, I know a chap in the War Office who'd look up the records for you.'

Nigel's reply to this kindly offer was ungrateful, to say the least. In the friendliest, but most serious tones possible he said,

'Why don't you want me to meet General Shrivenham, Felix?'

'I – you're being absolutely ridiculous. I haven't the least objection to your meeting him. I was merely suggesting a more practical way of getting the information you want.'

'All right. Sorry. No umbrage taken, I hope, where none meant.'

There was an awkward pause. Nigel was quite obviously unconvinced, and knew that Felix knew it. After a moment Felix smiled.

'I'm afraid that wasn't quite true. The fact of the matter is, I'm rather fond of the old boy. I suppose I was unconsciously fighting against the idea of his finding out the sort of person I really am.' Felix laughed bitterly. 'A murderer who can't even pull it off.'

'Well, I'm afraid it will become public sooner or later,' said Nigel reasonably. 'But, if you don't want Shrivenham to know about it yet, I can easily ask him about Cyril Rattery without dragging you into it. If you'll just give me an introduction to him.'

'All right. When were you thinking of going over there?'

'Tomorrow some time, I expect.'

There was another long silence – the uneasy silence that weights the air when a thunderstorm has threatened and passed over without breaking, but is already on its way back again. Georgia could see Felix trembling all over. At last, flushing painfully, his voice burst out unnaturally loud as though he were a lover who had at last screwed up his courage to declare his love.

He said, 'Blount. Is he going to arrest me? I can't stand this suspense much longer.' His fingers curled and uncurled, hanging down on either side of his chair. 'I'll start confessing soon, just to get it over.'

'That's not a bad idea,' said Nigel ruminatively. 'You confess and, as you didn't do it, Blount'll be able to pull your confession to pieces, and thus convince himself you're not the murderer.'

'Nigel, for God's sake don't be so cold-blooded!' exclaimed Georgia sharply.

'It's just a game to him. Like spillikins.' Felix grinned. He seemed to have recovered his composure. Nigel felt rather ashamed; he must cure himself of this habit of thinking out loud.

He said, 'I don't think Blount has any idea of arrest yet. He's very painstaking and likes to be sure of his ground. You've got to remember, a policeman's not allowed to forget it if he arrests the wrong man – it doesn't do him any good at all, at all.'

'Well, I hope when he does make up his mind, you'll send up a Very light or something, and then I can shave off my beard and put on a limp and slip through the police cordon and take a boat for South America – that's where escaping criminals all go in detective novels.'

Georgia felt tears pricking her eyes. There was something intolerably pathetic in the way Felix tried to joke about his predicament. Yet it was embarrassing too. He had courage, but not the kind of gallantry needed to carry off a joke like that. It was too near the bone, and he showed that he felt it. He was obviously in dreadful need of reassurance; why didn't Nigel give it to him? It wouldn't cost very much. An association of thought made Georgia say, 'Felix, why don't you ask Lena to come up this evening. I was talking to her – today. She believes in you, you know. She loves you, and she's simply wearing herself away wanting to help you.'

'I can't have anything to do with her while I'm under suspicion of murder. It's not fair to her,' said Felix, obstinately and a little aloofly.

'But surely it's her job to decide what's fair on her. She wouldn't care a hoot even if you had killed Rattery, she just wants to be with you, and – honestly – you're hurting her horribly. She doesn't want your chivalry, she wants *you*.'

While she was speaking, Felix's head twisted from side to side, as though his body was bound fast to the chair and her words were stones flung in his face. But he would not admit how they hurt him. He withdrew into himself, saying stiffly, 'I'm afraid I can't talk about that.'

Georgia shot an imploring glance at Nigel. But just then there was the sound of feet on the gravel drive, and all three looked up, secretly relieved by the interruption. Inspector Blount, with Phil at his side, was walking up the drive.

Georgia thought, Thank goodness here's Phil; he's the David to charm the surly mood of our Saul here.

Nigel thought, Why has Blount brought Phil? Violet Rattery was going to. Does this mean that Blount has found out something about Violet?

Felix thought, Phil – what's the policeman doing with him? God! he can't have arrested Phil? Of course he hasn't, don't be absurd, he wouldn't be bringing him here if he had. But the mere sight of those two together – I shall go mad if this lasts much longer.

14

'I had a very interesting talk with Mrs Rattery,' said Blount when he and Nigel were alone.

'Violet? What did she say?'

'Well, I asked her first about this quarrel she had with her husband. She was quite open about it – at least, that was the impression I got. They quarrelled, apparently, on the subject of Mrs Carfax.'

Blount paused for dramatic emphasis. Nigel examined attentively the end of his cigarette.

'Mrs Rattery asked her husband to give up his liaison – or whatever it was – with Rhoda Carfax. According to her account of it, she stressed not her own personal feelings, but the harm it was doing to Phil, who – it seems – knew what was going on, though no doubt he couldn't understand it all. Rattery then asked her point-blank if she wanted a divorce. Now Violet Rattery, so she says, had just been reading a book, a novel about two children whose parents were divorced – she's a woman, I'd say, who took fiction very seriously; there *are* people like that, aren't there? Anyway, the children – these two children in the book I'm referring to – suffered a great deal of mental torture as a result of their parents' divorce; one of them was a wee boy, who reminded her of Phil. So she told her husband that on no account would she consent to a divorce.'

Blount took a deep breath. Nigel waited patiently. He was only too well aware that Blount, being a Scotsman, would leave nothing to the imagination in his narrative.

'This attitude of Mrs Rattery's made her husband become exceedingly violent. Particularly about Phil. He resented, no doubt, the way the boy's affections were all given to Violet. But I think he resented even more the fact that Phil was so different from himself – of finer clay, if I may put it that way. He wanted to hit at Violet, and he knew he could hit at her best through Phil. So he suddenly said he'd decided not to send Phil to a public school, but to put him into the garage as soon as his legal period of education had expired. Whether Rattery meant this seriously, I don't know but his wife took it seriously, and that was where the real quarrel began. At one point she said she'd see him dead before she let him spoil Phil's chances in life – and this, no doubt, is what old Mrs Rattery overheard. At any rate, there was a fearful dust-up and in the end Rattery lost his temper altogether and began to beat his wife. Phil heard her crying out, and rushed into the room and tried to stop his father. There were terrible ructions. Uh-huh,' Blount concluded unemotionally.

'So Violet is still in the running?'

'Well, no, I'd say not. You see, it's like this. After that scene, she appealed to old Mrs Rattery to persuade George not to go through with this scheme of putting the wee boy into the garage. The old lady is a bit of a snob, as I daresay you've noticed, so for once she was of the same mind as Violet. I asked her about it, and she says she got George to promise to let Phil continue with his education. So that motive for Violet's killing her husband no longer holds good.'

'And it wasn't likely to have been jealousy of Mrs Carfax for, if so, she'd have poisoned her, surely, and not George?'

'That is reasonable, though of course it's only theory.' Blount continued on his ponderous progress. 'In the course of my interview with Violet Rattery another piece of information came to hand. I was asking her about Saturday afternoon. Apparently, after his talk with old Mrs Rattery, Carfax had a few words with Violet, and she saw him off the premises. So he had no opportunity of poisoning Rattery's tonic just then.'

'But why did he tell us an unnecessary lie, in that case, about his having gone straight out of the house?'

'Well, he didn't exactly. You remember, he said, "If you mean, did I make a detour on the way, for the purpose of putting strychnine into Rattery's medicine, the answer is in the negative." '

'But that's a quibble.'

'Oh yes, I agree. But I think it more than likely he quibbled because he didn't want his little conversation with Violet Rattery to be brought up.'

Nigel pricked up his ears. Now they were getting somewhere.

'And what was this conversation about?' he asked.

Blount paused impressively before replying. Then, his face grave as a judge's, he said, 'Infant Welfare.'

'You mean, Phil's welfare?' said Nigel, puzzled.

'No, I mean Infant Welfare. Just that.' Blount's eyes twinkled. He did not get many openings to pull Nigel's leg, and when he did get one, he liked to make the most elaborate possible use of it. 'According to Violet Rattery – and I see no reason to disbelieve her – there are plans for starting an Infant Welfare centre here. The local authorities are giving a grant towards it, and the rest of the money will be raised through private subscriptions. Mrs Rattery is on the committee formed for the purpose of getting these subscriptions, and Mr Carfax came in to tell her that he wished to give a considerable sum, anonymously. He's the kind of man whose left hand is not allowed to know what his right hand is doing. That's why he kept dark about his little conversation with Violet Rattery.'

'Dear me. "The sweet converse of an innocent mind." So Carfax is out. Or could he have slipped into the dining room on his way to old Mrs Rattery?'

'That possibility has been eliminated too. I had a word with the wee boy on the way up here. As it happens, he was in the dining room when Mr Carfax entered the house. The door was open, and he saw Carfax go through the hall and straight upstairs.'

'So it boils down to old Mrs Rattery, then,' said Nigel.

They were pacing up and down the waterfront of the hotel garden. On their left, a dozen or so yards in front, was a small shrubbery of laurels. Nigel idly noticed a slight stir of the bushes, unusual on so windless an evening; a dog in there, probably, he thought. Had he gone to investigate that movement, it is just possible that the course of several people's lives might have been profoundly altered. But he did not.

Blount was saying, his voice raised a little argumentatively, 'You're stubborn, Mr Strangeways. But you'll not convince me that all the evidence so far doesn't point at Felix Cairnes. There's a case to be made out against old Mrs Rattery, I'll admit, but it's too theoretical, far too fanciful.'

'You're going to arrest Felix, then?' said Nigel. They had turned and were walking past the shrubbery again.

'I see no other alternative. He had the opportunity; he had a far stronger motive than Ethel Rattery; he has practically convicted himself out of his own mouth. Of course, there's still a certain amount of routine work to be done – I've not lost hope that someone may have seen him taking some of the vermin-killer from the garage, or we may yet find microscopic traces of it in his room at the Ratterys', though admittedly we've not been able to so far. The fragments of the bottle may yield fingerprints – though, again, that's unlikely after its exposure in the gutter, and besides a detective writer would be the last person to leave fingerprints. So I shall not be arresting Cairnes at once, but he will be watched, and – as you know very well – it's after the murder, not before, that a criminal often makes his worst mistake.'

'Well, that's that, I suppose. But tomorrow I'm going to see a chap called General Shrivenham. And I shouldn't be at all surprised if I didn't return bringing my sheaves with me. You had better start reconciling yourself to the idea of being foiled again, Chief Inspector Blount. You know, I'm convinced that the solution of this problem can be found in Felix Cairnes' diary, if we only knew where and how to look for it. I believe it's been staring us in the face all the time. That's why I want to find out more about the Rattery family history; I've a notion it'll throw a spotlight on to something in the diary that we hadn't noticed before.'

15

The same night, Georgia had gone to bed. She knew better than to fuss Nigel when he was in one of his intense, abstracted moods and stared through her as though she was a bit of glass. But I wish to God, she thought, he'd not come down here at all, he's tired out, and he'll be in for a nervous breakdown if he's not careful.

Nigel was sitting at a desk in the hotel writing room. It was one of his more remarkable eccentricities that his brain functioned quite efficiently in the writing rooms of hotels. There were several sheets of notepaper in front of him. He began slowly to write . . .

Lena Lawson

Opportunity to obtain poison?

Yes.

Opportunity to poison tonic?

Yes.

Motive for murder?

(a) Affection for Violet and Phil: to remove George Rattery who was ruining their lives. Inadequate. (b) Personal hatred of G. R. Result of previous liaison with him and/or shock of manslaughter of Martin Cairnes. No, *ridiculous*. Lena was quite happy with Felix. (c) Money. But G. R. left his money to his wife and his mother in equal shares, and he hadn't much to leave anyway. L. L. is definitely out.

Violet Rattery

Opportunity to obtain poison?

Yes.

Opportunity to poison tonic?

Yes.

Motive for murder?

Fed up with George (a) because of Rhoda, (b) because of Phil. But the Phil business had been smoothed over, and V. had put up with G. for fifteen years, so why should she suddenly break out like this? If jealousy of Rhoda was motive, she'd have poisoned her, not G. V. R. is out.

James Harrison Carfax

Opportunity to obtain poison?

Yes. (Far more opportunity than any of the others.)

Opportunity to poison tonic?

Apparently none. Went straight up to Ethel Rattery's room on Saturday, evidence of Phil. Came down from there to talk to Violet, who saw him off the premises, evidence of Violet. Has sound alibi from then onwards, viz. Colesby's investigations.

Motive for murder?

Jealousy. But, as he pointed out to us, if he had wanted to stop affair between G. and Rhoda, he could have done so by threatening to end partnership with G., over whom he had the whip hand financially. C. seems to be eliminated.

Ethel Rattery

Opportunity to obtain poison?

Yes. (Though she was very much less often in the garage than the others.)

Opportunity to poison tonic?

Yes.

Motive for murder?

Insane family pride. Anything to end scandal of George–Rhoda affair, and particularly to prevent scandal of divorce. She begs Carfax to put his foot down, but C. tells her he is determined to divorce Rhoda if Rhoda wishes it. Her behaviour towards Violet and Phil shows that she can be completely ruthless, the autocrat for whom might is right.

Nigel looked over each sheet of paper carefully, then tore them up into very small pieces. An idea had struck him. He took another sheet and began to write . . .

Have we possibly missed a tie-up between Violet and Carfax? It's interesting that, to a certain degree, they give each other alibis – both factual and psychological. Carfax could, most easily of all four, have abstracted the vermin-killer; Violet could have put it in the tonic. It's not inconceivable that each of them, disillusioned by the behaviour of his own mate, may have turned to the other. But why not simply go off together? Why anything so drastic as poisoning George?

Possible answers: that George would have refused to divorce Violet, and/or Rhoda ditto Carfax; that, by going off together they would have left Phil in the hands of George and Ethel Rattery, a thing Violet would surely have shrunk from. Plausible. We must investigate the relations between V. and C. more thoroughly. But, unless it was sheer coincidence that the poisoning took place on the same day as Felix's attempted murder (which is almost unthinkable), the murderer must have been wise to Felix's plan – either through being taken into George's confidence or having discovered the diary independently. The former is unlikely in the case of Violet and Carfax, but V. might have found the diary.

Conclusion. One cannot disregard a possible conspiracy between Carfax and Violet. It's noticeable, by the way, that whenever I've been at the Ratterys' house, Carfax was *not* there. As her husband's partner and a friend of the family, Carfax might have been expected to be in attendance – giving Violet all the help and comfort possible. The fact that he has not been doing so may suggest he is unwilling to give us any opening for suspecting a guilty relationship between them. On the other hand, Carfax's attitude when interviewed by Blount was remarkably open, candid and consistent, and at the same time sufficiently unusual to compel credence. It is difficult for a criminal to carry off *consistently* a false moral attitude towards his recent victim – much more difficult than the mere carrying through of a prearranged plan (alibi, concealment of motive, etc.) I am inclined, provisionally, to believe in Carfax's innocence.

That leaves Ethel Rattery and Felix. The case against Felix is superficially by far the stronger. Means, motive, everything – even a confession of intent. But it is just there, at the diary, that it breaks down. It is just – but only just – conceivable that Felix should have prepared a second weapon (the poison) to work in case his dinghy plan failed. I cannot, in fact, bring myself to believe that he is either cold-blooded or mad enough to indulge in such complex strategy. But suppose for a moment that he did. What is absolutely inconceivable is that, after having had the tables turned on him in the dinghy, and after being told by George that his diary was in the hands of solicitors and would be made public in the event of George's death, Felix should allow the strychnine plan to go through.

To do so was simply to put his head into a noose and jump off into thin air. If Felix had doctored the tonic, he would inevitably – once he knew George's death meant his own destruction – have either told George about the poison or else have slipped into the house before dinner and removed the bottle. Unless, of course, he was so crazed with hatred against George because of Martin's death that he did not mind committing hara-kiri in the process as long as he killed George. But, if Felix had no regard at all for saving his own neck, why should he take all the trouble to work out a murder plan which would look like a drowning accident, and why should he get me down here to save his bacon for him? The only possible answer to all this is that Felix did not put the poison in the tonic. I do not believe he murdered George Rattery; it's against all probability and all logic.

Which leaves Ethel Rattery. A wicked, wicked woman. But did she kill her own son? And if, as I think, she did, will there ever be any way of proving it? George's murder is typical of the sort of egotistical high-handedness one associates with Ethel Rattery. No attempt on her part to trail red herrings – though to be sure there was no need for that, since she knew that all suspicion would fall upon Cairnes. No attempt to create an alibi for herself for Saturday afternoon, when the bottle was tampered with. She just dopes the medicine and sits back on her excessive haunches till George drinks it. And then issues an edict to Blount that the affair had better be called an accident. 'Disposer supreme and judge of the earth' is the role she sees herself playing. There's an almost aggressive lack of subtlety about George's poisoning that squares very well with Ethel Rattery's character. But is the motive strong enough? When it came to the point, would she act upon her own dictum that 'killing is no murder where honour is at stake'? Maybe I shall get enough material from old Shrivenham, or one of his cronies, to decide on that point. In the meantime . . .

Nigel sighed wearily. He glanced through what he had written, grimaced, and set a match to the sheets of paper. The grandfather clock in the hall outside gave a long, bronchial wheeze, gasped, announced that the time was midnight. Nigel took up the folder in which was fastened a carbon copy of Felix Cairnes' diary. Something caught his eye on the page at which it fell open. His body stiffened, his tired brain became suddenly alert. He began to flick the pages, looking for another reference. An extraordinary idea began to build up in his head – a pattern so logical, so neat, so convincing, that he had to distrust it. It was too like one of those marvellous poems one composes on the edge of sleep and looks at again in the disillusioned light of morning and finds commonplace, meaningless or mad. Nigel decided to leave it till the morning; he was not in a state now to test its truth; he shrank from its harsh implications. Yawning, he got up, put the folder under his arm and made for the door of the writing room.

He turned off the electric light and opened the door. The hall outside was dark as death. Nigel groped across the hall towards the electric light switches on the opposite wall, feeling his way with his hand on the front door. I wonder is Georgia asleep, he thought, and at that moment there was a swishing sound in the darkness and something came out of the darkness and struck him on the side of the head . . .

Darkness. A black velvet curtain against which painful lights flared, danced, dithered and went out. A firework ballet. He watched it without curiosity; he wished these lights would stop fooling about, because he wanted to open the black curtain and they got in the way. Presently the lights stopped fooling about. The black velvet curtain remained. Now he could walk forward and open the curtain, though he must first remove this hard board which seemed to be strapped to his back. Why was there a board strapped to his back? He must be a sandwich-man. For a moment he remained still, delighted by the brilliance of this deduction. Then he started to walk towards the black curtain. Instantly a blinding pain shot through his head and the firework ballet started up again with furious empressement. He let it dance to its finish. When that was over, very gingerly he allowed his brain to begin working: let the clutch in too suddenly and the whole damned contraption would fall to pieces.

I cannot walk towards that beautiful, black velvet curtain, because because because because I am not on my feet and this board strapped to my back isn't a board at all it's the floor. But no one can have the floor strapped to his back. No, a very sound point, if you allow me to say so. I am lying on the floor. Lying on the floor. Good. Why am I lying on the floor? Because because because – I remember now – something came out of the velvet curtain and caught me a crack. A very dirty crack. Joke. In that case I am dead. The problem of whatjercallit is now solved. Problem of Survival. Life after death. I am dead, but aware of existence. *Cogito, ergo sum.* Therefore I have Survived. I am one of the Great Majority. Or am I? Possibly I am not dead. The dead, surely, do not suffer from bloody awful headaches. It's not in the contract at all. So I'm alive. I've proved it by incontro – uncontro – whatever it is, logic. Well, well, well.

Nigel put his hand to the side of his head. Sticky. Blood. Very slowly he dragged himself to his feet, felt his way to the wall and switched on the lights. Their sudden glare stunned him for a moment. When he could open his eyes again, he looked round the hall. It was empty. Empty except for an old putter and the carbon copy of the diary which lay on the floor. Nigel became aware that he was cold. His shirt was all unbuttoned. He buttoned it up, bent down painfully to collect the putter and the diary, and struggled upstairs carrying them.

Georgia regarded him sleepily from the bed.

'Hello, darling. Did you have a nice round of golf?' she said.

'Well, as a matter of fact, no. A bird wonked me with this. Not cricket. Not golf, I mean. On the head.'

Nigel beamed fatuously at Georgia and slid, not without grace, to the floor.

16

'Darling, you're not to get up.'

'I certainly am going to get up. I've got to see old Shrivellem this morning.'

'You can't get up when you've got a hole in your head.'

'Hole or no hole, I'm going to see old Shrivellem. Get them to send up some breakfast. The car'll be here at ten. You can come with me if you like and see that I don't tear the bandage off in my delirium.'

Georgia's voice trembled. 'Oh, my sweet, and to think I kept on reminding you to get your hair cut. And it was your thick hair saved you – and your thick head. And you're not going to get up.'

'Darling Georgia, I love you more than ever, and I *am* going to get up. I began to see the light last night, before that bird made a pass at me with the putter. And I've a feeling old Shrivellem will be able to – besides, it'll be no harm to put myself under the protection of the military for a few hours.'

'Why – you don't think he'd try it again? Who was it?'

'Search me. No, I don't anticipate a repetition of the outrage. Not really. Not in broad daylight. Besides, my shirt was unbuttoned.'

'Nigel, are you sure you aren't wandering?'

'Quite sure.'

While Nigel was having breakfast, Inspector Blount was shown in. The Inspector looked rather worried.

'Your good wife has been telling me you refuse to stay in bed. Are you sure you're quite up to – ?'

'Yes, of course I am. I thrive on blows from putters. By the way, did you find any fingerprints on it?'

'No. The leather's too rough to take impressions. We found a queer thing, though.'

'What's that?'

'The French windows in the dining room here were unlocked. The waiter swears he locked them up at ten o'clock last night.'

'Well, what's queer about that? The bird who clouted me must have got in and out somehow.'

'How could he get in if they were locked? Are you suggesting he had an accomplice?'

'He could have got in before ten o'clock, and hidden himself – or herself, couldn't he?'

'Well, it's just possible. But how could any outsider know that you'd be sitting up till all hours – till the lights had been turned off in the hall and he could attack you without being seen?'

'I see,' said Nigel slowly. 'Yes, I see.'

'It doesn't look too well for Felix Cairnes.'

'Have you any explanation why Felix, having paid for the services of a not inexpensive detective, should then proceed to bat him over the head with a golf club?' asked Nigel, examining a piece of toast. 'Wouldn't that be – as they somewhat inelegantly express it – fouling his own nest?'

'Maybe – mind you, it's only a suggestion – maybe he had some reason for wanting you disabled just now.'

'Well, presumably there *must* have been some such idea at the back of my – er – assailant's head. I mean, he wasn't just practising strokes in the hall,' Nigel chaffed the Inspector. But he was thinking, Felix did seem rather obstructive about this little visit of mine to General Shrivenham. Blount still looked harassed.

He said, 'But that isn't really the queer thing. You see, Mr Strangeways, we've found fingerprints on the key and inside handle of the French windows and also on the handle and glass outside. As though someone had closed it with one hand on the glass and one on the handle.'

'I don't see anything so bizarre about that.'

'Wait a minute though. The prints are not those of anyone on the hotel staff, nor do they belong to anyone so far connected with the case. And there are no visitors but yourselves staying here now.'

Nigel sat up with a jerk that sent a twinge of pain through his head.

'So it couldn't have been Felix after all.'

'That's what's so queer. Cairnes would have struck you down, and then unlocked the French window – using a handkerchief when he turned the key – to suggest you had been attacked by someone from outside. But who left those prints on the outside of the window?'

'This is too much,' groaned Nigel. 'Dragging a mysterious unknown into the case just when – oh well, I'll leave that to you. It will give you something to do while I'm talking to General Shrivenham . . .'

Half an hour later, Nigel and Georgia were tucking themselves into the back of the hired car. And it was just at that moment that a housemaid, belated in her work as a result of Blount's early-morning investigations in the hotel, entered the bedroom of Phil Rattery . . .

A little before eleven o'clock their car drew up outside General Shrivenham's house. The front door was opened and they entered a spacious lounge-hall whose walls and floors were covered with tiger skins and other trophies of the chase. Even Georgia recoiled slightly from the ferocious, white-fanged jaws that grinned at them from all sides.

'D'you think one of the servants has to clean their teeth every morning?' she whispered to Nigel.

'More than probable. Mine eyes dazzle. They died young.'

The maid opened a door on the left of the hall. From it there proceeded the faint, whinging aerial music of a clavichord; someone was rendering, with rather moderate skill, Bach's Prelude in C Major. The tiny, dainty notes seemed drowned by the voiceless roaring of all the tigers in the hall. The prelude closed in a long, quivering whine, and the unseen player launched out industriously upon the fugue. Georgia and Nigel stood fascinated. Finally the music ended. They heard a voice say, 'Who? What? Oh, why didn't you show them in? Can't have people standing about in the passage.'

An old gentleman appeared at the door, clad in knickerbockers, Norfolk coat, and a tweed fishing hat. He blinked at them mildly with his faded blue eyes.

'Admiring my trophies?'

'Yes. And the music too,' said Nigel. 'The most lovely of the preludes, isn't it?'

'I'm glad to hear you say so. I think it is, but then I'm quite unmusical. Unmusical. 'S matter of fact, I'm still teaching myself to play. Bought this instrument a few months ago. Clavichord. Beautiful instrument. The kind of music you'd expect fairies to dance to. Ariel's spirits, you know. What did you say your name was?'

'Strangeways. Nigel Strangeways. This is my wife.'

The General shook hands with them both, eyeing Georgia with a markedly flirtatious look. Georgia smiled at him, fighting down an almost irrepressible desire to ask this charming old gentleman whether he always wore a tweed fishing hat to play Bach. It seemed to her the most entirely suitable wear.

'We've got a letter of introduction from Frank Cairnes.'

'Cairnes? Yes. Poor fellow, his little boy was run over, you know. Killed. Terrible tragedy. I say, he hasn't lost his reason, has he?'

'No. Why?'

'Extraordinary thing happened the other day. Extraordinary. In Cheltenham. I go over and have tea there every Thursday, at Banners'. I do a flick and then have tea. Best chocolate cakes in England at Banners' – you ought to try 'em. Make a pig of myself. Well, anyway, I went into Banners' and I could have sworn it was Cairnes sitting at a table in the corner. Smallish fellow, with a beard. Cairnes went away from the village here a couple of months ago, you know, but I rather think he was starting his beard before he left. Don't like beards myself. Wear 'em in the navy, I know, but the navy haven't won a battle since Trafalgar, don't know what's wrong with 'em, look at the Mediterranean now. Where was I? Oh yes, Cairnes. Well, this chap who I thought was Cairnes – I went over to speak to him but he shot away like a stoat, he and this other fella who was sitting with him, big fella with a moustache, looked a bit of a bounder to me. I mean Cairnes – or the chap I thought was Cairnes – shot away like a stoat and hustled the other fella, the bounder, along with him. I called out his name after him, but he didn't pay any attention, so I said to myself, that fella can't be Cairnes at all. Then afterwards I thought, well maybe it was Cairnes and he's lost his memory, like those chaps in the BBC – you know the SOS messages. That's why I asked you if Cairnes had lost his reason. Always was a bit of a queer fish, Cairnes, but I can't understand his going about with a bounder like that fellow in Banners' if he was in his right mind.'

'Do you remember what date that was?'

'Let me see. It was the week – ' The General consulted a pocket diary. 'Yes, here we are, August the 12th.'

Nigel had promised Felix that he would keep the Rattery affair dark when he talked with the General, but the General seemed to have landed himself unwittingly into the middle of it. For the present, he felt inclined to relax in this charming, Alice in Wonderland atmosphere, where a retired warrior played the clavichord and accepted as the most natural thing in the world the arrival of a stranger with a bandaged head and a famous wife. General Shrivenham was already deep in conversation with Georgia, on the subject of bird life in the valleys of Northern Burma. Nigel sat back, trying to fit into his tentative pattern the odd little episode which had befallen the General in Banners' tea shop. His thoughts were interrupted at last by the General saying, 'I see your husband has been in the wars lately.'

'Yes,' said Nigel, feeling his bandage tenderly. 'As a matter of fact a chap hit me over the head with a putter.'

'A putter? Well, I'm not surprised. Get all sorts of rag, tag and bobtail on golf courses today. Not that it was ever much of a game – stationary ball, like potting at a sitting bird, not a gentlemen's game at all. Look at the Scotch – they imported it – the most uncivilised race in Europe – no art, no music, no poetry to speak of, Burns excepted of course, and look at their idea of food – haggis and Edinburgh rock. Show me how a nation eats and I'll show you its soul. Polo, now – that's a different matter. Used to play a bit myself in India. Polo. Golf is just polo with all the difficulty and excitement taken out of it. A prose version of polo, a paraphrase of it; typical of the Scots, reducing everything to their own prosy level

– they had to paraphrase the Psalms even. Horrible. Vandals. Barbarians. I bet this fella who hit you with the putter had Scottish blood in his veins. Fine troops they make, mind you. About all they're good for.'

Nigel unwillingly interrupted the General's polemic, and explained the reason for his visit. He was concerned in the Rattery murder case and wanted to find out more about their family history. The dead man's father had been in the army – Cyril Rattery; fell in the South African War. Could General Shrivenham put him on to somebody who might have known Cyril Rattery?

'Rattery? Good Lord, he *is* the chap then. When I saw about this case in the papers, I wondered if the fella had anything to do with Cyril Rattery. His son, you say? Well, I don't wonder. There's bad blood in that family. Look here, have a glass of sherry and I'll tell you what I know about it. No, no trouble at all. I always take a glass of sherry and a biscuit in the middle of the morning.'

The General trotted out of the room and returned with a decanter and a plate of Romary biscuits. When they were all provided with refreshment, he began to talk, his eyes lighting up with a certain relish of reminiscence.

'There was a scandal about Cyril Rattery, you know. I wonder the papers haven't dragged it out again; it must have been hushed up at the time better than these things usually are. He went through the early part of the war with gallantry, but, when we began to get the upper hand, he cracked. One of those fellas who keep a stiff upper lip, y'know – scared to death, really, like the rest of us, only they won't admit it even to themselves – and then one day the whole thing blows up. I came across him once or twice, in the early days when the Boers were teaching us our job. Magnificent fellows, the Boers. Mind you, I'm only an old cut-and-thrust, but I know a rare type when I see one. Cyril Rattery was. Too good for the army. Ought to have been a poet: But even then he struck me as a bit – what do they call it nowadays? – a bit neurotic. Neurotic. Conscience, too. He had too much conscience. Cairnes is another fella like that, but that's by the way. The breaking point came when Cyril Rattery was sent out in command of a detachment to burn some farms. I don't know all the details, but apparently the first farm they came to hadn't been evacuated in time – there was some resistance and one or two of Rattery's men were killed. The rest got a bit out of hand, and when they'd mopped up the opposition they set fire to the buildings without enquiring too carefully if there was anyone left in them. As it happened, there was a woman there, who'd stayed behind with her sick child. They were burnt to death, both of them. Mind you, in war those sort of accidents are bound to happen. Don't like it myself – horrible. Nowadays you bomb non-combatants as a matter of course. Glad I'm too old to get mixed up in that sort of thing. Well anyway, this finished Cyril Rattery. He led his men straight back, refused to destroy the rest of the farms.

Disobeying orders, of course. He was broken for it. Disgraced. That was the end of him, poor fellow.'

'But I'd got the impression from old Mrs Rattery that her husband was killed in action.'

'Not a bit of it. What with the incident at that farm, and the disgrace – he was genuinely keen on his profession, y'know – and the state of his mind, which must have been getting rockier and rockier all through the war, well, he went right off his head. Died in a madhouse some years later, I believe.'

They talked for a little longer. Then Nigel and Georgia tore themselves reluctantly away from their delightful host and got into the car. As they drove back through the rolling, small hills of the Cotswolds, Nigel was very silent. He could see the whole thing now, and he hated the sight of it. He wanted to tell the driver to drive them straight back to London, right out of this sad and damnable case, but it was too late now, he feared.

They were back in Severnbridge, crunching up the gravel drive to the Angler's Arms. There seemed to be an unusual agitation around this quiet hotel. A policeman by the door: a knot of people gathered on the lawn. A woman broke away from this little gathering when their car approached; it was Lena Lawson, her ash-blonde hair streaming as she ran towards the car, her eyes wild with anxiety.

'Oh, thank God you're back,' she cried.

'What's the matter?' said Nigel. 'Has Felix—?'

'It's Phil. He's disappeared.'

Part Four

The Guilt is Seen

Inspector Blount had left word for Nigel to come down to the police station as soon as he returned. As the car took him there, he reviewed the disappearance of Phil, pieced together from the almost incoherent words of Lena and Felix Cairnes. In the confusion from last night's attack on Nigel, no one had noticed that Phil had not been in the hotel for breakfast. Felix assumed he had already had breakfast before he himself came down; Georgia had been too busy attending to Nigel; the hotel waiter thought the boy must have gone to his mother's house for breakfast. So it was not till the housemaid entered Phil's bedroom at 10 a.m., and found the bed had not been slept in, that anyone realised he was gone. She had also found, on the chest of drawers, an envelope addressed to Inspector Blount. What this envelope contained Blount had not yet divulged, but Nigel thought he could make a pretty accurate guess.

Felix Cairnes was almost distraught with anxiety. Nigel had never felt so deeply sorry for him. He wished he could spare him the tragedy which must ensue, but he knew that was impossible now. Things had started to move, and one had no more hope of stopping them than of checking a landslide or the launching of a liner when the button has once been pressed. The tragedy had begun when George Rattery ran down Martie Cairnes in that country lane. It had begun, you might even say, before Phil Rattery was born. These latest events were its catastrophe. There remained now only the epilogue. But that epilogue would be long and painful. It would not be finished till whatever span of life was left to Felix Cairnes, to Violet, to Lena and Phil, was also ended.

Inspector Blount, when Nigel found him in the police station, had an air of subdued triumph. He told Nigel of the steps that had been taken to find Phil: railway and bus stations watched, AA men warned, lorry drivers questioned. It was only a matter of time. 'Though,' he added very seriously, 'it may turn out to be a matter of dragging the river.'

'Oh God, you don't think he'd do that?'

The Inspector shrugged his shoulders. The silence between them became intolerable to Nigel. He said, a little feverishly, 'It's just Phil's last quixotic gesture. It must be. You know, I thought I saw a movement in the shrubbery. It must have been Phil. He heard you say that you were going to arrest Felix. He's passionately devoted to Felix. No doubt he thought, by running away, to divert suspicion from him. That's what was in his mind.'

Blount looked at him, shaking his head gravely.

'I wish I could think that was so, Mr Strangeways. But it's no good now. *I know that it was Phil who poisoned George Rattery*. The poor wee boy.'

Nigel opened his mouth to speak, but the Inspector went on, 'You said yourself, the solution of this affair must lie somewhere in Mr Cairnes' diary. I was reading it through again last night and I got a glimmering of an idea; what's happened since proves it. I'll take the clues in the order they came to my mind. First, Phil was awful upset by the way his father treated his mother: George Rattery used to bully her and knock her about; Phil complained to Mr Cairnes about it one time, but of course Mr Cairnes could not do anything. Now carry your mind to that dinner party he mentions in his diary. They were talking about the right to kill. Mr Cairnes says one is justified in killing a person who makes life miserable for everyone around him. And then, you remember, it's written down in the diary, Phil had piped up with some question, and Mr Cairnes wrote in his diary – 'We'd all forgotten he was there, I think. He'd only just been promoted to late dinner.' We've all been forgetting that the wee boy was there, I'm afraid – all the time. I did not even take his fingerprints. Well now, think of the effect on an impressionable, neurotic child of that chance remark of Cairnes' about getting rid of social pests. There was Phil, brooding about the way his father treated his mother, and then the man whom Phil admires most in the world says openly that one has a right to kill people who make life miserable for others. Remember Phil's implicit confidence in Cairnes – and you know there's nothing a boy won't do if it seems to be sanctioned by someone he worships like that. And remember that he had appealed to Cairnes to do something about it, and his appeal had failed. You've said yourself, often enough, that the environment in which Phil was brought up was enough to make any child mentally unbalanced. Well, there's your motive and your state of mind.'

'General Shrivenham told me this morning that Phil's grandfather – Ethel Rattery's husband – died in a lunatic asylum,' said Nigel softly, to himself.

'There you are. It was in the blood. Uh-huh. Now for the means. We knew that the wee boy would be down at the garage often enough, and then there's confirmation in Cairnes' diary: he says there that George Rattery told him Phil used to go potting with his airgun at the rats on the rubbish dump. Nothing easier than for him to take away a quantity of the vermin-killer. There had been an unusually painful scene between George and Violet last week; Phil had seen his mother knocked down and tried to protect her. That scene must have finally made up the poor laddie's mind for him – or turned his brain, whichever you like to call it.'

'But you're still up against the fantastic coincidence that Phil should have chosen the same day as Cairnes to murder George Rattery,' protested Nigel.

'Not so fantastic when you consider it was only a couple of days after this culminating scene between his father and mother. But it may not have been a coincidence either. The diary was hidden under the floorboards in Cairnes' room. Now Phil was always in and out of that room; he did his lessons there, for one thing, and a loose floorboard is just what you might expect a wee boy to discover or to have known of already. He may have kept his own secret treasures there once.'

'But surely, when Phil was so fond of Felix, the last thing he'd do would be to poison his father on the same day that Felix's own attempt was made; and thus incriminate Felix so obviously.'

'Ah, you're being too subtle, Mr Strangeways. Remember, it's a boy's mind we're dealing with. My theory is that, if it was not a coincidence, Phil discovered Cairnes' diary, found out that Cairnes intended to try and drown George, and when his father returned safe and sound from the river, put the poison in the tonic himself. It would never occur to him that he was incriminating Felix, because he had no idea that the diary had also been found by George and was already in the hands of solicitors. I know there are difficulties about this. That's why on the whole I'm inclined to believe the two murder attempts happening on the same day was a coincidence.'

'Yes, that all sounds reasonable enough, I'm afraid.'

'Now for some further points. After dinner on Saturday, when the poison had begun to work on Rattery, Lena Lawson goes into the dining room and notices the bottle of tonic on the table. She jumps to the conclusion that Felix is responsible for the poisoning and in a panic thinks only of getting rid of the bottle. She goes to throw it out of the window, *and she sees Phil's face pressed against the pane.* What was he doing there? If he was innocent, but knew that his father had been taken ill, he'd surely have been making himself useful, running messages, fetching things?'

'Knowing Phil's type, I'd say he'd more likely have run away as far as he could, up to his own room perhaps, trying to blot the horrible scene out of his mind – running away from it, anyhow.'

'I daresay you're right. In any case, one wouldn't expect to find him staring in at the dining-room window, unless he had put the poison in the bottle and wanted to make sure the room was empty before he came in to take the bottle away and hide it. It'd be natural for a wee boy, knowing he's done something wrong, to try and hide the evidence of his guilt. Well then, he told you later where the bottle was hidden and climbed over the roof to get it.'

'Why, if he'd poisoned it and hidden it to protect himself?'

'Because he now knew that Lena had told you she'd handed it on to him. He couldn't pretend now that he knew nothing about the bottle. What he could do was to destroy it. And he tried his best. He chucked it off the roof and, when he found that I'd collected up the fragments, he went for me like a little fury – you noticed how worked up he was about that. I thought for a moment he'd gone mad. I realise now, he *was* mad – he was mad already. The only thought in his poor, crazed little head was still to get rid of the bottle somehow or other. You see, all along we've been explaining his queer actions by his devotion to Felix

Cairnes. It never occurred to us that it was himself he was trying to protect.'

Nigel sat back, fingering the bandage on his head. It reminded him of something.

'How d'you square up Phil's guilt with your belief that it was Felix who dented my skull last night?'

'It wasn't though. The wee boy did that for you. Listen, this is how I reconstruct it. He made up his mind to run away. He creeps downstairs after midnight, in the dark. Just as he gets to the bottom of the stairs, he hears the door of the writing room open. He knows there is someone between him and the front door by which he'd intended to leave the hotel. He knows, too, that whoever it is has just come out of the writing room will likely switch on the hall lights, and then he'll be discovered. As he cowers close to the wall, his hand touches that putter which has been left leaning against it. He's desperate and terrified – the poor laddie – in a trap. He takes up the putter and swings it blindly in the darkness, hitting out towards this invisible person who stands between him and escape. He hits you and you fall. Phil is horrified by what he's done. He's afraid to turn on the lights, afraid of the body that lies between him and the front door. He remembers the French windows in the dining room, and slinks out that way instead. It was his fingerprints on the French windows, we compared them with the prints he'd left in his bedroom.'

'He was afraid of the body?' said Nigel dreamily. 'He ran away from it out of the hotel?'

'Well, what's wrong with that?'

'Nothing. Nothing. Yes, I'm sure that's what he would have done. I shall always take up the cudgels for you in the future, if anyone says to me that Scotland Yard has no imagination. By the way, you must meet General Shrivenham some time – you might make him alter his opinion about the Scotch.'

'The Scots, please.'

'But seriously, Blount, your case is brilliantly worked out; it's all theory though, isn't it? You haven't a scrap of material evidence against Phil.'

'A scrap of paper,' said the Inspector sombrely. 'A wee scrap of paper. He left it for me in his room. A letter for me. A confession.'

He handed across to Nigel a sheet of lined paper torn out of an exercise book. Nigel read,

Dear Inspector Blount,
this is to tell you it wasn't Felix, it was me who put the poison in that medicine bottle. I hated Dad because he was cruel to Mummy. I'm going to run away where you can't find me.
yours sincerely
Philip Rattery

'The poor boy,' muttered Nigel. 'What a pitiable affair this is. God, what a set-up!' He went on urgently, 'Look here, Blount, you've got to find him. Quickly. I'm afraid of what may happen. Phil's capable of anything.'

'We're doing all we can. Maybe, though, it'd be a better thing if we – e-eh – found him too late. He'd be sent to a home, you know: a mental home. I hate to think of it, Mr Strangeways.'

'Never mind about that,' said Nigel, looking with a strange intensity at Blount. 'Find him. You've got to find him before anything happens.'

'We'll find him all right, trust me. I'm afraid there's no doubt about that. He can't get far away. Unless he's gone by the river,' Blount added with sad significance.

Five minutes later Nigel was back at the Angler's Arms. At the door Felix Cairnes was awaiting him, his eyes dark with anxiety, unspoken questions trembling on his lips.

'What have they—?'

'Can we go up to your room?' said Nigel quickly. 'I've a lot to tell you, and it's a bit too public here.'

Upstairs, in Felix's room, Nigel sat down. His head had begun to ache again; for a moment the room swam before his eyes. Felix was standing by the window, looking out upon the gracious curves and shining reaches of the river upon which he and George Rattery had embarked. His body was tense. He felt an intolerable weight on his tongue and on his heart, preventing him from asking the question that had been growing within him all day.

'Did you know that Phil had left a confession?' asked Nigel gently. Felix spun round, his hands gripping the window sill behind him.

'A confession that it was he who poisoned George Rattery.'

'But it's crazy! The boy must have gone mad,' exclaimed Felix, in a wild, random kind of agitation. 'He'd no more kill – look here, Blount's not taking it seriously, is he?'

'Blount has worked out an extraordinarily convincing case against Phil, I'm afraid, and this confession put the lid on it.'

'Phil didn't do it. He couldn't have done it. I know he didn't do it.'

'So do I,' said Nigel, in level tones.

Felix's hand stopped short in the middle of a gesture. For a second he stared at Nigel uncomprehendingly. Then he whispered:

'You know? How d'you know?'

'Because I've found out at last who really did do it. I shall need your help to fill in the detail of my theory. Then we can decide what's to be done.'

'Go on. Who was it? Go on, tell me, please.'

'You remember that phrase of Cicero's – it comes somewhere in the *De Officiis*, I think. "*In ipsa dubitatione facinus inest*"? – "The guilt is seen in the very hesitation." I'm very sorry, Felix. You're too good a chap to commit a successful murder. As Shrivenham said to me this morning, you've got too much conscience.'

'Oh. I see.' Felix swallowed hard, and dropped the words into the shocking silence that gaped between them. Then he tried to smile. 'I'm sorry I've been all this bother to you. It can't be much fun for you, after all your efforts on my behalf, having to come to this conclusion. Well, I'm glad, in a way, that it's over. I'm afraid Phil queered my pitch with that confession of his. I'd have had to tell the police. Why *did* he do it?'

'He was devoted to you. He overheard Blount say he was going to arrest you. It was the only way Phil could help you.'

'Oh God. If it had been anyone else. He reminded me of Martie, of what Martie would have been.'

Felix sank into a chair and buried his face in his hands.

'You don't think he's done – anything foolish? I'd never forgive myself.'

'No. I'm sure he hasn't. I honestly don't think you need worry about that.'

Felix looked up. His face was pale and tense, but the worst suffering had gone out of it.

'Tell me. How did you find out?' he asked.

'Your diary. It was a mistake, Felix. You gave yourself away. As you wrote at the beginning of it – "that strict moralist within who plays cat-and-mouse with the furtive, the timorous or the cocksure alike, forcing the criminal into slips of the tongue, luring him into overconfidence, planting evidence against him, playing the agent provocateur." You intended your diary to be a kind of safety valve for your conscience, but then, when you changed your plans, *when you found you could not kill a man whose guilt was unproved,* the diary became the chief instrument in your new plan – and that's where it gave you away.'

'Yes. I see you know everything.' Felix gave him a twisted smile. 'I'm afraid I underestimated your intelligence. I ought to have called in a more obtuse champion. Have a cigarette. The condemned man is allowed a last smoke, isn't he?'

Nigel was never to forget that final scene. The sun pouring in on Felix Cairnes' pallid, bearded face; the cigarette smoke wreathing up in the sunlight; the quiet, almost academic way in which they discussed Felix's crime, as though it had been no more than the plot of one of his own detective novels.

'You see,' said Nigel, 'up till the moment when you failed in your attempt to push Rattery over into the quarry, your diary was deeply concerned about the fact that you could not prove it was he who killed Martie. But, after this point, you seemed to take his guilt for granted. It was that discrepancy which first put me on to the right line.'

'Yes, I see.'

'We had been going on the assumption that your failure at the quarry was due to Rattery's having come to suspect your intentions. Why did he lie and say he was subject to vertigo? Because, we argued, he'd become more or less vaguely suspicious of you, and wanted to play for time. But last night, when I read through your diary again, it suddenly occurred to me that perhaps it was you after all who had lied. Supposing you had got Rattery to the edge of the quarry and, just as you were on the point of tripping and falling against him and pushing him over, you found you simply couldn't do it – because you had no real proof that he was the murderer of your son. Wasn't that what happened?'

'Yes. You're quite right. I was too damned soft,' said Felix bitterly.

'Not an altogether unworthy characteristic. I'm afraid it betrayed you, though. It betrayed you later, too, when you refused to have anything more to do with Lena – even after you had told us in the garden that evening about the diary and your real hatred of George. You wanted to break with her, because you didn't like the idea of her being linked up any longer with a murderer. Phil's not the only absurdly quixotic creature in this case.'

'Don't let's talk about Lena any more. It's the one thing I'm ashamed of. I did come to be very fond of her, you see. And I'd used her as a pawn – forgive the cliché.'

'Well, to go back. I reviewed all your actions after the quarry episode in the light of this hypothesis that they were aimed first at extracting the truth from George – and only then, if he admitted to having run over Martie, at killing him. The guilt was seen in the hesitation to murder a man who might conceivably be innocent. You could not ask him point-blank whether he'd killed Martie. He'd merely have denied it and turned you out of the house. So you deliberately set out to make him suspicious of you, to make him inquisitive, to tell him in devious ways that you intended to kill him.'

'I don't see how you could have arrived at that.'

'First, you got yourself invited to stay in the Ratterys' house, although, only a short time before, you'd said nothing on earth would induce you to live under his roof, and although the risk of your diary being discovered was thus enormously increased. But suppose an integral part of your new plan was *that George should discover the diary.* And, by your own account, you deliberately provoked him to look for it, remember. At that lunch party when Mr and Mrs Carfax were present, you told them you were writing a detective novel. You pretended to get very het up when someone suggested you should read aloud and you cleverly conveyed to George the suggestion that you'd put him into the story. After that, no man of the George type could resist poking about after the ms – especially when, only a few days before, you'd very neatly allowed him to discover that your real name was not Felix Lane.'

Felix stared at him for a moment in genuine incredulity. Then comprehension showed on his face.

'General Shrivenham told me this morning that on August the 12th, a Thursday, he had seen you – or thought he saw you – in a Cheltenham tea shop. You were with a big man in a heavy moustache – a bounder, as the General unerringly designated him. Obviously Rattery. Now Shrivenham goes to this tea shop regularly every Thursday afternoon. Being a friend of his, you would be likely to know that and, knowing it, the last thing on earth you'd do would be to go to that shop with Rattery on a Thursday afternoon – unless you wanted to be recognised and hailed by the General as Cairnes. Which is exactly what happened. Rattery hears the General calling out "Cairnes" after your retreating figure, and at once he begins to wonder if you may not be something to do with the Martie Cairnes he ran down in his car. As soon as Shrivenham told me that – by the way, he came out with it of his own accord – I quite understood why you didn't want me to talk to him.'

'I'm awfully sorry about that crack on the head I gave you. I really lost my own yesterday. It was just a futile attempt to postpone your conversation with Shrivenham. He's such an old chatterbox – I was afraid he might tell you about the tea shop incident. But really, I tried not to hit you too hard.'

'That's all right. We aim to take the rough with the smooth. Blount thought it was Phil who had hit me on his way out last night. Blount'd got it worked out very neatly, but his theory didn't explain why I found my shirt buttons undone when I came to. You don't open a chap's shirt to feel if his heart is still beating unless you're afraid you've hit him too hard. Phil would have been far too terrified of the body to come near it – as Blount himself admitted. And if George's killer had been anyone else but you, and felt I was getting too near the truth for his comfort, he'd have hit to kill;

he'd certainly have hit me again, if he'd opened my shirt and found my heart still beating.'

'Ergo, the man who felt your heart was me. Ergo, I was the murderer of Rattery. Yes, I'm afraid that was a bad stroke on my part.'

Nigel offered Felix a cigarette and struck the match for him. His hand was shaking far worse than his friend's. He could only go through with this conversation by pretending to himself that it was an academic discussion of an imaginary crime. He went on, piling detail on detail, though each of them knew all about it, and thus delaying the inevitable moment when he or Felix would have to decide on the next – the last – step.

'August the 12th was the day you met Shrivenham in the tea shop. There's no account of that meeting in your diary. You mention that you had a pleasant afternoon on the river. It's interesting – I'm afraid I'm being damnably cold-blooded about this – that you should have falsified this entry. There was no point in doing so, as George was intended to read the diary anyway, and it was dangerous to pretend you'd not been in Cheltenham, when the police might go into your movements and discover the discrepancy.'

'I was excited and upset the evening I wrote that. The business in the tea shop had been the first move in my new campaign against George, you see, and it was a touch-and-go business. It must have clouded my judgement.'

'Yes, I thought it must have been something like that. Your entry of August the 12th had already struck me as slightly out of key, you know. You develop a theory about Hamlet's procrastination. You protested too much. It was somehow a little false and literary. It suggested that you wanted to conceal from the imaginary reader the real reason for your own procrastination – that you couldn't bring yourself to kill a man till you were certain of his guilt. That, of course, was the real reason for Hamlet's indecision, too. But, by working up this theory about prolonging the "sweet anticipation of revenge", you hoped to head any inquisitive person away from the idea that your actual motive was a too sensitive conscience.'

'It was clever of you to see that,' said Felix. There was something extraordinarily pathetic to Nigel in the way Felix admitted this – admitted it in quiet yet faintly disappointed tones, as if Nigel had found a flaw in one of his books.

'You came back to the same point in a later entry. It went something like this, "The still, small voice, you think, gentle reader. Don't deceive yourself. I haven't the faintest qualm of conscience about killing George Rattery." You tried to pretend you had no conscience, but conscience was written large in your actions and between the lines of your diary. I hope you don't mind my going on like this. You realise I have to get everything cleared up – in my own mind, at least.'

'Go on as long as you like,' said Felix with another twisted smile. 'The longer the better. Remember Scheherazade.'

'Well then. Assuming that you now intended George to read the diary, it followed that your dinghy plan must have been a blind. If you had really meant to drown George in the river, you would not have written down all the details in your diary and then encouraged him to read it. So I asked myself, why this business in the dinghy at all? And the answer was that you did it in order to wring a confession out of George. Is that correct?'

'Yes. By the way, I was already pretty sure that George had taken the bait. I'd found the diary one day replaced in a slightly different position under the floorboard. Obviously it would not be enough for George to realise that I was Cairnes and out for his blood. Owing to the threat of manslaughter which hung over his own head, he wouldn't dare to expose me unless it became a matter of life and death for him. That's why he allowed me to go through with my plan right up to the point when I'd taken him up the river and proposed he should sail the boat downwind. He safeguarded himself, of course – as he thought – by sending off the diary to his solicitors before starting out. I was pretty certain he'd do that. It was rather a tense business for both of us in the dinghy. George was wondering, no doubt, whether I'd really have the nerve to go through with my plan, and I was on tenterhooks, waiting to see if he was really aware of his danger and if at the last moment he could be forced into admitting that it was he who'd run over Martie. We were both nervous as cats, I can tell you. Of course, if he'd accepted my suggestion that he should sail the boat downwind, it would've meant that he'd not read my diary at all: and in that case, I should have emptied the bottle of tonic when we got back to his house.'

'He caved in, then, at last?'

'Yes. When we turned round, and I asked him to sail the boat, he broke out properly. Said he knew what I was up to, had sent the diary to be opened by his solicitors in the event of his death, and then tried to blackmail me into buying it back from him. That was my worst moment. You see, I was pretty sure he must have killed Martie, or he wouldn't have left it so late to call my hand. I wasn't the only one whose hesitation showed his guilt. But I had no absolute proof. And when I pointed out to him that the diary, on account of its explanation of Martie's death, was just as dangerous to him as it was to me, he could have bluffed it out – could have pretended he knew nothing about Martie at all. But, as it happened, he caved in. He admitted the position was a stalemate, and thus tacitly admitted his responsibility for Martie's death. That signed his own death warrant, as they say.'

Nigel got up and walked over to the window. He was feeling dizzy, and a little sick at heart. The emotional strain, so severely repressed, of this conversation was telling on him. He said:

'From my point of view, the theory that the drowning plan was a fake and never meant to be put into practice was the only theory that could explain another difficult point.'

'What was that?'

'It involves talking about Lena again, I'm afraid. You see, if the dinghy accident was really meant to go through – if it was your bona fide and only plan to kill George – you'd inevitably have been compelled to disclose your real identity at the inquest. Lena would then have known you were the father of Martin Cairnes, and she would at once suspect that the "accident" was not as genuine as it looked. Of course, she might not have given you away, but I couldn't see you putting your life in her hands like that.'

'I'm afraid I deliberately blinded myself all along to the strength of her love for me,' said Felix soberly. 'I had started by deceiving her, and I could not really believe that she was not deceiving me – making up to me for my money. It shows what a worthless creature I am. I shall be no loss to the world – or to myself.'

'On the other hand, if you poisoned Rattery and knew that the diary would become evidence, you'd be accepting the idea that the whole Frank Cairnes story should come out. You relied on no one's doubting that the plan to drown George was a genuine one. Since you intended to drown George that afternoon, and had only been prevented by his unexpected knowledge of your plans, it was unthinkable that you should have made the preparations for him to be poisoned on the same evening – that's the way you expected the police to argue, wasn't it?'

'Yes.'

'It was a brilliant idea. It took me in all right. But it was a bit too subtle for Blount, you know. X admits having planned to kill Y; Y is killed; therefore the odds are that X did it. That's the way his mind worked. It's always dangerous to overestimate a policeman's sublety – or to underestimate his commonsense. And another thing: you gave the police very little chance to suspect anybody else of the murder.'

Felix flushed. 'Oh, look here, I'm not as bad as that. You don't really think I'm capable of trying to incriminate some innocent person, do you?'

'No. Not deliberately. I'm sure not. But your diary contained material which made me think for a while that old Mrs Rattery was the murderer, and Blount based a great deal of his case against Phil on the diary, too.'

'I wouldn't have minded Ethel Rattery getting hung, I admit. She was twisting up Phil's life so abominably. But it didn't occur to me that I was throwing suspicion on her. As for Phil – well, you know I'd have died rather than let any harm come to him. As a matter of fact,' Felix went on in lower tones, 'it *was* Phil who killed George Rattery, in a way. I might've become discouraged or frightened, and given up the idea of killing George, if I hadn't been seeing every day the damnable effects he had on Phil. It was like seeing my own Martie being warped and tortured. Oh God! And if I've done it all for nothing! Supposing Phil really has—'

'No, Phil's all right. I'm quite sure he's not done anything foolish,' said Nigel, trying to put into his voice greater conviction than he felt. 'But how did you mean Rattery's death to be taken, then?'

'Why, as suicide, of course. But Lena took the bottle away and got Phil to hide it. Poetic justice, I suppose.'

'But where was George's motive for suicide?'

'Well, I knew he would come in from the river that evening very agitated. People would notice that. It's the sort of question a coroner always asks – was the deceased in a normal frame of mind? I imagined the police would think he'd done it in a kind of brainstorm – afraid of the facts about Martie's death coming out. Something like that. And I knew he would call the garage to get his car on the way back, so he could easily have got the poison then. I really didn't worry about motive much, though. All I wanted was to get Rattery out of the way before he could do any more harm to Phil.' Felix paused. 'It's a queer thing. I've been worrying myself sick all this week, but now I know I'm for it, I don't seem to mind.'

'I'm damned sorry it's had to turn out like this.'

'It's not your fault. You just carried too many guns for me. Does Blount want to take me along now?'

'Blount doesn't know anything about it yet,' said Nigel slowly. 'He still thinks Phil did it. Which is all to the good – it'll make him all the more zealous in his search for Phil. He's got his reputation to keep up.'

'Blount doesn't know?' Felix was standing by the chest of drawers, his back to Nigel. 'Well, I wonder. Perhaps you didn't carry too many guns for me after all.' He opened a drawer and turned round, a feverish excitement in his eyes, a revolver in the palm of his hand.

Nigel sat quite still, relaxed. There was nothing he could do. There was the whole breadth of the room between them.

'When Phil disappeared this morning, I went down to look for him at the Ratterys'. I didn't find him, but I found this gun. It's George's. I thought it might come in useful.'

Nigel screwed up his eyes, looking at Felix with an interested, slightly impatient expression.

'You're not thinking of shooting me, are you? Really, there'd be no point in—'

'My dear Nigel!' exclaimed Felix, smiling at him sadly. 'I don't think I deserve that. No. I was thinking of my own convenience. I attended a murder trial once; I don't much fancy having to attend another. Would you object if I declined the invitation and used this?' He grimaced fastidiously at the revolver. Nigel was thinking, He's doing it all with a monstrous effort of will, his pride is terrific. Pride and a kind of artist's sense of climax are enabling him to rise to the occasion, to subdue his shrinking flesh. Under an intolerable stress we are all inclined to dramatise a situation – it's our way of softening the hard reality, of making bearable an extreme agony.

After a minute he said, 'Look, Felix. I don't want to hand you over to Blount, because I think George Rattery was no loss to the world. But I can't keep quiet about this either. There's Phil to think of, and besides, Blount has trusted me in the past. If you'll write a confession – I'd better dictate it to you so that all the vital points are covered, and post it to Blount in the hotel letter box, I'll go to sleep for the rest of the afternoon. I need a sleep, the way my head's buzzing.'

'The British genius for compromise,' said Felix, glancing at him quizzically. 'I ought to be grateful to you for that. But am I? . . . Yes, I am. Better than a revolver – messy, squalid business. To go down fighting, in my element.'

Felix's eyes were lit with excitement again. Nigel looked at him questioningly.

'If I could get to Lyme Regis. My dinghy's there. They'd never expect me to try and escape that way.'

'But, Felix, you wouldn't have a chance of reaching—'

'I don't really think I want a chance. My life ended with Martie. I know that now. I just came back to life for a few weeks to save Phil. I'd like to die out at sea – fighting a clean enemy for a change – the wind and the waves. But will they ever let me get that far?'

'You've got a good chance. Blount and the police are all looking for Phil. If he had a tail on you, he's probably taken it off by now. You've got your car here, and—'

'And I can shave off my beard! By God! I might get through. I said I'd be shaving off my beard one day and slipping through the cordon – that evening in the garden, you remember.'

Felix tossed the revolver back into the drawer, put out scissors and shaving tackle and set to work. Then, with Nigel standing at his elbow, he wrote his confession. Nigel went with him to the head of the stairs and saw him drop the envelope into the postbox. They were alone together in the room for a minute.

'It'll take me about three and a half hours to get there in my car.'

'You'll be all right if Blount doesn't return here till this evening. I'll tip off Lena to keep quiet.'

'Thanks. You've been good about this. I wish – I'd like to know that Phil was safe before I pushed off.'

'We'll look after Phil for you.'

'And Lena – tell her it's a far, far better thing, and all that. No. Give her my love. She was kinder to me than I deserved. Well, goodbye. Tonight or tomorrow should see the end of me. Or is there anything after death? It'd be nice to understand the reason for all these damnable things that happen.' He grinned quickly at Nigel, 'Then I'd be Felix *qui potuit rerum cognoscere causes.*'

Nigel heard the car start up. Poor chap, he muttered, I really believe he thinks he's a chance, in a dinghy, with this wind getting up. He went off to find Lena . . .

Epilogue

Press cuttings from Nigel Strangeways' files of the Rattery case.

Extract from the *Gloucestershire Evening Courier.*

Philip Rattery, the boy who has been missing from his home at Severnbridge since yesterday morning, was found today at Sharpness. Interviewed by a *Courier* reporter, Mrs Violet Rattery, the boy's mother, stated, 'Philip stowed away on one of the Severn barges. He was found when the barge was unloaded at Sharpness this morning. He is none the worse for his escapade. He had been worrying about the death of his father.'

Philip Rattery is the schoolboy son of George Rattery, the prominent Severnbridge citizen whose death is being investigated by the police. Chief Inspector Blount, of New Scotland Yard, the officer in charge of the investigation, informed our representative this morning that he is confident of an early arrest.

There is still no news of Frank Cairnes, who disappeared yesterday afternoon from the Angler's Arms at Severnbridge, where he had been staying, and whom the police wish to question in regard to the death of George Rattery.

Extract from the *Daily Post*.

Yesterday afternoon the body of a man was washed ashore at Portland. The body has been identified as that of Frank Cairnes, the man for whom the police have been searching in relation to the Rattery murder case. Subsequent to the discovery of the shattered remains of Cairnes' sailing dinghy, the *Tessa*, washed ashore during the southerly gale of last weekend, the investigation had been centred upon this stretch of coast.

Cairnes was well known to the reading public as a crime novelist, under the pseudonym of Felix Lane.

The adjourned inquest on George Rattery will take place at Severnbridge (Glos.) tomorrow.

Note by Nigel Strangeways

This is the end of my most unhappy case. Blount still regards me with some suspicion, I fear. In the politest possible manner, he intimated that it was 'a great pity Cairnes slipped out of our hands like that,' accompanying the words with one of those shrewd, chilly glances that are much more disquieting than any accusation. Still, I'm glad I gave Felix the chance to go out in the way he wanted to go. A clean ending, at least, to a dirty, dirty business.

In the first of Brahms' four Serious Songs, he paraphrases Ecclesiastes 3, 19, as follows: 'The beast must die, the man dieth also, yea both must die.' Let that be the epitaph for George Rattery and Felix.